Cotswold

Debris

Book 1 of the Brenscombe Series

By RR Gordon

Brenscombe. Book 1. Cotswold Debris

Copyright © 2019 by RR Gordon
iv

Dedication

This book is dedicated to my daughter Alexandra Gordon, who inspired the story. She also came up with the characters, the names, the locations on a long drive up to Newcastle one day. I suppose it's her story really ... but if we just keep it between ourselves then she'll never know ...

Map Of Brenscombe

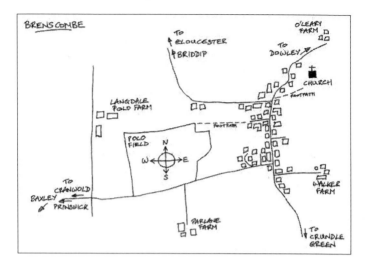

1. The Beginning Or The End

"My name's Uros." He pronounced it *Oorosh*, with a guttural rolling of the *r* like a Russian, but the rest of his speech was pure Gloucestershire.

"I know. You gave your name to my colleague and she wrote it on the big whiteboard over there."

The man glanced over at the wall and then looked back at her again. An intense stare, but a wrinkle of amusement around his eyes. He was around thirty years old with dark, cropped hair. He was slim and wiry, and the muscles in his neck stood out slightly as he turned his head. And he was tall. Before he had sat down, she'd noticed that he was a head taller than her.

He snorted in the general direction of the whiteboard. "That's a bit low tech isn't it?"

"I don't know if you've noticed, but there isn't any electricity."

"I thought hospitals were meant to have their own generators or something."

"The diesel ran out yesterday. Hold still."

She tied off the final stitch and put a bandage around his hand to help prevent infection. She sat back and rubbed her eyes tiredly.

"Your name's Sophia."

"You can read," she said glancing down at her badge. She would have smiled, but she didn't have the energy.

"You're a good doctor. I've had stitches before and you did a much better job than the last bloke."

"I'm not a doctor."

"Nurse then."

"I'm not a nurse. I'm a healthcare assistant."

"What's a healthcare assistant?"

"We assist the nurses. Fetching stuff and whatever. Do you know when you last had a tetanus injection?"

"No idea."

"Have you had one since you were at school?"

"I don't think so." He shrugged.

"How old are you? Thirty?"

"Thirty one."

"I'd better give you one just in case then." She stood and removed a needle from a box on the shelves. It was the last one and she threw the box in the bin.

"You sound like you know what you're doing for a healthcare assistant. How long have you been doing it?"

"I've been here two weeks."

She slid the needle in and pressed the plunger. The needle followed the box into the bin.

"What were you doing before that?"

"I was in sixth form."

"Sixth form. You're just a schoolkid? But you just put ten stitches in my hand."

"Twelve actually."

"How many times have you done stitches?"

"Did you see that five year old girl who was in here before you?"

"Yes?"

"She was the first. She just had a couple though."

"What? I'm only the second person you've done?"

"I've watched it a lot over the last couple of weeks. You'd be surprised how many times people come into A&E with cuts at the moment." She sighed. "I'm hoping to go to medical school next year and you've got a better chance of getting in if you have some experience so I volunteered to be a healthcare assistant for a few months."

"You're just a schoolgirl doing her work experience?" He laughed. "Where are all the real doctors?"

"Same place as everyone else. Looking after their home and families. We've had fewer and fewer doctors and nurses coming in each day. Good experience for me though."

"Well, you're better than that miserable old guy I had last time. He couldn't have cared less. You did a neat job."

"You're all done anyway."

"What time do you finish work tonight, Sophia?"

"I don't know. Another million years probably. I've been here for about twenty-six hours already I think. Or is it twenty-eight?"

"Do you want to come for a drink when you've finished?"

"A drink?" She laughed. "I just want to sleep for a week. Right, you've got to go. There are some more patients in the waiting room."

"I might just come back in a couple of hours and see if you've changed your mind." He smiled, stood and walked to the door. "You didn't ask where I'm from."

"Pardon?"

"Most people ask where I'm from when I tell them my name."

"Does it matter where somebody is from?"

"I like you," he smiled. "I'll see you later."

She forced a smile through her tiredness, not believing that she'd ever see him again. Well, maybe the next time he came back in after a fight. The cut looked like it had been inflicted by someone else. It was at a strange angle for him to have done it himself.

He closed the door, after a final glance back at her, and she leant back in her chair. Maybe she'd just grab five minutes rest.

The door opened. It was Jane, her colleague. A real nurse with fifteen years' experience.

"Hey, Sophia, you can go home now. You look exhausted."

"I can't leave you on your own," she said, standing up.

"Don't worry, I'm heading off as well. Bob - Dr Chapman - has just come in and Heather finally arrived ten minutes ago. I can't blame her, I suppose. She has two young boys and she didn't want to leave them until her husband got back. Are you okay to get home? You live out in a village somewhere, don't you?"

"Yes, Brenscombe, up near Briddip."

"Oh, you can't walk back there. It'll take you hours. It's about ten miles, isn't it?"

"My dad said he'd come along this afternoon to pick me up. He said he'd drive over again at the end of the day to see if I was finished."

"In a car? Has he still got petrol?"

"Oh yes," she nodded with a faint smile. "For the last year he's been keeping loads of canisters of petrol in the garage. And hundreds of tins of baked beans. We thought he was mad and kept making jokes about it. Anyway he said he'd come back around now and see if I was ready to go back home."

"I'll wait outside with you until he arrives. Let's go before they ask us to treat another patient. Sometimes you just have to get out when you can."

Sophia picked up her backpack from the reception area and followed Jane out of the hospital. They walked out to the car park exit and sat on a low stone wall.

Jane looked around anxiously, but the road was empty. "The world's gone mad," she said softly, more to herself than Sophia. She continued looking up and down the road. "At least it's quiet at the moment. It was mayhem last night."

"My dad thinks it's going to get worse. Well, it's obvious I suppose. Hardly anything in the shops and everybody fighting for the scraps that are left."

"We were thinking of going to live with my sister. She lives in a little place on the coast in Scotland."

"That sounds like a good idea."

"I think we've left it too late now," Jane shrugged. "The trains aren't running anymore and the buses don't have any petrol. Nobody has any petrol. Well, apart from the police and the army. And your dad."

"You should walk."

"Walk to Scotland?"

"My dad says it's going to be bad when the food finally runs out. You don't want to be in a big town then. You could come up to Brenscombe? You can stay with us. My dad thinks we might have enough food - there's farm land all around us. And he has his tins of baked beans." She laughed tiredly.

"That's kind of you, but how would your mum feel if we just turned up on your doorstep one day?"

"I think the rules will be changing soon. Anyway she likes having visitors."

Once again Jane glanced up and down the road nervously. There was still nobody about.

"At least it's peaceful without all the cars," she said.

"It won't be like this in a week from now." Sophia stood and stretched herself like a cat. She yawned. "You know what I would love? Some chocolate. I'm just going to pop over to that shop and see if they have any left."

"You'll be lucky. It's been closed for a couple of days." Jane leaned forward and peered towards the small corner shop fifty yards away. "It still looks shut to me."

"I thought I saw somebody at the window a moment ago. I'll just go and see. You never know."

"I'll come with you. It's better to stay together." Jane stood up and they walked over to the shop together.

"Look, it says *Closed* on the door," Jane said, as they arrived at the shop.

Sophia leaned her forehead on the window and cupped her hands around her eyes to see through the glass. "I think there's someone at the back of the shop."

She knocked on the door and tried the handle.

"You can't - " Jane started, but Sophia had already opened the door and was walking inside.

"Hellooo," she called. "Is anyone here?" She looked around and called again. "I hope you don't mind me coming in like this? I just wondered if you had any chocolate left?"

There was silence for a moment and then somebody spoke, a voice she thought she recognised.

"Well, Sophia," said the voice, "it's good to see you again."

Uros came around the end of the aisle and walked over to her with a smile. "You've finished work then?"

"What are you doing here? Is this your shop?"

"It is now."

"What do you mean?"

"The paki who owned it said he didn't want it anymore."

"You can't call him that. Anyway why did he say that? Where is he now?"

"He's lying down at the back of the shop."

Sophia made to walk past him, but Uros held out a hand. There was blood on the bandage she had just put on him.

"You've pulled your stitches out," Sophia said, sighing. "I worked hard on those."

"Don't worry, it's not my blood."

"What? Oh." She looked at him, seeing the man he really was. The man she had suspected he was.

"Come on, Sophia. Let's go." It was Jane, standing in the doorway.

"I just want to look at the owner," Sophia replied, trying to push past Uros once more.

"There's no point." He held out his arm again. "But look on the bright side, I've found his stockpile, the stash that he was keeping for himself. And there's loads of chocolate in there. Why don't you and I go to the back room and have some."

"We're not going anywhere with you," Jane said, walking forward and holding out her hand towards her friend. "Come on, Sophia."

"Don't worry, I wasn't inviting you." Uros smiled at Jane, a smile without warmth.

"I want to see the owner of the shop," Sophia repeated firmly.

Jane moved forward and grabbed Sophia's arm to pull her from the shop but, before they could move, Uros caught hold of Jane and yanked her towards him. She struggled and tried to break free, but he struck her hard across the side of the face and she fell backwards into a freezer cabinet. Her head hit the door handle as she fell and she collapsed heavily onto the floor, her skull striking the tiles with a sickening thud. Blood seeped from the side of her head, pooling on the stained black and white floor.

"Jane!" Sophia cried, moving towards her, but Uros seized hold of her arm.

"Why don't you come with me," he said.

Suddenly there was a huge explosion and plaster fell from the ceiling above him. Sophia's ears were ringing, but she took the moment to pull her arm free.

She turned to see her father, John, in the doorway walking towards her. He was holding a shotgun.

"Are you okay, Sophia?" he said, levelling the gun at Uros, who was brushing the ceiling fragments out of his short hair.

"Where on earth did you get a gun from, Dad?" Without waiting for the answer, she bent down and held her fingers against Jane's neck.

"Anthony next door. I asked if I could borrow it, just in case."

"Anthony has a shotgun? He's a teacher." She didn't take her eyes off Jane as she spoke. Her colleague groaned and Sophia breathed a sigh of relief. Jane opened her eyes and groaned.

"He goes clay pigeon shooting. It's his hobby."

"Don't point that gun at me, old man." Uros had now recovered his composure and although he hadn't moved, his demeanour was more aggressive.

"Are you okay, Jane?" Sophia asked. Jane mumbled a yes, but her eyes still looked unfocussed.

"Get on the floor," her father said to Uros. "Lie on your back."

Uros didn't move. There was silence. Sophia examined the back of Jane's head, parting her hair to see the cut.

"It only looks like a small cut, half an inch perhaps, but there's so much blood."

"I'm okay," Jane said woozily, starting to sit up. "The scalp can sometimes bleed a lot. I'm okay."

"Get in the car. The engine's still running," her father spoke calmly, not taking his eyes from the man in front of him. "Take your colleague with you."

"The owner of the shop!" Sophia said, suddenly remembering, and stood up. She ran round the other aisle towards the back of the shop.

The two men remained standing, five paces apart, the double-barrelled shotgun still pointing at Uros's chest.

"You've just got one bullet left," he said.

"Cartridge," John replied.

"What?"

"It's not a bullet, it's a cartridge filled with dozens of tiny ball bearings. They spread out when fired. At fifty yards the ball bearings are in a pattern the size of a dinner plate. I suppose at this distance they'll be smaller than the lid of a jam jar when they hit you."

Uros didn't reply. He looked like he was considering making a move for the gun. "You don't want to shoot me. You'd have done it by now."

"Correct. I don't want to shoot you. I'd like you to lie on the floor but I'm not willing to shoot you just for that. However I'm prepared to shoot you to protect my daughter. If you make a move either backwards or forwards I'll pull the trigger. The only way you can move without me shooting you is downwards."

"What do you do?" Uros smiled.

"My job? I'm not sure if jobs exist any more. Until recently I ran a small software business."

"You're not going to shoot me."

John didn't reply and they simply stood in the centre of the aisle looking at each other. There was just the sound of Sophia at the back of the shop.

Eventually she came slowly back up the other aisle and stood next to her father.

"He's dead."

"I'm sorry," her father replied softly, "but we need to go. Please could you get in the car, Sophia?"

"We need to take this man to the police."

Uros laughed.

"I don't think he's prepared to go with us." Her father shrugged. "Are you?"

Uros laughed again.

"Therefore our only choice is to shoot him or leave. Would you like me to shoot him? It's unlikely to kill him – unless I get lucky – but he would be injured enough that we could probably take him to the police station. Or I could shoot him in the leg perhaps. I should be able to re-load before he recovers."

Sophia looked at Uros, considering. He looked worried for the first time.

"No," she replied, hanging her head slightly. The smile returned to Uros' face. "But we should report him to the police on the way back home," Sophia continued.

"Go and jump in the car. Shout when you're in. I don't want to take my eyes off him."

Sophia turned to help Jane up and they walked out of the shop with Jane leaning on her. They climbed into the old Mercedes estate that was sitting outside, the engine chuntering.

"Okay, Dad," she shouted. "We're in."

Her father walked backwards out of the shop, keeping the gun trained on the other man. Uros walked slowly forwards, keeping the same distance between them.

The driver's door was open on the near side of the car and John slid onto the seat whilst keeping the shotgun trained on his target. Uros was now standing in the shop doorway, waiting for an opportunity to make a move.

Without closing the door, still holding the gun at the man, John put the car into gear and drove off. When he was twenty yards up the road he passed Sophia the gun and pulled the door closed.

From behind them, she heard a faint shout, fading as they drove away: "I'll see you again one day, Sophia."

-o-o-o-

The drive back from Gloucester was uneventful, aside from people staring in surprise that a car was still on the road. Returning to Brenscombe village, John started to edge the old Mercedes estate slowly onto the drive, but his two teenage boys were standing in the way. They seemed to be having a heated discussion.

Lewis, the elder of the two, was more stockily built and already as tall as his father, even though he was only sixteen years old. Reid, despite being the younger of the two at nearly fifteen, was actually an inch taller than his brother and father, his slender build and unruly hair accentuating his height.

John rolled down the driver's window. "Open the garage door for me please, Reid."

"Lewis just kicked the football into next door's garden and won't get it back."

"It came off you last," his brother retorted.

"Only 'cos you blasted it at me. And it only skimmed my shoulder. Go and get it." Reid pushed his older brother vaguely in the direction of the neighbour's house. Lewis returned the push, but harder so that the younger Reid stumbled backwards onto the front of the car.

"Boys," said John quietly but firmly. "I've got someone in the car who has hurt their head. Lewis, please fetch the ball and – "

"But, Dad – "

"I don't care. Go." He turned to his youngest son. "Reid, open the garage door please. I'm wasting petrol here. Quickly please."

Lewis started trudging up the road to the neighbour's house and Reid ran through the back door of the house to heave up the large double garage door from the inside.

John drove the car in and switched off the engine quickly. He and Sophia helped Jane into the house. Fortunately she had recovered a little during the twenty minute drive and the support was now more symbolic than necessary.

John's wife, Emilia, was preparing the evening meal and turned as the newcomer was brought into the kitchen.

"What's happened? Who's this?" she exclaimed worriedly on seeing the blood, then glanced from John to Sophia. "Are you two hurt?"

Reid came in, having closed the garage.

"Where's Lewis?" Emilia asked quickly, looking over Reid's shoulder. "Wasn't he with you?"

"Relax, Mum. He's just gone next door to get the football. He kicked it over the hedge and then wouldn't get it, but Dad told him – "

"Reid, be quiet," John interrupted curtly. "Don't worry, Emilia, we're not hurt. This is Jane, Sophia's colleague from work. She was attacked near the hospital and we brought her back here to get cleaned up. She'll be staying with us tonight. Longer if she wants." They sat Jane down at the kitchen table.

"What on earth happened?" Emilia fetched a cloth and started cleaning up the back of Jane's head. Sophia came over to help.

John explained his version of the events and Sophia completed the missing details.

"That's terrible," Emilia said, as she fussed over their visitor. "Something should be done about that man."

"I've been thinking of calling a meeting of everyone in the village and this has made my mind up," John said. "We need to get prepared in case we have unwanted visitors. People like this bloke today who will take what they want if there's no law and order. We need to do something to ensure our safety."

"What do you mean?" his wife said as her daughter assessed the wound on Jane's head. "That's what the police are for."

"Emilia, you haven't been into town for a few weeks. Nobody's being paid any more so nobody's working – and that includes the police. It's anarchy."

"Don't be so melodramatic, John. Surely it's not that bad."

"There were riots in Gloucester last night," Jane interjected. "It's been happening more and more over the last few weeks. They smash shop windows, take what they want, set fire to abandoned cars. It's just not safe to go out at night now."

John nodded. "We need to post guards on the outskirts of the village in case these people come up here. And work out what we're going to do about food. I'm going to talk to some of the local farmers like Peter Parlane. I imagine they might need some help in the fields if they run out of diesel for their tractors and perhaps we can organise a workforce in exchange for some of the produce. What do you think?"

"Yes, I suppose so," his wife replied distractedly, concentrating on the task at hand. "But I can't believe things are going to be that bad though."

"We need to sort something out before we eat all our food reserves. The world's changed, in just a couple of months it's transformed unbelievably and if we don't change with it then there simply won't be enough food in a very short space of time."

That was the day that it all began for us – or rather the old way of living ended. That was the moment, many years ago, when I realised that a new order had begun and I needed to accept it. As John said to us many times, adapt or die.

You're all here around this fire tonight because you fight to stay alive – and sometimes we need to fight with every last fragment of our souls.

I can see it in your eyes, the spark of life, the steel, the granite, the fight. We are Brenscombe. It's not a place, it's a way of living, a way of being, an idea, a family, an army, a tribe, a group of warriors that slides a knife into a small crack in the world and widens it to build a safe home for its people.

2. Mark And Rachel.

Many hundreds of years ago there were tribes similar to ours called Vikings. Each clan had a skald, a storyteller who kept the history of his tribe in his head and told the legends around the camp fires each night as we are doing now.

It is important to know where you are from and to teach the young about the path we have travelled so that they don't make the same mistakes as us. The education of our people is essential to our ability to remain superior to our enemies, our competitors, those that wish to steal our food. That, and a sharp sword of course.

I am your skald, but I am growing old. This telling, over the coming nights, may be my last but when I'm gone my daughter will take my place. I am worried that I will forget something, some important fact or idea, but I will try to make sure that every word is right for her.

Does anyone have any questions before I begin tonight's telling? Yes, John? What's chocolate? Ha, that's a good question, young John. I talked about it last night, didn't I? Well, you remember that honey we had last year? Chocolate is sweet like honey but solid like a biscuit. Yes, it is nice. Was nice. Hopefully you'll taste chocolate one day.

Let me continue where I left off last night. This is our story. The story of how the Brenscombe tribe was started many decades ago when I was young, many hundreds of miles from here, how it grew out of the debris of the old society ...

"What's the point?" Rachel said.

"I told Andy I'd go back in today." Mark pulled his jacket on.

"You're joking. Nobody's going to work anymore. And it's dangerous out there."

"Nobody's going to pick on me." Mark smiled. He was six foot one and nearly sixteen stone. He was perhaps carrying an extra stone around his waist, but he hid it well. "And I thought I might pop into the supermarket on the way back in case they've got any more food in."

"Well, that's not a bad idea, but be careful. It was like a riot last time."

"If the office is closed then I'll just go straight over to the supermarket and be back in an hour or so. I thought I'd go on my bike."

Rachel nodded pensively, glancing down at her breakfast. She looked up again. "Mark?"

"Yeah, I'll be careful."

"No, I was going to say … do you think we should go up to your mum and dad's house?"

"What do you mean?" He looked at her. "To visit? Or permanently?"

"For a while at least." She shrugged. "Your father said it might be safer up at Brenscombe. What are we going to eat when the last of the food is gone? At least your dad has all those tins of baked beans."

They both smiled.

"But all our stuff is here," Mark replied. "And things might get sorted out."

"We could just come back if it does."

"But we need to be here to look after the flat," he insisted. "Look, I've got to go. Let's talk about it later."

"Okay, but be careful."

"Of course I will." He gave his girlfriend a kiss and headed out of the door.

-o-o-o-

Ten minutes later Mark rode his mountain bike through the entrance gate to his office car park and looked around. There was one solitary car on the far side – the same VW Golf which had been there for nearly three weeks. He wondered who owned it.

Mark glanced at the large office building in front of him. All quiet.

He rolled over to reception and, without climbing off his bike, pulled at the door. Locked.

After a final look up at the windows, he shrugged and decided to leave.

At least we can come here if we need any wine, he thought to himself. Mark worked in the call centre of Braithwaites Wine, the largest merchants in the country, and behind the office was their main warehouse with over a million bottles of wine.

I'm surprised it hasn't been broken into already, he thought.

He cycled over to the supermarket on the other side of the business park. The roads were quiet but when he turned into the car park he saw dozens of people going in and out of the store.

Only they weren't using the doors. All the way along the façade, the huge plate glass windows had been smashed and people were simply stepping over the low sill, their shoes crunching on the shards of glass.

Mark shook his head. Why were they doing it? he wondered. Every last morsel of food was sold last week. Or had there been another delivery? Then he saw a man with short, red hair step through of one of the windows carrying a huge pack of nappies. There were obviously other essentials that people needed.

The man carrying the nappies was caught up by another, a man in his early twenties, long dark hair tied back in a ponytail. He had just come out of the shop as well with some smaller items in his hand. "Oi mate," said the ponytail. "Can I have some of them? You got the last pack."

The red-haired man stopped and looked the other man up and down. All around them people were coming and going. Mark debated looking round the supermarket himself, but food was the only thing they really needed and there was an air of tension about the place. He was glad he was still forty yards away from the front of the building. He saw a teenager step out of the shop carrying a stack of DVDs and shook his head. What was the point when there was no electricity?

The red-haired man finally came to a decision. "These are mine," he said and started backing away from the larger man. "I got them first."

"I'm a reasonable guy," said the ponytail man, walking forward. "Let's just have half each. There's forty eight in that huge pack. I'll give you half of this cotton wool."

"I don't want any cotton wool. And that packet is tiny. That's not a fair swap."

"I need those nappies. Either give me half of them or I'll take the lot."

Mark wondered if he should intervene, but he didn't know what he would do. What was fair? Should he encourage them to share the nappies? Then he saw the man with the ponytail pull out a knife. It looked like a large kitchen knife.

"Okay, okay," said the red-haired man, "you can have half of them."

"Too late, mate. Give me the whole pack."

Mark saw the man consider his options, glancing over his shoulder to the edge of the car park where the housing estate began.

The man with the ponytail stepped forward and made a grab for the pack of nappies. The two men wrestled with them for a second and then the bag split, nappies spilling all over the floor.

Another man walked over to them and said "Would you mind if I had some of – " and then he saw the knife. "Don't worry," he muttered, backing quickly away.

The man with the ponytail stepped forward again to stand amidst the scattered nappies and the red-haired man retreated a dozen paces. Ponytail put his knife in a small home-made sheath that was attached to the back of the waistband of his trousers and crouched to pick up the nappies. The red-haired man just watched.

The man with the ponytail stood up, his arms full. "You can have the rest," he said, nodding at half a dozen of the white items lying on the floor. He turned and started walking towards the houses.

The red-haired man stood looking at his assailant walking away. *Don't do it*, Mark thought. The red-haired man then obviously decided that six nappies was better than being stabbed and he bent to scoop them up.

Mark glanced around and saw that other arguments were breaking out here and there. There was a feeling of tension, people raising their voices, becoming more agitated as the supermarket shelves emptied. *Time to leave*, he thought.

-o-o-o-

Mark let himself back into the flat. Rachel looked up at him.

"Oh, you're back," she said. "Thank goodness. I've been worried the whole time."

"We're going to Brenscombe. Right now. You were right."

"Right now?"

Mark told her what had happened at the supermarket as he took a backpack out of the cupboard and started putting some clothes in it. "There's no more food. There's no more anything. People are becoming desperate."

"That's why I told you not to go out," Rachel said.

"Let's go up to Mum and Dad's place. Like you said, they've got food – and we'll be safer up there. Let's get packed."

"Right now?"

"You should have seen those people at the supermarket. It won't be long before they're going into each other's houses looking for food. We have to go before it's too late."

Rachel nodded and walked over to pull a suitcase out from under their bed.

"You can't take that," Mark said as he glanced over. "It's five miles. And up Briddip hill."

"You're right," Rachel nodded thoughtfully.

"Why don't you pack your rucksack? I'll carry that and you can carry my backpack. You should be able to get quite a lot into your big rucksack."

"Can we come back for more of our clothes another day?"

"Sure."

Rachel looked around the room, realising that she would have to leave the majority of her clothes behind. Then she had a thought and looked over at the kitchen. "The most valuable thing in the flat is our food. We have to take all of it. Maybe just one change of clothes."

It was Mark's turn to pause. He looked at the new fifty-inch television that had been dormant for the last week. He looked at his Xbox, his iPod and its docking station. He took his mobile phone out of his pocket. He had carried it around for a week even though the battery was flat and he didn't know why. Habit. He threw it on the bed.

"You're right," he nodded. "Just the food then."

He pulled half of his clothes out of his backpack and moved over to the kitchen. They didn't have any fresh food left but they had plenty of flour, rice, couscous, pasta and tins of soup and tuna. After some discussion, they even packed spices ahead of a change of clothes.

A short while later they were ready to leave.

"Hold on," said Mark. "Let's tie a spare pair of shoes onto the outside of the bags."

Rachel nodded her agreement and reached for her hiking boots. While she concentrated on attaching the boots onto the bag, Mark slipped into the kitchen, took the largest kitchen knife, wrapped it in a tea towel and slid it into the side pocket of the rucksack. He then tied a spare pair of shoes onto the bag.

They walked out with a final glance around the flat. Mark wondered if they really would ever come back to fetch their clothes.

They decided to take the bikes. It took them just five minutes to cycle through the Brockton suburb of Gloucester where they lived and they were soon out into the countryside. Ten minutes later they reached the foot of Briddip Hill, but, weighed down with the heavy backpacks, they were soon walking up, pushing the bikes beside them.

"At least there's nobody about," Mark said and immediately wished he hadn't. Two men emerged from a small country road fifty yards ahead of them, each man carrying what looked a stick. After a moment Mark realised that they were golf clubs.

"Maybe they're just going for a game of golf somewhere," Mark smiled to Rachel. He didn't believe that for a second. "Just keep walking."

As they neared the men, Mark shouted a cheery "Good morning", but there was no response – other than the two men spreading out across the road in front of them.

"Keep walking," Mark said under his breath again. "There are only two of them."

Mark made to walk to one side, but the larger man held up a hand and said. "What's in those bags?"

Mark and Rachel stopped. Mark assessed the two men. They were in their forties, one looked in good shape, but the other looked overweight. He looked them in the eye, one at a time, but the overweight man glanced away immediately. The leader held his gaze.

"What have you got in those bags?" the man asked again."Any food?"

"Rachel, could you hold my bike please?" Mark leaned his bike towards her and she held the handlebars in her spare hand, wondering what Mark was doing.

He took the large rucksack off his back and put it on the ground. He slowly unzipped the side pocket and pulled out the rolled up tea towel. The two men leaned forward expecting food to be unveiled, but he unwrapped the nine-inch kitchen knife and stood up.

"Mark! Where did you get that from?" Rachel cried.

He didn't answer her, but turned to the two men. "You have one chance to move out of our way. You should have chosen better weapons. They're too unwieldy. As soon as you start your swing, I'll step inside."

The larger man looked him up and down, considering his chances with Mark, who was a couple of inches taller and a couple of stone heavier. He glanced at his friend. "We can take him together."

"No, Kev, let's leave them," the other man said, shaking his head. "I didn't want to do this anyway."

"But we need food for our kids," the larger man said.

"Not like this," his friend replied and started to move to the side of the road. After a second the larger man grudgingly decided to follow suit. He wasn't going to tackle Mark on his own.

With one hand Mark carefully pulled the rucksack back on, took his bicycle back from Rachel and, keeping to the opposite side to the two men, they started up the road again. Mark kept his eyes on the men, walking backwards up the road for a while until he saw the two men disappear off down the hill.

"Why on earth did you bring that knife?" Rachel asked when Mark announced that the men were out of sight.

"It's a good job I did."

She shook her head. "Aren't you going to put it away now?"

"I think I should hold on to it. Just in case."

They continued up Briddip Hill, as the road curved from side to side, increasing in steepness before turning a sharp right-hand corner. On this section of road the trees grew tall on both sides and almost overlapped above their heads. Occasionally there was a break in the trees on their right and they could see away to Gloucester in the distance.

"This is the last bit, isn't it?" Rachel asked. "It looks different when you're walking. I didn't realise the hill was so long."

"Briddip is just around the next bend. We're nearly there. Then we can get back on our bikes for the last couple of miles to Brenscombe."

Mark glanced up the road and saw two figures appear at the top, four hundred yards away. In the reduced light of the trees he couldn't see anything more than their outline.

"Not again," Rachel said.

Mark clutched the knife tighter and she noticed the movement.

"I think you should put the knife away. They'll think *we're* threatening *them*."

"We need it close to hand."

"Put it behind your back at least."

Mark did as his girlfriend asked, but kept his eyes on the two people ahead of them.

"I think one of them is a woman," he said.

"Are you sure?" Rachel peered up at the figures.

"And the other person looks a bit older from the way he's walking. Definitely a man. He's holding something behind his back."

"If one of them is a woman they're less likely to attack us," Rachel said.

"Do you think so? Women need to eat too."

"The world would be a much safer place if it was run by women – and we probably wouldn't have screwed up the global economy."

Mark decided this wasn't the time to argue. He looked more intently at the two figures that were now only two hundred yards away.

"Hold on," he smiled. "I know that walk." He watched a little longer, noticing the man favouring his left leg.

"You know someone from their walk?"

"Yes, it looks like Dad. He's always complaining about his left hip and his left knee after his Monday night 5-a-side." He called up the road: "Dad?"

The two figures stopped. "Is that you Mark?"

"Yeah."

"Thank goodness," came the reply as they all started walking towards each other again. They covered the remaining distance quickly.

"I'm so relieved it's you," said John. "You looked like you were holding something behind your back and I wasn't sure if you might attack us."

"It's just a kitchen knife," Mark replied, bringing the blade out in the open. "I thought the same about you."

John sheepishly pulled out his shotgun. "Sorry."

"Wow, that beats my knife," Mark said in astonishment. "Where did you get that from?"

They both exchanged stories and John introduced Jane, explaining that he was escorting her back to her home on the edge of Gloucester.

"She lives about a mile past your house," John said. "And then I was coming to see you. I was going to ask if you wanted to move up to Brenscombe, but you've beaten me to it. Mum will be so pleased to have you both at our house."

"It was Rachel's idea."

"You're lucky to have her," John said with a smile. "Why don't you two carry on to Brenscombe and I'll be back in a couple of hours when I've taken Jane home.."

"Shall I come with you, Dad?"

"No, no, you've got all that stuff. I've got the gun anyway." He was about to set off, but then turned back. "But you can help me with something. I'm organising a village meeting tomorrow afternoon and I've asked your brothers and your sister to knock on everyone's door. Can you help them?"

"Sure. What's the meeting about?"

"We need to work out some kind of rota for a watch at each of the roads into the village. So that people like the ones you just met – and the man I met yesterday – can't attack us or steal our food. We need to get everyone there. Tell them three o'clock at the village hall tomorrow afternoon. I'll tell you more about my plans when I get back and perhaps you can come with me to chat to the local farmers tomorrow morning."

"What about?"

"I'll tell you later." He and Jane started walking down the hill. "See you in a couple of hours," he shouted over his shoulder.

"Be careful, Dad," Mark shouted. His father simply raised a hand in acknowledgement as he continued down the road.

3. Village Meeting

John glanced at his watch. It was 3 o'clock. He stood up and walked to the front of the village hall. "Shall we get started?" he said loudly. Conversation ebbed away and people looked over at him expectantly.

He considered the assembled faces. The hall was full. Every seat was taken and there were dozens standing at the back. He guessed that there were more than two hundred men, women and children in the room.

"Thanks for coming," John started. "I invited everyone along this afternoon, because I think we need to get organised. We need to ensure the safety of our families and work out what we're going to do about food. In the coming months those are the two things we need to worry about: food and defending ourselves. And we'll be stronger if we do it as a community. That's it really."

He paused, realising that he should have prepared a little more, but the morning had been so busy.

"That's it," he re-iterated and then stopped. He'd run out of steam. "What does everyone think?"

There was silence for a few seconds. Everyone had obviously been expecting him to talk a little longer.

Melissa Dacourt spoke up first. "What are you talking about? It's John, isn't it? It's just a power cut. They're on strike, aren't they? I thought we were just meeting to agree how to make the electricity board do something about it."

Melissa and Hamish Dacourt lived in a large house in the centre of the village and, like most of the inhabitants, John had only ever seen them as they passed each other in their cars on their way to work. He had never spoken to the couple before.

"Sorry I should have introduced myself at the start. Yes, my name is John Strachan. We live in Ingleby House at the top of the village, opposite the turning to Cranwold." He paused for a moment. "Some of you know me, but some of you don't. We've all lived busy lives working in the towns nearby, but I assure you those lives are over. The electricity board can't do anything about the power because there's no money. Their staff stopped turning up to work some time ago. Why would they go to work if they hadn't been paid for three months? It's same for those of you here who work. You haven't been paid for months so you don't go any more. Or do you?"

"But they'll get it sorted out soon," Melissa insisted.

"Who will?"

"The government? The army? The police?"

"The day before yesterday my daughter saw somebody murdered in Gloucester. We only just managed to get away from the man who did it and went straight to the police station. Gloucester's main police station is a huge building, with a large staff normally, but the whole place was closed. Locked up. We banged on the doors and looked through the windows but the office was empty."

"That's terrible," Melissa muttered. "What do we pay our taxes for?"

"I don't blame them really," replied John. "They too haven't been paid for months and they want to be at home to keep their families safe. We need to organise our own community to provide our own protection and I'm suggesting that we place guards at each of the roads coming into the village."

A voice at the back shouted: "Who do we need to be protected from?"

"People will be coming out of the towns to look for food in the coming weeks."

"But we're ten miles away from Gloucester or Cheltenham – and an hour's drive from Birmingham or Bristol."

"And up a steep hill," somebody else shouted. "They'll be too lazy to walk up here when there are nearer places that are easier to get to."

"A friend of mine lives in a small village the other side of Gloucester," John replied, "and a few days ago half a dozen men walked into the village, broke into three of the houses and took as much food as they could carry. In broad daylight. While the owners were in their homes. Do you want that to happen here?"

He looked around the audience, letting the tale sink in before continuing.

"There are a hundred thousand people in Gloucester and they don't have enough food," John said. "They're starting to fight amongst themselves for what little food they have and when it's gone what do you think they'll do? They'll explode out of the towns and cities like a horde of ravenous dogs. Most of them are normal, rational people, not thugs, but they'll decide rationally and logically that in order to live they need to get some food from somewhere. And they'll scour everywhere to get it – so we need to have guards on the entrances to the village. You saw on the news what happened in Greece when their economy collapsed and it happened in Spain and Italy when they went as well."

"This isn't Spain," Melissa said.

"Do you think the English are any more civilised? When they haven't eaten for a week?" John paused and looked around. "Over the last year, the global economy has completely collapsed. National economies have evaporated. Other countries have tried to bail them out and then their money has run out. Like a line of dominoes, one by one, the countries of the world have toppled over into darkness."

"You're being melodramatic. As my wife said earlier, the electricity people are just on strike, aren't they?" This question was from Hamish, Melissa's husband. "That's what they said on the news. Before the telly stopped working."

"Do you think they're going to go back to work if there's no money? Would you?"

"People could take it in turns. The government should get it organised."

There was some laughter in the room and Hamish looked quickly round to see who it was, but it melted away under his gaze.

"Okay," said John. "I'll accept, for the sake of argument, that it's *possible* that the government will create a rota for people to work at the electricity companies," – more laughter – "and maybe the police, the army and everywhere else. But shouldn't we get organised ourselves – just in case the government don't sort it out or if there's a delay. Just in case another couple of weeks passes and everybody from the nearby towns turn up on our doorsteps demanding our food."

"We haven't got much food ourselves," said another man that John recognised, but whose name he couldn't remember.

"I know," John agreed. "We all have a little food in our cupboards but that will be gone soon. However we're fortunate that we live in a small village and there are rabbits, pheasants, even deer in the countryside around us."

"And Peter's cows," somebody shouted from the back of the room. There was forced laughter.

"Yes, Peter has cows." nodded John, "And Pat and Neil have a few too. But nobody would stoop to stealing these animals, would they? We're English." He smiled and looked at the awkward faces of some of the audience.

"What are we going to do when our food runs out though?" Hamish asked. "There are fields of wheat all around the village as well. Surely there's too much for Peter, Pat and Neil. Can we buy some food from them?"

"That's up to them I suppose. Although what are you going to buy it with? If you have any money, it's worthless." John paused. "However I have a suggestion and I took the liberty of sounding out Peter, Pat and Neil this morning. The land, the animals and the crops belong to the farmers, but without diesel or electricity they aren't going to be able to harvest the wheat or turn it into flour. And cows will now need to be milked by hand. I don't have all the answers, but I know that the farmers will need manpower. Perhaps we can work out a fair trade. Perhaps we should work out that rota you were talking about earlier, but for working in the fields."

There were some shrugs of agreement from the assembly and even some nods.

"And for providing protection," John continued.

"What do you mean?" Hamish asked.

"As I said earlier, I think we should have guards at each of the roads into the village. For example, between here and Briddip there's that dip in the road and if you stand at the top of it, you could probably see someone coming from half a mile away.

That's the main route in from the Gloucester and Cheltenham side of the village."

More nodding of heads.

"And," John continued. "We need to keep watch throughout the night as well. Everyone will need to take a turn."

The heads stopped nodding.

"Peter, Pat and Neil's crops and animals need protection as well," John continued. "They don't want anyone stealing them in the night. A by-product of this guard rota is the protection of their crops. It's the community working together to provide a safe environment for ourselves and for the food that is growing here."

He looked around the room, letting his words sink in.

"And finally," he started again, but then paused. He wanted to make sure that he hadn't lost anyone. "I know it's a lot to come to terms with. Perhaps up until today, you've just been a bit annoyed that there isn't anything to watch on television, but that will pale into insignificance over the coming months. Food and security will be our main worries, followed by heating during the winter, fetching water from the stream at the bottom of the valley and other pragmatic concerns like those."

He paused again and then continued: "I keep saying it, but we need to get organised. I know it sounds harsh, but it's going to be survival of the fittest and we need to get a system in place before anybody else. And we need to work out a system that's effective and fair, but we're not going to do it tonight. We can't have a committee of two hundred people. I think we should conclude tonight by voting for a village leader who can then appoint half a dozen people to run things."

"I suppose you mean yourself?" Melissa Dacourt commented caustically.

"God no. I'd hate to do it. I was going to suggest Peter actually. Peter Parlane who owns one of the farms on the edge of the village. Most of you know him, I imagine?"

"But my husband is the chairman of the parish council," Melissa pointed out. "Aren't you, Hamish?"

She nudged her husband, who jumped to his feet. "Yes, I'd be happy to put my name forward as village leader."

"Why do we even need a vote for village leader?" Melissa said. "The parish council is already in place so why waste time with voting all over again."

"That's an interesting point," John replied, "but the local elections were run last year and things are completely different now. We're now voting for someone who will hold our lives in their hands and not, with all due respect, just someone to arrange for the fixing of the potholes in the road."

"But – " Melissa began, but John ignored her and continued:

"In fact I was going to suggest that we appoint someone for a trial period, say three months. We're creating a new way of running the community and we should have a review fairly soon. I propose we have a vote tonight and then vote again in three months. Maybe have an informal village meeting once a week though. What do you all think?"

There was silence from the sea of stunned faces.

"I'll tell you what," continued John once more. "Let's have a break for twenty minutes. You probably need to chat to your family or friends and neighbours before we dive into a vote."

John sat down and the room immediately erupted noisily into dozens of small discussions.

-o-o-o-

It was nearly midnight before John and Emilia slipped into their bed.

"That meeting took a lot longer than I expected," John said.

"You shouldn't have let them discuss it amongst themselves. It was two hours of argument, squabbling and disagreement. You should've just gone straight into a vote."

"Hmmm, maybe. At least Peter got voted in. Eventually. After all that talking it was nearly unanimous."

"I don't think Melissa and Hamish were pleased," Emilia smiled.

"Peter said he might give Hamish a role on the new committee or council or whatever we're going to call it."

"Is that a good idea?" Emilia mused. "I've never liked them. Hamish or his wife Melissa."

"You've never spoken to them before tonight."

"No, but I never liked the look of them. Don't laugh. You've complained about them as well."

"When?"

"Whenever they park their big Range Rover in the middle of the road while they open and close their gates. They never leave enough room for people to get past and you just have to sit and wait for them."

"Perhaps we should give them the benefit of the doubt. We're creating a new community now and we all need to get along."

"Perhaps ... " Emilia didn't sound so sure. She leaned over and blew out the candle. "It's a good job you bought all those candles."

"We're going to have to re-discover how things like that are made. I'm glad we've still got that old Encyclopaedia Britannica set in the loft. I knew we shouldn't chuck it out."

"Do you really think we're returning to the dark ages, John? Surely somebody will sort things out."

"I can't see how you can patch the system. Too many countries had too much debt. Maybe we just need to start again from scratch."

"But that could take years."

"Centuries maybe," he nodded.

Neither spoke for a moment. The room was quiet aside from the sound of the wind blowing against the window.

John was about to speak again but he held back for fear of worrying his wife. *It's cold out there tonight*, he thought to himself, *What must it be like out in the open? I just hope we're able to stay in this house*.

4. The Watch

*Far away from here, down towards the south-west of England,
there is an area called the Cotswolds, a rambling landscape of
soft hills and green valleys, with small villages tucked away in
hidden corners. In the southern end of the region is Brenscombe,
a cluster of stone-built houses, not the honey-coloured stone of
the north Cotswolds, but a deep grey, which becomes flecked
with white lichen as the years roll by.*

*Brenscombe is perched near the edge of the Cotswold
escarpment, a high ridge which runs for many miles along the
eastern edge of the wide Severn valley. The village seemed to
have a climate of its own, always two degrees colder than the
valley below, offering cooler summer days and snow in winter
when there was just rain on the lowlands.*

*Four villages surround it on the points of the compass: Briddip
to the north, Dowley to the east, Crundle Green to the south and
Cranwold to the west.*

*We lived there as children not knowing the simple beauty of the
place, an unremarkable, quiet settlement set back from the main
highways. It is only now that I know how lucky we were to live
there. All around us were verdant fields rolling down to
woodland, broken only by meandering streams.*

*That is Brenscombe, my childhood home and the place where my
heart lives still.*

The following day John had already gone out by the time the
rest of the family came down for breakfast. He came back home
around mid-morning, bustling into the kitchen with a quick
"good morning" and asked Mark to come out with him.

"Sure," his son replied. "Where are we going?"

"Down the road to see somebody on the village committee.
Things are starting to get organised, even faster than I'd
expected." He moved to the doorway. "Let's go, I'll explain on
the way."

It was a gloomy late March day and a light drizzle was falling as
the two walked along the main village road.

"What's this all about, Dad?" Mark asked.

They turned left into the small side road called Knapp Lane.

"Peter asked me to speak to Sandy Woodall. Do you remember him?"

"I'm not sure …"

"His house is just up here on the left. He used to be in the army so Peter's put him in charge of the security of the village. And Sandy said he needs a fit young man and I thought of you. Well, you're young, at least."

Mark looked at his father and saw that he was smiling.

"I'm fitter than you, Dad," Mark laughed.

"True enough," his father said, as he patted him on the shoulder. "Anyway Sandy's a nice guy and seems to know what he's doing. He used to be a major in the Scots Guards, but retired a few years ago. Here we are."

They walked up the drive and John knocked on the door. After a few seconds it was opened by a silver-haired man wearing glasses. "Hi John, come on in," he said. "You must be Mark." They shook hands.

The man's welcoming smile reminded Mark that he had indeed seen him around the village over the last few years. He had often encountered Sandy running and cycling around the nearby hills and the man had always waved cheerily as he sped past. The man looked to be in his early sixties and Mark had always marvelled at his fitness.

They sat down at the kitchen table.

"Your father said you played rugby," Sandy commented.

Surprised at the question, Mark simply said: "Er, yes. Just a team in the Gloucester league."

"What position did you play?"

"Outside centre normally."

"Good," he nodded. "Most rugby players can handle themselves well in a physical encounter. I've been asked to set up a watch rota and have a think about how we can make the village more secure. I'm putting a temporary system in place while I consider the longer term strategy."

"Okay."

"Do you know the old fort by the church?" Sandy asked him.

"Fort?" Mark thought for a second. "You mean the over-grown ditch?"

"Yes, it was a small fort in the 12th century. There are no walls anymore, but the earthworks might be a starting point for us. I'm planning to clear the trees and bushes from the ditch that runs all the way around the central area, but leave the trees in the middle for now. Step two will be to build a fence or stockade around the central section, but initially we can use the trees for shelter if we're under attack."

"Do you really think we might be attacked?"

"Hopefully not," replied Sandy, "but we need to be ready. Anyway, building the stockade might take a few weeks and then we'll need to build shelters inside the fort."

"Okay."

"We've got Tim Butterworth in day-to-day charge of the work at the fort. He's a landscape gardener – or used to be."

"Do you mean Tim who lives round the corner from our house?"

"That's right," Sandy nodded. "Also, we're setting up a guard rota. Everyone in the village will take a turn. I'm initiating a four-hour watch system at the roads into the village. That's to say each person will be on duty for four hours. People can't stay effective for longer than this at night. Or even during the day really. Each watch is two people and therefore we need forty eight people in total every twenty four hours."

"Right …" Mark did the sums in his head.

"So everyone in the village will need to do one watch every four or five days. Women as well as men. Old as well as young. Alternate day and night watches."

"Are we just guarding the roads? What if somebody comes across the fields?"

"We have line of sight across most of the fields from the watch locations, but I agree there are points of weakness if somebody is prepared to climb fences and push through hedges. But there are other demands on our time so there's only so much we can do."

"When you're not on watch," John chipped in, "each person needs to give four hours each day to other community tasks, clearing the ditch, helping with farm work and so on. That leaves the rest of the day for jobs around your own home. Growing vegetables in the garden, home security, hunting for food, and the normal tasks like cooking and cleaning."

Mark's notion of lounging around the house was evaporating fast.

"Getting back to security," continued Sandy, "I need half a dozen watch commanders. People who can do an eight-hour shift making sure that the right people are on the right watch, filling in if somebody is ill, making sure they don't fall asleep, generally cracking the whip. The watch commander is in overall charge of the village for that eight hour period. Your father suggested that you might be interested in doing the job."

"Sure," said Mark, thinking it sounded better than farming and clearing bushes from the ditch. "I'd have thought you might give it to someone older and more experienced though?"

"Most of the people living in this village are over fifty and a watch commander will need to go backwards and forwards between all of the watches. Two of the watch posts are three hundred yards outside the village and the Briddip post is half a mile past the village boundary. If you visit each watch just once every two hours then you'll cover around six or seven miles in the eight hours. We're planning to use bikes – even at night if we can – but I still need people who are quite fit. Or I need more people or radios, which we don't have. For now, I'm looking for fit, young adults. You are currently the only person in the village who is in their twenties. That I know of."

"Okay, I'm keen to help," Mark said, and then smiled. "And it sounds better than all the other work."

"You'll still be helping with the other work" replied his father, returning the smile. "Farming, cleaning, vegetable garden."

"Did you say hunting earlier? I could do hunting."

"We all need to do the hard jobs as well as the fun jobs."

Mark turned back to Sandy. "So what do we do if someone attacks?" he asked. "Run to the fort?"

"It depends on the threat. Level One is minor threat: for example there may be one or two people walking towards you along the road from Briddip to Brenscombe. You should simply inform them that the village is closed to outsiders and either suggest that they return the way they have come or direct them along Blacklanes which will take them around the outside of the village. One guard should be twenty yards back from the other and fetch help if the first is attacked."

"Fair enough, what if twenty people are coming down the road towards us?"

"I'm calling that Level Two. Sorry if this sound all very formal, but we might as well do it properly. Level Two is a threat from between three and fifty people. One guard is to remain to talk to the potential hostiles – who hopefully won't be hostile and can be diverted around the village as before. Meanwhile the other person immediately raises the alarm, which is done by ringing the church bell three times. On hearing the bell, everyone in the village is to either support the watch or move to the fort and ready themselves to defend the position."

"That seems over the top if it's four people."

"I'm going to leave that to the watch, but if in doubt then raise the alarm. At the very least they should fetch the watch commander and more men. But there's no harm in raising the alarm – we need to practice the drill repeatedly anyway." Sandy paused for a moment. "Then there's Level Three, that's the highest level. If there are more than fifty people – or they have guns – this is a threat that is larger than we can handle. The watch should raise the alarm by continuous ringing of the church bells, which signifies that everyone needs to disperse from the village into the surrounding valleys and woods."

"You mean run away?"

"I have estimated that with our numbers – around two hundred adults – and range of personnel, that is to say primarily elderly and certainly untrained, that we can't fight a force greater than fifty young males. If we're in the fort we'll ultimately be over-powered, despite the strong position. Our best hope is therefore to scatter and then return to our homes when they've gone."

"Hmmm." Mark wasn't sure.

"I can understand your scepticism, but this is our initial strategy. Let's see what the fort looks like in a couple of months. If it looks like it can be defended against higher numbers then we'll modify the procedures."

Mark nodded. "When do you need me to start?"

"Tonight at midnight. We're splitting the hours of darkness between two watch commanders."

"Midnight? Tonight?"

"Is that okay?"

"Sure, sure." Mark was regretting having agreed so quickly. Too late now.

Sandy stood up. "Report back here at 2330 and I'll run through your other instructions."

"Okay." Mark and his father rose from their chairs as well.

"You'll be fine. Don't worry, I'll be alongside you for this first shift." Sandy smiled and shook his hand. "Good to have you on board."

Mark turned to leave, then then a thought occurred to him and he turned back.

"My girlfriend, Rachel, came up to Brenscombe with me today," he said. "She's a couple of years older than me. What I mean is, she's another person in the village who's in her twenties."

"Is she fit?"

"She runs half-marathons."

Sandy nodded, impressed. "Perhaps you could ask her to pop round for a chat. I'd like to see what she's made of."

-o-o-o-

After their meal that evening, John and Emilia went through to the lounge with a cup of tea. Sophia was already sitting in an armchair in the corner of the room, reading a book on anatomy by candlelight. She didn't look up and John smiled at her commitment. His daughter still held out hope that one day the world would resume its normal course and she would be able to go to medical school.

He and Emilia sat down on the sofa, which still faced the dormant television. John sipped his tea and leaned back with a contented sigh.

"What are you going to do when we run out of teabags?" teased Emilia.

"We should use each one half a dozen times," he replied, playing her joke with a straight bat. He did some arithmetic in his head, whilst having another sip. "Mind you, one teabag per day would still mean we only have enough for three years. I should have bought more."

"You bought plenty of everything. We must have a thousand cans in the garage, along with hundreds of boxes of pasta and rice. Everything will be past their sell-by date before we finish using them."

"Dried foods like that can keep for years. They're just covering themselves with the sell-by dates. We'll have to start hunting soon though. Rabbits and things. We should try to just use one can each day."

"There are seven of us now though."

"That's what I mean. We need to start working out a way of being self-sufficient rather than using our reserves."

"You have the shotgun still, don't you?"

"No, I gave it back to Anthony. Anyway he only has so many cartridges." John sipped his tea. "I'm planning to go over to Dowley tomorrow. There's a man over there who used to run an archery club. I thought I might be able to buy a bow from him."

"There's an archery club there? A tiny little village like that?"

"Don't you remember Sophia and I went there a couple of times? Must be a few years ago now. The man who runs it is involved with the Girl Guides camp there. Caretaker or something. Anyway he uses their land for the archery. I remember him telling me that his daughter shoots for Great Britain juniors. She's probably not a junior anymore though."

"How would you pay him for a bow?"

"I thought I might trade him for some of our food. Maybe a dozen tins and a few packets of rice."

"You're going to give away some of our food?"

"Well, I'm hoping that a bow will give us the means to hunt for more food."

"But do you think a few cans are enough for him? Surely a bow is worth hundreds of pounds?"

"I think the value of food has increased dramatically now. A second ago you seemed very reluctant to give any of it away." He paused a moment, considering all the things he needed to do. "I've been thinking that we need a trade. Something that we can exchange for the items that we need. In this new society everyone will need a trade. I wish I'd got some bees last year."

"Bees?"

"When I was stocking up it crossed my mind to get a couple of beehives. We'd then be able to trade honey."

"John, you stockpiled food, diesel, medicines, clothes, shoes, even toothpaste and toothbrushes. Our house is packed full of stuff. I'm not sure if I would want thousands of bees round the house as well."

"Hmmm, what about electricity ..." he mused. He took a sip of his tea. "We could trade that somehow."

"I've been telling you to set up that bloody wind turbine since you bought it."

"There never seems to be time."

"John, you spent £5,000 on that thing and you can't leave it in a box in the garage forever."

"Ah, so you're glad I bought it now?"

"I'd rather have had a summer holiday last year, but the least you could do is set it up as we spent so much money on it."

"Maybe I could do it tomorrow."

"Before you go to Dowley."

"It'll take half the day though."

"You'd better get up early then, hadn't you? You're lucky I don't get you to do more work around the house."

John smiled. "Thanks for the meal tonight. I know it isn't easy cooking over a log fire."

"Do you think I'll be able to use the cooker again when you have the windmill set up?" she asked hopefully.

"The maximum output is a couple of kilowatts."

"What does that mean?"

"I think it might be enough to power a cooker if it's windy. I don't know. We'll try it."

"The kids could use their Xbox again."

"Great," he replied sarcastically. "That gives me a nice incentive to spend all day putting it up."

"It gives them something to do in the evenings."

"It's good that they're all playing a real game in the kitchen. A bit of social interaction. I don't think this new way of living is all bad."

"The children are helping around the house during the day while you're out on your adventures," she smiled. "We dug up the bottom section of the lawn today and planted all the seeds we had. Some in the greenhouse as well. Actually I did a few swaps with Fran next door so we've got potatoes, corn, cabbage, lettuce, cauliflower, radishes, carrots, peas and beans."

"That sounds good," he nodded. "What are you doing tomorrow? Actually has Hamish told us when we're meant to be working on one of the farms?"

"Yes, you and I are both working at Neil's place the day after tomorrow. I asked him to put us down for the same day."

"It must be a complicated rota if people have all sorts of requests like that. It's good that Peter put him in charge of it."

"Yes, but he and Melissa aren't down to do anything."

"What?"

"I was chatting to him this afternoon and asked when he was working. He said that he and Melissa were in charge and therefore they didn't have time to work in the fields."

"They're not *in charge*. It's not meant to be like that. Everyone's meant to take a turn."

"I said that to him, but he wouldn't have it."

"I'll have a word with Peter tomorrow."

"After you've done the windmill."

"Okay, okay. Before I go over to Dowley."

Emilia had a thought. "Are you going to walk over to Dowley tomorrow? Carrying a dozen cans and whatever else. It's four or five miles isn't it?"

"I'm planning to go over on my bike with the food in a backpack. By the way I asked Lewis and Reid to come with me to carry some of the stuff. Reid's coming, but Lewis said he'd rather work in the fields. Maybe I'll ask Sophia to come instead."

His wife looked at him in surprise. "Lewis is going to work in the fields? He's on the rota for the day after tomorrow – same as us."

"Apparently he told Peter he'd help him with something."

"He'd rather do extra work in the fields than come with you to buy a bow? There must be more to it."

"What do you mean?"

"I wonder if Peter's daughter is working in the fields tomorrow," she mused.

"You mean little Annie?"

"She's not so little anymore, John. She's only a year younger than Lewis." Emilia smiled at her husband. "You're so busy looking years into the future, you don't see what's under your nose."

John sipped his tea and thought for a moment, realising his wife was right: he sometimes didn't see what was right in front of him. He patted her knee fondly.

Life was shifting radically, he thought, but some things never changed. His wife was still the boss and boys continued to chase girls. The more life changes, the more it stays the same.

5. Work In The Fields

Those were the first days of our tribe. I realise now that our community was like a small child tottering around, learning to walk. We were understanding how to work together, how to create a new type of community.

Yes, young John?

Ha, don't worry, we'll have stories about battles soon enough. Plenty of them. Too many.

It's important that first you understand how our tribe was created and the younger days of the person who is now your leader. Your experiences as a child form the mould for the adult you will become. Your leader is strong and intelligent, driven and loyal, fearsome in battle, yet loves peace more than war, loves an ear of corn as much as a well-crafted arrow.

Let me start tonight with a tale about my brother, when he was simply my little brother and not the legendary warrior he became. Ah, Lewis, he always liked the girls, even when he was sixteen ...

Lewis gently closed the door of the house behind him. The rest of his family were still asleep, but he had promised Peter Parlane that he would be there shortly after dawn. He wanted to impress Peter, but more importantly his daughter. Step one was arriving on time.

He started along the Cranwold road and looked ahead to the watch post which was just past the entrance to Peter's farm, positioned at the perfect vantage point for the long straight road running out to the west of the village. He was surprised to see three people at the post rather than two, but quickly realised that the third was his brother Mark, whose bike was leaning against the tree beside him.

As Lewis walked up to the watch station, he heard Mark's voice, loud and ebullient even at this early hour.

"… and then I ran the ball into the right corner. Seventeen-nil. They weren't going to – " He stopped in mid-sentence and whirled round. Mark's face went from worry to pleasure at seeing his brother and then to anger, albeit mild. "Lewis, you shouldn't sneak up on the watch like that."

"I wasn't sneaking. I was just walking."

"What are you doing up so early?" Mark looked at his watch. Six thirty. Only an hour-and-a-half until he could go to bed. He started to yawn, but turned it into a cough.

"I'm going to help Peter feed his animals."

"At this time? That's good, I suppose."

"Did anything happen during the night?" Lewis asked. He would quite like to be a watch commander, but he didn't envy Mark the night shift.

"No, all quiet, wasn't it Fran? A bit cold though. At least it didn't rain." Mark looked around. "Actually we'll get soaked if it rains. I'll have a word with Sandy about getting some kind of shelter put up."

"I'd better go," Lewis said, glancing over to the Parlane farmhouse. He didn't want to be late.

"See you later," Mark said and turned to Fran and Jonathan. "I'm going to head over to the Briddip watch to see how they're getting on. Shall I bring you anything back?"

"A bacon sandwich would be nice," Jonathan smiled. "Thanks for popping over to see us. It was nice to have a chat – it helped keep us awake."

Lewis set off down the farm track. Peter and Annie were just coming out of the farmhouse door and he gave them a wave, jogging forward to meet them.

Peter was an amiable, well-built man in his early fifties. Everybody in the district knew Peter Parlane, simply the mention of his name bringing a smile to their lips. His daughter, Annie, had inherited her mother's quiet personality, but a careful observer could see glimpses of her father at times.

"Morning, Lewis," said Peter, slapping the young man on the back. "I like a man who's punctual."

"Morning," Lewis replied, pleased at the compliment. Step one successfully completed. "What would you like me to do?"

"Annie will show you the ropes. I've got to get out to the fields and set things up for those who are arriving to help at eight o'clock. There's a lot to do – they won't know what's hit them." Smiling, he clapped Lewis on the back again and set off, shouting over his shoulder: "We'll stop for breakfast in a couple of hours when I've got people started. Clare will sort something out for us."

Lewis turned to Annie. "Er … hi," he said, not sure what else to say. He was pleased that she would be working with him.

"Hi, Lewis," she smiled and walked over to the barn. Lewis followed.

"What are we doing?" he asked.

"Feeding the animals to start with," she said. "You can do the chickens while I do the pigs. Then we need to check on the goats and sheep."

"I thought you just had cows …"

"We've got about fifty cows and two pigs, a dozen goats and three sheep. And thirty or so chickens." She picked up a bucket and held it out for him. "Fill that with chicken feed from that bag over in the corner."

"Right," he said, looking around.

"I'll get the food for the pigs. You saw the chicken run outside, didn't you? You just walk around throwing some on the ground for them and then put the rest in the small trough at the end."

He hadn't been looking at anything but Annie as they walked across the yard. However he went out through the barn door to look for the chicken run. How hard could it be to find some chickens in a farmyard?

-o-o-o-

At three o'clock that afternoon John, Sophia and Reid finally set off on their bikes to Dowley. The first part of the journey was slightly downhill and they rolled eastwards out of the village. John stopped to chat briefly to the two people on watch and said they'd be back in two or three hours.

Freewheeling down the road, Sophia asked: "Why did you get back from Peter's house so late after lunch, Dad? It'll be getting dark in a couple of hours." She took one hand off the handlebars to adjust the strap on her backpack, which was heavy with food.

"We should be okay until about six o'clock tonight."

"5.57 actually," interjected Reid.

"Accountant," muttered Sophia, deliberately loud enough for her brother to hear.

"She called me an accountant again, Dad."

"Reid, does it matter if I'm three minutes out?"

"Well, you don't want to think you have more time than you really have."

"Actually how do you know it's 5.57 tonight?"

It was Reid's turn to sigh. "It was 5.54 last night and at this time of year it alters by 3 minutes each day."

"Accountant," muttered Sophia again.

"Dad!"

"Try to save your breath for this hill," his father replied, knowing Reid would probably be at the top before he was halfway up.

"In answer to your question, Sophia, it took me a lot longer than I thought to set up the wind turbine on the garage roof and I still don't know how to hook it into the wiring in our house. I'm going to ask around the village to see if anyone can help."

"And then can we play Xbox?" Reid called over his shoulder, already ten yards ahead.

John ignored the question. "And then I went over to Peter's house, thinking that I would just be there for ten minutes."

"You were there for nearly two hours." She pedalled easily up the incline, staying alongside her father.

"We needed to talk about a couple of things. For example Hamish Dacourt is in charge of the farm work schedule, but he has omitted himself and his wife Melissa from the rota."

"That's not fair. Other people won't do it if they don't."

"Exactly," panted John. They were halfway up the hill now. He glanced ahead. Reid was nearing the top. "They're also saying that their son Noah is too young."

"He's twelve, isn't he? I think he just started secondary school this year."

"That's right. He can probably do more in the fields than some of the older villagers. Peter's going to have a chat with Hamish." He paused for breath. "Then we started talking about what we should do if people don't help out or" – pant – "or break other rules that we've agreed." – pant – "In Hamish's case we could remove him from the village council, but he might still say he doesn't want to work in the fields." – pant – "We could withhold food, but you can't just have one person making decisions like that, you need a fair system with a panel of a dozen people."

They reached the top of the hill where Reid was waiting, using a stick as a sword to attack unsuspecting bushes. As his father and sister cycled past he jumped back on his bike and was soon in front of them again.

"That sounds like a jury," Sophia said.

"I know. We realised we were almost working out a complete legal and judicial system, so we decided to leave it for another day, perhaps when the village council is convened. And then we started talking about how often the council should meet. It's never-ending."

"Did Mum tell you that we were thinking of starting a school for the younger children?"

"Yes, she did," her father nodded. "That's another thing for the village council to discuss actually." John sighed. "There are only a dozen children in the village, but obviously they need to continue their education. We just need to fit it in with all the other work."

"I was talking about it with Mum this morning. We thought that we could run it ourselves. Mum can do English, French and German. I can do biology, chemistry and physics and we thought that Rachel could teach geography. Her degree was geography, wasn't it? After that we just need maths and history, but I'm sure we could find someone to do them."

"Sounds good to me."

"Mum and I thought we could start running the lessons next week. Maybe at the village hall."

"That would be wonderful," her father said. "I'm sure Peter would be pleased that you're organising it yourselves."

They whiled away the rest of the cycle ride discussing how the school could operate and thirty minutes later they entered the village of Dowley. They turned down a small side road and presently John stopped at the entrance to a driveway which opened out into a car park in front of a cluster of small buildings.

"This is the place, isn't it?" he asked, glancing at his daughter. To their left was a Cotswold stone house, ahead was a low, ramshackle red-brick building and a small stone barn was to their right.

"Yes," Sophia nodded. "I remember that store room over there. That's where the targets and bows are kept."

They rolled their bikes across the car park to the main house and leaned them against the wall. John knocked at the door.

There was no answer. They looked through the windows, but couldn't see anybody. Everywhere was quiet, but John had the feeling that he was being watched.

"I'll try again," he said. "I'm sure there's somebody here."

John knocked once more and then heard a noise from behind them. He turned round quickly to see a tall grey-haired man and a young woman. They were standing in the middle of the car park and he wondered how they had appeared there so quietly. He also noticed that they were both holding bows, an arrow notched on the string but pointed at the floor.

"Can I help you?" the man asked.

John recognised him as the man they had come to see. The young woman must be his daughter. She looked around twenty years old now. She was tall and willowy like her father.

"My name's John Strachan. I don't know if you remember us, but my daughter and I came to your archery club a few years ago. We live in Brenscombe."

"I remember your daughter. She was promising, even after just two sessions, but she stopped coming." He sounded disapproving.

"You know how it is. Life is so busy and there's only so much time for out-of-school activities. We both enjoyed it though."

"It was good that you stopped coming so quickly. I wouldn't have wanted to waste more time on you if you were going to give up in the end."

"Oh, right."

"We only wanted dedicated archers. People who would be willing to put in the hours to get to the top."

John shook his head. "Look, I'll get to the point. The reason we're here is that I'd like to buy a bow from you."

"A bow? You?"

"Yes, do you think that would be possible? I have something to trade."

"What would you do with one of my bows?"

"Er ... I'd like a weapon both for hunting and for protection. You know, with things as they are right now."

"Get a stick."

"A stick?" John was confused.

"As a weapon. A bow isn't a gun. You can't just buy a bow and fire it at something. You need years of training. And what would you hunt?"

"I don't know. Rabbits perhaps?"

"Rabbits!" The man laughed, but it was more of a snarl. "You know how hard it is to hit something that small? When it's moving at full speed?"

"I hadn't really thought about it. I suppose I'd lie in wait and shoot when they're sitting still."

"Ha!" The man laughed again. "The movement of drawing your bow will set the rabbit off. You need to stand with the bow drawn. Do you know how much strength it takes to keep a bowstring drawn for a minute? Or ten minutes?"

This time John didn't answer. This wasn't going as he'd envisaged.

The man continued: "Do you know why our archers were so successful in the Hundred Years War? At Agincourt? Because they were trained from young boys. It was only after two decades of conditioning that they had the strength to draw the string on a longbow. You wouldn't even be able to move it a few inches."

"Surely you have simple bows that you can sell us. What about the bows that we used in the club when we came along for those two sessions?"

"Those are little more than toys that we use for beginners."

"Well, can we buy one of those?" asked John, starting to get a little exasperated.

"You'd have more chance of hitting someone with the arrow if you ran up and poked them with it. I don't want to waste any of my bows on someone who just thinks they can pick it up and fire it without any practice."

"I've brought food to offer as a trade."

"I don't need it."

"You don't need food?"

"I don't need your food. I can catch the food that I need."

"What if we promised to practice?" Sophia said suddenly. "How many hours a day would you like us to practice?"

The hint of a smile appeared at the man's mouth. "I said she had potential. Where do you live?"

"Brenscombe," Sophia replied. "Why?"

"I'll give you a beginner's bow if you tell me that you'll practice two hours a day."

"You'll give me a bow?" Sophia asked in surprise. "That would be great."

"And you don't want any of our food?" John said. "You'll just give us a bow?"

"I don't want any of your food and I'll give your daughter a bow if she tells me that she will practice for two hours a day. Not you, but your daughter. I'll even give her three arrows. But I have one other condition."

"What's that?"

"She has to hit one of my targets. Over in the shooting range now."

"What? Why?"

"I only have a limited supply of bows. I've started making some more, but they take time. Why should I waste one of my bows on someone from another village who can't use it properly? The people of my village might need these bows one day soon."

"Perhaps our two villages can provide protection for each other?" John suggested.

"That's the only reason that I am even considering this. You said you live in Brenscombe."

John looked at his daughter. "What do you think?"

"I'm happy to have a go," she replied. "What's the worst that can happen? I miss and he says no."

"Follow me." The man led the way around the main building to a large field. On the way, they picked up a bow from the store that Sophia had indicated earlier.

In the field were half a dozen targets set up at different distances. Each was a large straw wheel around five feet in diameter with a paper target tacked to the front.

The man tapped the ground with his own bow. "Stand here."

Sophia did as she was told and the man handed her the smaller bow. He placed three aluminium arrows in the ground beside her.

"You just have to hit the target with one arrow out of the three," he said. "You can choose your target. You can either hit the gold in the nearest target – that's thirty yards away – or hit any part of the furthest target, which is eighty yards away."

Sophia looked at the two options for a second. "I'll take the further target."

"The right choice," the man smiled. "Fire when ready."

It had been a few years since she had done this, but Sophia remembered the instructions the man had given her at the time. She notched the arrow on the string. She remembered which eye was her dominant eye, closed the other. She picked a point on a tree behind the target. The first arrow was going to be her range finder. The point she was aiming for was five yards above the target.

She loosed the arrow and watched it sail in a perfect arc across the sky. It fell a couple of yards short and a yard to the left.

"I thought my direction was okay," she said. "Why did it go left?"

The man simply smiled.

"The wind obviously," Reid interjected. He had simply watched in silence up to this point.

"There's no wind," Sophia replied.

"Not down here," her brother said. "Look at the tops of the trees. Actually there's a very slight breeze down here as well."

Sophia bent, picked a few blades of grass and tossed them into the air. They drifted slowly to the left.

She picked up her second arrow and selected a point slightly higher on the tree behind the target, and a yard to the right. She held for a second, breathed out and released the arrow, trying only to move her fingers and thumb.

The arrow arced towards the target. Sophia felt good about this one. It was on line but what about the distance? It accelerated towards the target as it lost height and thumped into the left leg of the wooden easel that held the large straw wheel.

"Yes," shouted John. "You hit it. Does that count?"

Sophia looked at the man, who simply shook his head.

She picked up the final arrow. She wasn't nervous, it was a simple case of picking a higher point on the tree behind. She now knew exactly how much higher, and maybe a hair to the right.

She loosed the arrow and watched it sail beautifully and mathematically towards the target. It landed with a thunk in the red circle, just outside the gold bullseye.

"What a shot!" shouted her father. "That's amazing."

The man snorted. "Is it amazing, Sophia?"

"Actually I was disappointed not to hit the gold. My two range finders should have been enough to work it out."

"You should concentrate on replicating everything exactly every time you shoot. Your stance moved an inch to the right on the last shot. Don't move your feet next time. Draw the bow until you feel the notch on the exact same point of your cheek, it's easier if you touch it to your lips. And your elbow was at a different height each time. Just slightly."

"Okay," she nodded, understanding the logic of it all.

"Nevertheless, that was good shooting." He shook her hand and then continued: "This is now your bow." He made a show of presenting it to her. "The three arrows are yours as well, but before you collect them from the target …"

He turned slowly to Reid who was standing a few yards away.

"… may I ask your name?"

"Er … Reid," the teenager replied nervously, surprised that the man had turned to him. "Reid Strachan."

"Good to meet you. I'm Neville Forrester. Would you like to take a shot, Reid? If you think you can hit the target in two shots I'll give you three arrows. If you hit it in one then I'll give you a bow and three arrows. But you have to choose what you're going for in advance. Oh, and if I give you a bow you have to commit to practicing for two hours each day like your sister."

Reid was silent for a few seconds and John was beginning to wonder if his son had heard the question.

"Am I allowed to talk to Sophia before I shoot?" he said finally.

Forrester nodded. Reid was quiet again.

"One," he said finally.

He stepped forward and took the bow from his sister. They debated the exact position for his feet while Forrester put an arrow in the ground in front of him.

Reid asked his sister what point she had been aiming for on the tree and they discussed how much adjustment there should be for his height. She explained how to notch the arrow and draw it back. He drew the string back gradually and then, without firing, released it again very slowly. He asked her if there was anything he should change about his movements, but she shook her head.

And then he was ready. He drew the bow back, took aim and released.

John, Sophia and Reid held their breath as the arrow arced through the sky, clipped the edge of the target and embedded itself into the turf behind.

Reid stamped his foot on the ground in frustration.

Forrester smiled at his annoyance. "You're obviously a perfectionist, but that's good enough for me," he said. "For today at least. I think you may have a different dominant eye to your sister. However I was more interested in the process that you went through rather than the final result. You had obviously paid attention and have a feel for the adjustments that are required. We'll get you a bow from the store in a moment."

"Thank you," Reid replied proudly.

"However, I've another question for you." The old man paused for a moment. "I'm looking for an apprentice. Someone who can help me make bows and ultimately become a bow-maker themselves. I actually have two apprentices already, but I don't think their hearts are in it. Their father arranged it on their behalf and I think they would rather be playing in the woods. I think you might have the right mentality, but I only want you if you're willing to commit wholeheartedly."

"What would you want me to do as an apprentice?" Reid asked. John was surprised that his son hadn't just declined immediately.

"You would be my assistant, initially just fetching and carrying, but looking and learning. Then I'll set you to making arrows. Selecting good wood, fashioning it, fletching the feathers. Then the same process with the bow, I'll teach you about the wood, the string, how to create different types of bows, longbows, short bows for firing from horseback."

"Can you teach me to shoot as well?"

"Absolutely, I would want to instruct you for an hour each day with another hour of practice on your own. You're already over six feet but with three years of growth yet and you have a large frame. Your muscles are small but that we can improve. We might be able to turn you into one of the few men in modern-day England who can draw a full length longbow."

"Can *you* fire a longbow?"

"Barely. I started too late. It's nearly too late for you, but with hard work who knows?"

Reid turned to his father. "What do you think, Dad?"

"It's up to you. I think it would be a good trade, even if the world comes to its senses."

"Could I come home each evening? It's not too far to cycle each day, is it?"

"Of course you should come home. Your mother wouldn't stand for anything else."

Reid turned back to Forrester. "Can I think about it?"

"Perhaps I can make an alternative suggestion: how about a one month trial? For both of us. You can decide if you wish to continue or, if you're not up to scratch, I'll suggest that you stop."

Reid considered this suggestion for a moment. "Okay."

"We'll start on Monday. You get weekends off, but you still need to do your practice."

Forrester reached out a hand and Reid shook it.

-o-o-o-

"You did what?" said Emilia that evening. "It sounds to me like you've sold our youngest son into slavery in exchange for two bows and a handful of arrows."

"It's an apprenticeship. He'll be learning a trade."

"How much is he getting paid?"

"He's not being paid anything."

"That's slavery."

"No, it isn't. In fact hundreds of years ago, fathers actually had to pay for their sons to be apprenticed to a master craftsman. Anyway I said it was up to Reid. It was his choice."

"He's too young to make a decision like that. He can't even tidy his room."

"Emilia, I know he's your baby." John put a hand on his wife's shoulder. "He'll be okay though."

"What if he gets attacked on the way home?"

"The road just runs from Brenscombe to Dowley. There can only be people from one of the two villages on the road, but just in case there are problems, on the way back today I showed him the footpath through the woods."

"Will you take him to Dowley on Monday?"

John sighed. "Yes, okay."

"And fetch him at the end of the day?"

"Okay, but just Monday. I'm not going there and back twice every day. I'm forty eight years old, you know."

"And why didn't you bring the food back? I thought you said he didn't want it."

"His daughter, Caitlin, said she wanted it. She was silent the whole time, but just as we were about to leave, she said that she was bored of rabbit."

"You gave him half of our food and our youngest son."

"It was about a hundredth of our supplies and he has to grow up one day, Emilia."

His wife sighed and looked out of the window. "I know, John," she nodded, after a few seconds. "It's just that I didn't think it would be for a couple of years."

"He'll be okay."

John put his arm around Emilia and she laid her head on his shoulder. "You promise he'll be alright?" she said quietly.

"Yes, of course. What could possibly go wrong between here and Dowley?"

6. Man Of The People

It is important to understand your enemy, to climb inside the mind of your opponent and look at the world through their eyes. Our first enemy was an unassuming, yet intelligent, man who wanted to create power for himself, which ultimately represented a threat to our community. We know how this all began because one of his people joined our tribe, became Brenscombe.

This is the story as seen through the eyes of our enemy and it will be a valuable lesson for you all. We thought we were ready so we sat there like cows waiting for it to rain.

Nigel Barkley was an accountant by trade, but he thought of himself as much more than that: an experienced advisor who could provide important financial help to businesses across many industry sectors. He had built up a small practice with three junior staff and then couldn't believe his luck when a larger firm, which was looking to expand, had offered him three times his annual turnover to buy the business – along with a partnership in the merged firm.

He only stayed with the new, combined business for a couple of years. Despite the partnership, it didn't feel like *his* business anymore and, with the pay-off and half a dozen rental properties amassed over the years, he had enough money to support his family. Coincidentally, during this restless period, a friend in a local political party said they were looking for businessmen to stand at the upcoming local elections.

Nigel was never particularly politically-minded, but he felt it might be good to put something back into the community – and it would look good to his friends – and so, two days after his fifty-first birthday, he was elected to the Kingsholm & Wotton seat of the Gloucestershire county council.

Local politics was even more tiresome and fruitless than he had expected and four years later he decided to call it a day. He had done his bit, he felt, and that was that. He looked forward to a little more golf and tennis with his friends – that was until the post of Mayor of Gloucester became free due to the death of the incumbent.

He was persuaded to take the largely ceremonial role for just six months until the next mayoral election, on the basis that he would only have to work a day a week, but be paid for three. It was too good an opportunity to turn down – which is why he was the man in charge when the triple-dip recession turned into a catastrophic global economic meltdown.

In the last few days before the power cuts he was working eighteen hours a day as, one by one, the county councillors disappeared off to look after their own problems. He tried in vain to resolve hundreds of competing issues, from un-collected refuse to blocked drains to hospital shortages. He felt like the boy at a party running around in circles trying unsuccessfully to find an empty chair when the music stopped – who was then asked to keep a hundred plates spinning on the ends of sticks.

When the electric companies finally went on strike, he breathed a sigh of relief. No more emails, no more phone calls, no more anything for a few days.

Nigel spent that time with his family, but then soon realised he hadn't been able to secure a future for them. He had been too busy with the county's problems to set aside any reserves of food for his wife and three children.

One night at the start of April his wife and eldest son, Harry, sat with him in the lounge discussing their problems by the light of one of the last three candles which they owned. His two other children, both young teenagers, had already gone to bed.

"We've nearly run out of food, Nigel" his wife said snappily. "You're the Mayor – can't you do something?"

"I've told you dozens of times, it's a largely ceremonial role. It would be nice if it was like five hundred years ago – then I would be in charge of the city guard and could order them to take some food from the local peasants and give it to me."

"You can't do something like that, Dad," his son said disgustedly. Six months earlier Harry had completed his maths degree at Leeds university and since then had been looking for a job, although his father had yet to hear of any interviews. It was too late for that now of course.

"Obviously I can't in this modern era of political correctness. I'm just saying it would be nice if a Mayor actually had some power."

"What are the real government doing?" his wife asked. "Surely they must have emergency source of electricity that would last for months. They must have plans in place for this sort of thing. You know, if an enemy country attacks and blows up all the power stations."

"I imagine they do, but they certainly didn't share those plans with the Mayor of Gloucester."

"Well, didn't they send some kind of message or instructions?"

"We didn't hear anything other than what was on the television. The prime minister with his platitudes about all being in it together. I bet he has plenty of food on his dinner plate tonight."

"What about the army?"

"What *about* the army?" Nigel sighed.

"They must still have guns and bullets."

"I'm sure they do, but there's no enemy. What do you want them to do? Shoot all the bankers who caused this economic catastrophe? Actually I'm quite open to that particular suggestion. If one was sitting here right now and I had a gun …"

"They should stop all this unrest. Put men on the street. Actually where have the police gone? They should be stopping the looting in the shops."

"I went to see the Chief Constable at his house a couple of days ago, but he said there was nothing he could do. The union had declared an indefinite strike until their members received their pay. The police union are one of the more militant, unsurprisingly."

"So we're all in the dark? Literally and figuratively." Even by candlelight, Nigel saw that his wife was quite pleased with that one.

"We saw situations like this in other countries before our power went, didn't we?" Nigel replied. "Greece, Spain, Italy, France. Africa, Asia, everywhere. The government was theoretically still in control, but it was every man for himself outside of the nucleus."

"Do you think there are any countries that are still okay?"

"Even Germany and USA were affected. Every industry was going on strike there as well. I'm sure electricity wouldn't be too far behind. To be honest, I would imagine that the only countries not affected might be the ones under military control. North Korea perhaps. Or places like Iraq and other Arab states."

"North Korea could invade us while we're in this state."

"They could in theory," Nigel sighed, "but they still need our staff in our power stations to run things. And they don't know where they live." He smiled at the idea of a North Korean officer walking round Gloucester knocking on doors.

"Somebody needs to do something."

"Like what?" Nigel sighed once more.

"Anything. The people need a leader to tell them what to do."

"And you think that's me?"

"Why not? You're the Mayor."

"I told you, it's largely ceremoni – "

"So you keep saying. Do you think Henry V said his role was largely ceremonial at Agincourt? No, he said attack the bloody French. Do you think Winston Churchill said his role was largely ceremonial in the war? No, he said we should fight them on the beaches."

"But that's different. Their roles *weren't* largely ceremonial. They actually had power."

"Okay, what about Martin Luther King, Ghandi, Oliver Cromwell, Sir Bradley Wiggins."

"Bradley Wiggins?"

"Well maybe not Bradley Wiggins, but the others led by the force of their personality and people followed."

"She's right, Dad," his son chirped up. "Nelson Mandela."

"You keep out of it. Do you think you're the first university student to say the name Nelson Mandela? What can I do? Produce food out of thin air?"

His wife and son became silent. Nigel realised his voice had been rising. He was just about to apologise for his outburst when his son spoke again.

"I've been wondering …" Harry said. "Do you think there's still any food at that Morrisons distribution centre?"

"What are you talking about?"

"That place where I did a few weeks' work before Christmas. It's the distribution centre for all the supermarkets in the county, isn't it?"

"Bloody hell," said his father, sitting up. "You're right. It's actually the hub for all the Morrisons stores between Bristol and Birmingham. And all the way over to Wales. I was on the planning committee that approved the building plans a few years ago."

"They had a lot of food there," said Harry, "but nobody even knows it's there. I didn't until I worked there."

"You're right. It's just a series of huge, nondescript warehouses with no windows." Nigel thought for a moment. "Surely the people who worked there must have taken the food by now."

"It's a big place. A few people can't have taken it all."

"There might be something in what you say. If there is still food there, then we could set up a system to distribute it methodically." Nigel didn't speak for a few seconds while he thought it through. "But we can't just open it up. People will loot it like everywhere else. We need security guards and then we can do it properly."

"What a good idea, Harry," his wife said.

Nigel ignored her. "And we can use this to kick-start the long-term strategy. If we initiate a new system of government using food as the basis of the power, then we can get things going in an orderly fashion in the countryside around Gloucester. There's obviously wheat growing in fields, cows producing milk, but we need a mechanism for people to bring it to market safely."

"I knew you could do it, Nigel."

"But first we need to check that the food is still in the distribution centre. Harry, first thing in the morning you're going to take me over there. You can show me where it is and together we can work out how to get in. And if it's still in place then we'll talk to the people of Gloucester."

"How are you going to do that?" his son asked.

"That's a good question. I'll have to think about that."

The more important question, Nigel thought to himself, was where he was going to find security guards and how he could get them to work for him.

After four years of interminable committee meetings to agree ineffective compromise agreements between a coalition council, he had come to firmly believe that power should be given to a single-minded individual who could drive new initiatives to a conclusion. That night as he lay in bed, Nigel Barkley decided, that with food as his mandate, he could be that individual.

7. Public Address

Uros Viduka had lived in England since he was ten years old. His father, Novak, an English teacher in Yugoslavia, had read Laurie Lee's Cider With Rosie and, twenty years ago, he brought his wife and young son on a long summer holiday to see the idyllic Cotswolds that he had read so much about.

Of course the Cotswolds presented the Serbian family with endless days of rain, but at least Novak had the opportunity to drink a pint of cider in The Woolpack in the Slad valley and they visited many of the other locations mentioned in the Laurie Lee classic. However, a few days before they were due to return home the simmering Balkans conflict had boiled over to such an extent that the United Nations sent in a peacekeeping force.

The peace-loving teacher could see what was going to happen to his home country and decided to seek asylum in Gloucestershire. One Monday morning he presented his family at Shire Hall in Gloucester to the consternation and bewilderment of the young girl on reception.

Three years – and half a dozen government-funded court cases later – the Viduka family was at last granted UK citizenship, just a few months before the final throes of the Balkan war.

However England was not the beautiful haven that Novak Viduka had imagined for his wife and son. For those three long years, the county council placed the family in the cheapest accommodation possible, in an undesirable suburb of Gloucester.

In this small, under-privileged community, the young Uros had learned the hard way that might was right. A desire to fit in had soon given way to a need to be top dog among the local youths. His father was distraught at seeing his lovely, polite, well-educated son grow into a thug who refused to go to school and prowled the streets of Gloucester during the night. By the time Uros was fourteen years old, he been arrested by the police on half a dozen occasions.

Uros, in turn, despaired of his father who, unable to find any other employment during the long legal battle, had worked for the city council, initially as a waste disposal labourer. Novak worked hard, as he always had, and soon found himself promoted sideways to the parks department where he cut the lawns and tended the flowerbeds. Gardening was one of his passions and, despite the low pay, this new role suited him.

Uros, however, saw the job as too menial for a man of his father's education and up-bringing. Father and son constantly argued about the way the other conducted his life. Novak's wife, Elena, attempted to perform the role of UN peace-keeper but to no avail.

Shortly after his seventeenth birthday, Uros moved out of the family home to share a house with five of his friends. And now fourteen years later, he hadn't spoken to his father since an argument six years ago. Uros couldn't even remember what the quarrel had been about, but it had been the last of many.

Still living in the same council house with the same friends, Uros woke shortly before midday and realised he was hungry. The last thing he had eaten was a packet of biscuits the previous evening, the final item from the secret store of the Pakistani shopkeeper that he had beaten up a few days before. He hadn't intended to kill the man, but it had happened somehow.

Lying in his bed, staring at the ceiling, he wondered if other shopkeepers had a similar hidden treasure trove. Perhaps he should find out and he knew just the place to start.

His housemates were still asleep after drinking the remains of a barrel of beer stolen from a pub in the city centre the previous night and he left without waking them. Food was in short supply so why share it? His route happened to take him past the steps of Shire Hall just as a man with bald head, glasses and thin moustache arrived at the top of the steps and started speaking in a loud voice. Uros smiled as the man attempted a presidential style speech to half a dozen bewildered people passing by, all of whom tried to avoid catching his eye.

He decided to stop and listen. This should be fun.

"People of Gloucester," the man started loudly, glancing around. Uros smirked as the passers-by averted their eyes from the madman and hurried on. "I am your Mayor, Nigel Barkley."

That made three or four of the people stop and look up at him. Buoyed by this small success, Nigel shouted the words that he knew would appeal to the others.

"I know you need food." The remaining people stopped and looked at him. Uros now looked at the young man standing beside the speaker. He wondered if it might be his son, yet to lose any hair. The young man was obviously nervous, wondering how this speech was going to turn out.

The word "food" seemed to have carried magically and another dozen people filtered out from alleyways, buildings and side streets.

"I can provide you with food," the orator shouted, warming to his task. Everyone in the small crowd stepped forward. Uros smiled as the man's son involuntarily took a step backwards at the top of the steps and then slowly moved forward once more to stand alongside his father. "But I need your help."

Uros sat down on a bench. This might be worth listening to.

Ten minutes – and a lot of words – later, the Mayor ended on his final message. "Tell all your friends that I will be here at midday every day to give you the latest news. Thank you for listening. Those that wish to help please come up and see me."

The small crowd dissipated as quickly as it had gathered. Only Uros remained, still sitting on the bench opposite the steps. He smiled as Nigel Barkley watched the people walk away. Nobody had stepped forward to work with him to build a new future. He wasn't surprised.

"Well, Harry, the people have voted with their feet," Nigel murmured to his son. "Pathetic individuals that they are."

"We could go round the streets asking people for help."

Nigel didn't answer. He watched the last remaining man, rise from his position on the bench opposite and start walking over. "Just a minute, perhaps we have a taker."

"Do you really have food?" Uros asked when he reached the top of the steps. He was taller that Nigel by a few inches and his tone was slightly threatening, but perhaps everybody was like that at the moment? Nigel didn't care, he had the power.

"I do, but, as I said, I need help to distribute it fairly."

"Oh yes, it needs to be done fairly," Uros smiled. "How much help do you need? I have some friends."

"What sort of friends?"

"Just some lads I share a house with."

"What's your name?"

"Uros Viduka." He waited for the inevitable question about his name.

"I'm pleased to meet you, Uros," Nigel pronounced the name correctly, much to Uros' surprise, and held out his hand. "My name is Nigel Barkley. What do you do for a job? What did you do?"

The handshake gave Uros a second to consider his answer. "I'm a gardener. I work for the council in the parks department, cutting the lawns and tending the flower beds."

"You're a gardener?" Nigel looked him up and down. Uros was tall, maybe six three or six four, his walk over to the steps just now had been more of a prowl and the man obviously had power in that slender frame, but it was the eyes that intrigued Nigel. Over forty years of watching people's expressions, in order to win new business or to assess an opponent's position in a negotiation, he flattered himself that he understood people. This man's eyes drilled into him. Uros looked straight at him, straight *through* him maybe, like he felt Nigel Barkley to be of little consequence.

Nigel turned to his son. "Would you mind locking up my office please, Harry?" He tossed the key to his son.

"Let's sit down a minute, Uros." Nigel sat down on the top step and waited for Uros to join him. He wanted the taller man to come down to his eye level.

When Uros sat down beside him, he looked him in the eyes and said: "You're not a gardener. What do you do really?"

Behind them, Harry had just stepped inside the grand front doors of Shire Hall, but on hearing this he paused and listened.

Uros smiled. "What do you think I do?"

"If I asked to see your hands, I'm sure you wouldn't have any dirt under your fingernails."

Uros didn't reply, his face giving nothing away.

"You don't look hungry to me," Nigel continued. "Not like the other people who were here a minute ago. Their eyes conveyed a different message to yours."

"You made a mistake in your pretty speech just now," Uros retorted. "You appealed to their better nature, but it's every man for himself now. You dangled a carrot in front of them, but you should have dangled a larger juicier carrot for those who might help you."

"And why did you step forward?" Nigel asked.

Uros shrugged. "Maybe I want to help my fellow man."

"I think you just want to help yourself." As he said the next words, Nigel studied the other man's face. "I think that once I tell you where this food is that you will believe you don't need me anymore."

Uros' expression didn't change. Not a flicker. But Nigel thought that was confirmation in itself.

"However you need to think about the long term," he continued. "I need someone like you – and your friends, if you feel that you can control them – but you also need someone like me. I have access to a large supermarket distribution centre, which can feed the city for a few weeks, but I want to use that to create some breathing space to build a system that will be in place for years."

Uros looked at him, waiting for more. He might as well hear the man out.

"If we can offer security to the people of the surrounding villages," Nigel said, "then we can ask for a contribution from them. In the past, they might have called it a tax, but I'd like to use the term contribution, which will of course be mainly in the form of food. The farms around Gloucestershire provide more than they can eat, but they need to know that they aren't going to be attacked constantly so that they can get on with the work in the fields."

Unaware that Harry was still listening to the conversation just inside the doorway, Nigel continued: "Here's the big, juicy carrot that I'm going to dangle in front of you. We will be at the centre of this system, in control of its success or failure. You can be my second in command, head of security, chief of the city guard, we need to come up with an official title that sounds friendly as well as secure. But the important point is that you will have as much food as you want. Not just for a few months, but if we do it right then for years. Forever."

"And why do I need you?" Uros asked. "Like you said, once I find out the location of this distribution centre. I can do all this myself. In fact I might start looking for it on my own this afternoon."

"You're obviously an intelligent, well-educated man, but I think you'll frighten people. Do you think that they'll trust you and hand over a fair proportion of their crops to you? You could probably work out how much is fair and all the other sums on which this new economy should be based, but do you want to? I'll do that. When they look at me they'll see the Mayor of Gloucester– or at the very least an accountant who is no threat, but is offering security."

Uros chuckled. "The sums would be easier if we let everyone in the city fight each other for a few weeks to thin out the population."

Nigel paused. "To be honest, the same thought has crossed my mind. I haven't actually worked it out yet, but it feels like the population in the city is too large to be supported by the current output of the local farms. Our farmers are geared up wrongly at the moment, growing large volumes of a few products for a global market. We need a wider spread of produce and more crops that people can eat, rather than rape seed oil and other products like that."

Uros thought for a moment. "You need an agricultural expert, who can advise the farms what to grow."

"Exactly," Nigel nodded. "I have a couple of business associates who might be able to help in that area."

"Let's say we do what you're proposing. What will we do if the real government sorts things out and they get the electricity back on, petrol in the pumps, food back in the shops?"

"Then we'll be heroes for having tried to create an interim solution and stopped the looting and fighting. You'll get a knighthood or something."

"Ha!" Uros laughed. "My mother would like that."

"So have we got a deal?"

There was silence for a minute as Uros considered the proposal. What did he have to lose? At the very least he would find out the location of the mountain of food and if Nigel didn't continue to deliver a successful scheme then he could walk away. Or he could make Nigel walk away.

Uros stood up and held out his hand. "You've got a deal, old man."

Inside the Shire Hall doors, Harry quickly headed off to lock up his father's office and didn't hear the final comments.

As Nigel shook his hand, Uros added: "And how many weeks are we going to leave it until we start distributing the food?"

"What do you mean?"

"The thinning out that I was talking about."

Nigel looked his new colleague in the eye and wondered if he wasn't biting off more than he could chew by getting into partnership with this man. Only time would tell …

8. Greater Than The Sum Of The Parts

We are one tribe, but many individuals who have their own thoughts, ideas, interests, dreams. What is it that keeps us together? For some it's simply habit or not having the wit to leave, but for most they recognise our community provides safety and they are happy to sacrifice some of their individuality for this. It's the price, and we're happy to pay it.

But sometimes, particularly in times of stress or doubt, individual feelings can spill out – with some people this happens more frequently than with others. This is fine if the damage is not permanent and it must be remembered that we are all responsible for repairing the damage. Each of you will occasionally need to ease tensions, help your friends or family get over an argument, re-build the sense of community. The leader of our tribe needs to do this more than most and it is his most important task, for if the tribe dissolves into its individual parts then all is lost.

Most people think a leader should be strong in battle, a fearsome warrior, a powerful force but the most difficult, yet most important job is talking to people and understanding their feelings. For our leader the price is greater than for any of us.

Your leader is the man who carries the village on his back.

John heard the back door slam and then saw his wife burst in through the kitchen door. She stood there with her hands on her hips.

"I just had an argument with Melissa," she said angrily. "In the middle of the village."

"What about?"

"Sandy's wife, Evelyn, told me that Melissa has refused to stand watch."

"After all that fuss about them taking a turn on the farm work? I thought we'd come to an understanding."

"We should kick them out," Emilia exclaimed.

"Come on, we can't do that," John replied calmly. "Did she give a reason?"

"She said she couldn't possibly stand watch for four hours in the middle of the night."

"Did you tell her – "

"Yes, I told her I did four hours a couple of nights ago. Stupid woman."

"What did she say to that?"

"She said that there was no point in women standing watch anyway, because we couldn't repel a force of dozens of bloodthirsty young men."

"Did you tell her that wasn't the point?" John said. "That the person on watch is just meant to raise the alarm if there's a large force?"

"Of course I did, John. She simply repeated her belief that men should stand watch and she couldn't possibly be out there in the cold all night. What are we going to do about it?"

"I don't know. It's difficult isn't it?"

"Well, I'm not doing watch duty again until she does. Nor will anyone else. Quite a few people were gathered round by the time I'd finished. Admittedly a couple took her side – wondering why we had a watch anyway – and others told her she should do it and they weren't going to until she did. She then stormed off, saying 'well I'm not doing it'."

"Did you hear that the watch turned somebody away yesterday afternoon?" John asked.

"Did they?"

"Yes, on the Briddip road. It was just a man and a woman who were walking to Swindon where the rest of their family live. I don't think they were any kind of threat but Ralph sent them around the village down Blacklanes. Anyway these people had been speaking to others in their area of Gloucester and many of them were aiming to get out of the city. I think we're going to see a lot more people here in the coming weeks."

"Well, somebody needs to talk to Melissa. What about having a word with Hamish?"

"Hamish has been stirring things up himself," John said. "Talking about the way the village is being run and trying to say that we're organising things badly. Anyway I think Melissa listens to Hamish least of all."

"That's probably true." Emilia agreed.

"Peter seemed to talk them round last time. I don't know how."

"Evelyn said Sandy has already told Peter. They were going to discuss the best approach. I think anybody who doesn't help out should be told to leave."

"Can we be that Draconian? What if there was something you disagreed strongly about? We need to think of another way of persuading them." He thought for a moment. "I'll tell you what: these doubters will soon change their mind when we start being approached by people wanting our food. It won't be long now, mark my words."

John hoped that he would be proven wrong, but he knew it was going to happen. As surely as birds flying south for winter or a dog lashing out when cornered. Nature takes its own course. It was just a matter of time.

-o-o-o-

It was Reid's fourth day as Forrester's apprentice. He hadn't realised it was going to be this hard.

Forrester was always shouting at him. Too slow, not good enough, take more care.

He had been quite looking forward to today: Forrester had told him that, for the first time, he was going to begin making arrows, but it was slow, painstaking work and nothing had gone right.

It was now mid-morning and he was only just finishing his second arrow shaft – and the first was in the bin. It hadn't been up to standard and Forrester had simply snapped it in half. Reid took longer over his second attempt and he was now beginning to think that it looked okay.

Reid stopped sanding the thin shaft of wood and took it over to Forrester's workbench, where he was working on the initial stages of a bow.

"Neville?" he said nervously. "How's this?" He placed the arrow shaft on the workbench.

Forrester looked at it for a second, picked it up, snapped it in half and threw the pieces into a large wicker basket beside his workbench. "No," he said curtly. "Try again."

The man returned his attention to his bow.

Reid didn't move. He didn't know what he was doing wrong.

"You're still here," said Forrester, not looking up from his work.

"I don't understand what was wrong with that arrow."

The bow-maker sighed and stood up from his work. "It wasn't straight. I told you earlier. An arrow needs to be completely straight otherwise it will veer off course in the air. You're aiming for a perfect cylindrical shaft which is the same diameter all the way along. Later we'll talk about tapering the fletched end to move the centre of gravity forward, but for now just give me a perfect cylinder."

"It looked straight to me," Reid said plaintively.

"It wasn't. Next time roll it on your workbench. You'll see the kinks more obviously then."

Reid trudged back to his bench and selected a long, slender stick from a basket on the floor. It was fairly straight already, but with a few knots and bumps where leaves had started to grow out of it. He measured its length. Forrester had told him that he only wanted arrows that were as long as the distance from his shoulder to his wrist.

He set to work and for the next hour he trimmed and sanded the stick until it was a perfectly cylindrical shaft of wood. He frequently rolled the arrow on the workbench and realised that his teacher had been right – the shaft initially bumped and jumped its way across the tabletop, but after a while he managed to make it roll true.

He looked up at the clock on the wall. Nearly lunchtime. Might as well go for it.

He walked over to Forrester's workbench and placed it in front of him. The man looked at the arrow, paused from his work and studied it more closely. "Not bad," he said to Reid's relief.

Forrester picked up the arrow and turned it over. He suddenly stopped and said: "No."

"What's wrong? It's okay isn't it?"

"Look at this knot here in the middle. It runs almost the whole way through the shaft. It's a weakness and it could simply snap as you pick the arrow out of the quiver. There's no point in finishing it." Forrester snapped the slender piece of wood in half and threw the pieces into the large wicker basket. Reid felt like a part of him had been broken in two – he had worked all morning and had not created a single successful arrow.

Forrester must have seen the look in his eyes because, for the first time, he offered some words of encouragement. "You did a good job on that shaft."

"Why are we using twigs anyway? Aren't they all going to have bits like that in them?"

"I'll tell you what, this afternoon I'll let you use some other sections of wood. These are pieces 1cm square that I've cut from sheets of wood that I bought a few months ago. However I warn you, this means that your starting point is harder. They are obviously cuboid in shape and you need to shave off the corners all the way down the shaft. It's more work but the end result is higher quality."

"Why didn't I use those from the start?"

"I'm not going to waste my good bits of wood on your first attempts. It takes time to cut them and I only have so much wood. In any case, we we're going to need to use those long, thin sticks in the future." The man glanced up at the clock and dusted his hands together. "Right, let's break for lunch. You get something to eat while I look for Barnaby and his brother and then we'll do an hour of training."

Barnaby and his younger sibling, Dominic, were the other two apprentices that Forrester had mentioned in their first meeting, but Reid had yet to lay eyes on them. Not that he blamed them for never turning up. Neville was a slave-driver.

He sat on the step outside and ate his sandwich, which was made from bread that his mother had baked that morning. Tuna again. The bread was nice, but he wished his father hadn't stockpiled so many tins of tuna.

Reid sighed. He wasn't actually looking forward to the training. Strangely, he hadn't actually been allowed to use any arrows yet – in fact on the first day he had spent an hour with Forrester simply going through the motions without even a bow. This was followed by an hour of 'practice' on his own, which on that day had simply been repeating the motions in the workshop as Forrester occasionally looked up from his work to point out his deficiencies.

Reid finished his sandwich and sat back for a few minutes peace. It was a lovely spring day, the sun shining and a crisp, clear freshness to the air.

"Come on then," came the voice of Forrester as he rounded the corner of the workshop building. "We'll forget about Barnaby and Dominic – again. Let's get going."

They went out to the field.

"Fifty press-ups," Forrester commanded.

Reid sighed and did as instructed. Unlike the first day, he was now able to complete the fifty without stopping.

"Have you been doing fifty every morning and evening at home?" Forrester asked him the same question every day.

"Yes," Reid nodded.

"And have you found some weights?"

"Sort of. We've got a bag of eight boules and I'm using that."

"Boules? French bowls?"

"They're quite heavy actually. Especially when you've lifted them for the fiftieth time."

Forrester simply handed him a bow.

"Show me that you remember what I said yesterday," he said simply.

Reid sighed internally once again and for the next hour they went through the motion of drawing the bow repeatedly, his teacher tweaking his position with a word or a tap of from his own bow.

"Right," said Forrester at the end of the hour. "Carry on practicing until I call you."

"When are you going to let me fire arrows, Neville?"

"Do you think this is interesting for me? You can have an arrow when you get everything right."

"But I'm doing everything you say."

"Yes, but you're not doing it without me saying it." Forrester shook his head. "You're lucky, you know. The South Koreans are the finest archers in the world and do you know why? They start them at the age of five and they're not even allowed to hold a bow until they're ten years old."

"Why do they bother doing it?" Reid shook his head in wonder.

"Because they have discipline." Forrester walked away to the workshop, leaving Reid to practice.

An hour later, the bow-maker called him and set him back to work preparing arrow shafts. He provided Reid with some 1cm square sections of wood and showed him how to file away the corners. He then left his apprentice to sand the shaft as he had done during the morning.

Reid spent a long time preparing the arrow, rolling it on the workbench surface to find any deficiencies and then sanding again.

Mid-way through the afternoon he was considering putting his head in the lion's mouth once again and taking the arrow shaft to his master, when the workshop door opened and two teenage boys entered.

"Hi Nev," said the elder boy. He was short but looked the same age as himself, Reid thought, and had wild, curly, blonde hair and a freckled face. The other boy had similar features but looked a couple of years younger.

"Barnaby and Dominic Deane as I live and breathe," said Forrester in a tired voice as he looked up from his work. "To what do we owe this pleasure?"

"We've come to work, Neville," replied Barnaby with a grin.

"You should have been here four days ago then."

"My father needed us to do some work for him."

"So why did Caitlin see you up in Ostrich Woods the other day?"

"We were collecting wood for my dad."

"She thought that you and Dom were playing hide-and-seek."

Barnaby grinned again. "We were just making the work more interesting."

"My arrangement with your father was that you would be here Monday to Friday. If you don't want this apprenticeship that's fine. There are others that are willing to put in the hard work. Let me introduce you to Reid, he started this week."

Barnaby turned to look at Reid, seeming to notice him for the first time. He looked him up and down and stepped forward to shake his hand. "It's an honour to meet a hard worker," Barnaby smiled.

"Right," said Forrester. "Let's get to work. Reid, you come and use the end of my bench. Barnaby and Dominic can share that one. Arrow shafts, boys. Shout if you get anything half-decent."

Reid gathered his tools and the arrow shaft on which he had been working and moved over.

As he placed the shaft on the tabletop, Forrester picked it up and examined it. "Not bad," he murmured, mostly to himself.

"Look at this shaft, Barnaby," Forrester announced, holding it up in the air. "Reid has only been here four days, in fact this is his first day working on arrow shafts and look what he's produced. You two have been here four months – when you can be bothered to turn up – and he's already better than you." He tossed the piece of wood to Barnaby, who glanced at it briefly.

"That's wonderful work, Reid," Barnaby said, not looking at it, his eyes instead on Reid. He wasn't grinning now. Barnaby threw the arrow shaft back to Reid.

"Get back to work," Forrester said.

All four of them worked hard for the remainder of the afternoon, in which time Reid created two more arrows, one of which Forrester simply snapped without a word and dropped into the basket. The second passed his high standards and was set alongside the first success on the workbench.

At last five o'clock arrived and the bow-maker announced: "Let's call it a day."

Barnaby and Dominic simply downed their tools and headed out. Reid cleared the sawdust and shavings into a wooden box on the floor at the end of the workbench as he had been instructed on his first day and laid his tools neatly in a line alongside the arrow shaft that he had just started.

"I like a man who keeps his bench tidy," smiled Forrester. Reid thought it was the first time he had seen the man smile.

"So," said the bow-maker, "don't forget to do your exercises tonight and I'll see you tomorrow."

Reid promised he would remember and headed out of the workroom. He walked over to his bike, pulled it away from the wall and sat on it. It was only as he started to pedal, and the front wheel skewed over to the right, that he noticed that the front tyre was flat. He glanced behind him and saw that the back tyre was also flat.

Oh no, he thought, *two punctures*. He was going to have to walk home.

As he lifted his leg back off the bike, he heard giggling from behind him and turned around to see Barnaby and Dominic looking at him over the top of a dry stone wall which ran along the side of the driveway.

"Nice work, eh, Reid?" shouted Barnaby and the two boys ran off over the field, laughing to themselves.

Reid sighed and looked down at the tyres. Barnaby had obviously let them down. He pumped up the front tyre again and waited a few seconds. It seemed okay so he pumped up the back tyre as well.

After waiting a short time, he squeezed both tyres again. They seemed fine so he finally set off, hot and bothered from the effort.

All the way home, Reid muttered to himself crossly. This apprenticeship in Dowley was no fun, the work was soul-destroying, the archery practice was stupid and now there was an annoying boy who was making his long journey home even more hard work.

What's the point? he thought to himself. *I'm not going back tomorrow.*

A dozen times he had the same thought as he pedalled along the hilly road back to Brenscombe, but when he was finally there he had calmed down a little.

When his mother asked him how his day had gone he simply said "okay", went straight to his room and practiced the motions of drawing a bow for an hour. Perhaps tomorrow he would be allowed to use an arrow if he did everything right.

9. Power Corrupts

Gloucester is not a bad place, it's simply that our enemies came from there at this time.

Two thousand years ago a people called Romans conquered much of the known world and created a settlement called Glevum where the city stands today. Its location was important as it offered the most southerly crossing for the river Severn and therefore the city was a significant trading point for England and Wales.

Gloucester will rise to prominence again when the world settles down, but for a time it represented a threat to our way of living and I will never feel easy there. Simply the word "Gloucester" sends shivers through me and it always will.

Nigel Barkley sat back and dabbed the corners of his mouth with a napkin. That was a delicious piece of ham. He had always liked a good, thick slab of ham, hand-carved, not the paper-thin slices that were usually offered up in a packet.

He was sitting in his office in Shire Hall, eating the hearty lunch that his wife had packed up for him that morning. His wife had been happy over breakfast, chirpy even, and it was all down to having a little food in the cupboards. Well, a lot of food actually.

His wife now thought that he was fulfilling the role of Mayor in a suitable fashion and she seemed to be looking at him differently, more appreciatively.

Little did she know that it was only the Barkley family and Uros Viduka and his friends that were benefiting from the stockpile of supermarket supplies that had been unearthed. Nigel had also been amazed to find that a generator was still running the refrigeration units in the distribution centre. Unfortunately the diesel was now starting to run low so they were going to have to find some more if they could.

There was a knock at the door, Uros walked in without waiting for an answer and slumped into the chair opposite. Nigel was actually surprised that he had knocked.

"That was the biggest one yet," Uros sighed. He looked more dishevelled than normal and tired, like he'd been running.

"Tell me the numbers," Nigel said simply.

"There were perhaps a hundred people involved in the riot. Mostly men, but some women and teenagers."

"What caused it this time?"

"I have absolutely no idea. It was on Southgate, by the shops. Maybe somebody thought there was food in one of the shops? By the time we got there it was already in full swing."

"Did you intervene?"

"Only when it was starting to peter out. There are only a dozen of us, you know."

"I know," nodded Barkley. "I've already told you to sign up a few more."

"I've got Lee doing that. He picked out a few people in the riot today, the ones who seemed strongest."

"How many dead?"

"Fourteen. Twelve men. Two women."

Nigel grimaced. "We don't want to lose all the men. We'll need them when we start going round the villages."

"There are plenty more where they came from."

"What are you doing with the bodies?"

"You don't want to know."

"Actually I do. We don't want to create a health problem."

"We're taking them to the tip."

"The tip? The refuse centre over by Hardwick?"

"That's right."

"Well, make sure they get buried, not just dumped."

"Okay."

"I'm serious."

"I said okay," Uros said angrily. "You don't need to give me orders. Don't forget that we're partners. You're not my boss. I'll get Brett to round up a few people to do it. Anyway there was something else I wanted to tell you," Uros paused. "Brett heard from one of his friends that something is happening at Baxley Castle."

"What do you mean?"

"There's a rumour that somebody is setting himself up there with a small army."

"What do you mean an army? A real army with guns?"

"No, like we're doing here. Recruiting local people into some kind of small force. And they've taken over Baxley Castle."

"Are they a threat to us?" Nigel asked.

"I don't know."

"Baxley's halfway down to Bristol, about twenty miles to the south of here. That's far enough away for the place not to be a serious worry unless they're building something on a larger scale. How many men do they have?"

"I don't know."

"You don't seem to know much. Have you ever been to Baxley Castle?"

"No, it's just a place people go for a day out, isn't it?"

"Yes, well, it used to before all this. We went a couple of times when Harry was young. However it's a proper castle, not just a stately home or a ruin."

"Should we do something about them?"

"Nobody's going to get them out of that castle in a hurry, not with baseball bats and sticks. Can you send someone to find out what they're doing? Someone you trust so we don't get Chinese whispers. We need to know the size of their force and what their plans are."

"Okay, I'll send Brett."

"Brett's an idiot. We need to send someone who can ask intelligent questions and who's not going to look like a threat." Nigel thought for a moment. "Actually … I might send Harry."

"Can he walk twenty miles on his own?" Uros asked sarcastically. "He'll have to sleep rough for a night or two – if he makes it there without getting attacked."

"It's about time he toughened up. He should be here soon actually. I'll talk to him."

"If you're sure."

"This development has made up my mind about something – we need to move forward. It's been about two weeks since we found the distribution centre and I think there's only enough diesel to keep the generators going another week. If we can't find more diesel, then the refrigeration units are going to stop working and we might as well get the food distributed."

"We've been looking but no joy yet. All the fuel has either been used or burned."

"We might as well start sharing out the food in a week from now then."

"Just another week? There are still too many people around."

"We need to accelerate the process."

"We could kick off some riots ourselves I suppose," Uros mused.

"No, we need to encourage people to leave the city. That'll be quicker and less messy."

"How are we going to do that?"

"I'll make an announcement at midday tomorrow. We now get quite a lot of people turning up to my little speeches each lunchtime."

"What are you going to say?"

"I'm going to tell them I've heard there's food in Birmingham. I'll say the government is dishing out food."

"Sounds good," Uros nodded.

"Your job is to get things ready for when we start distributing the food here next week. I want to get people signed up to work for the city guard in exchange for food and I want everything to run smoothly. No more riots from next week. An orderly society. We're going to start to re-build. I'll start thinking about how we're going to work with the farms and villages around Gloucester."

"That's easy. We just tell them to give us some food in return for protection." Uros smiled to himself.

"No, we need to offer them more. We need to offer them a safe, well-structured environment for them to trade. Farmers will need to sell their produce or at least trade it for other goods that they need. To start with we need to provide a weekly market where they'll feel safe."

"That sounds like hassle for us."

"And we'll for a small contribution each time they come to market of course."

"That sounds more interesting," Uros smiled.

"It's a shame that money is now worthless," Nigel was speaking more to himself now. "We need some way of paying for goods and services, rather than simply trading chickens for wheat or eggs for cabbages." He looked out of the window thinking of a solution to the problem.

"I'll leave that one to you, Mr Mayor," Uros said and rose from his chair. "I'll come back tomorrow lunchtime and see what the stupid people of Gloucester think of your announcement that the government is giving out food in Birmingham."

At that moment the door opened and Nigel's son entered the room. "What was that?" Harry said, glancing from Uros to his father. "There's food in Birmingham?"

"You think he can get to Baxley and back on his own?" Uros headed out of the door, shaking his head and chuckling to himself. Harry looked back to his father.

"No, Harry," sighed his father. "We haven't heard anything."

"But I thought Uros just said …"

"That's what I'm going to announce tomorrow, but it's not true. We just have too many people in the city and I want to encourage some of them to leave."

"You're going to lie to them?"

"They'll be no worse off in Birmingham than here. In fact, there might even be some kind of normal society up there with food in the shops."

"You don't really think that, do you?"

"Well, it's possible."

"I don't like what you're doing, Dad," Harry said. "We've had access to the distribution centre for two weeks now and you haven't started giving it to the people who need it. Just Uros and his mates."

"We need time to get a proper system set up and guards to make sure the people don't cause a stampede."

"That sounded fair enough two weeks ago, but you haven't done anything about it."

"I've been here every day working through these plans," Nigel said, pointing at the papers on his desk. It was partly true – he wanted a system that would work for the long term but it was taking longer than expected to work it all out. "We're nearly there now."

"How much longer?"

"Just a couple more days. Uros needs to recruit some more guards."

Harry snorted. "They're not guards. They're thugs and you've put them in charge."

"I'm in charge."

"Until they don't need you anymore."

"Do you think I haven't thought of that?" Nigel smiled. "I know the kind of men I'm dealing with, but they're a necessary evil until I can replace them."

"How are you going to do that?"

"Wait and see, son. Now sit down a minute, I want to ask you to do something for me. Do you remember Baxley Castle?"

-o-o-o-

"I'm exhausted," sighed John as he slumped onto the sofa next to his wife. "I'm working harder now than I ever have before. Twelve hours every day. At least. And at weekends."

It was nine o'clock in the evening and John and Emilia were having a cup of tea in the lounge. The sound of laughter was coming from the rest of their family in the kitchen.

"What are they doing in there?" Emilia wondered.

"Playing some sort of game," her husband replied. "It's good to have Mark home again, isn't it? Reid and Lewis love having their big brother around. Sophia too for that matter."

"You know, I quite like this new way of living," Emilia said, sipping her tea. "Helping out on the farms and then working with the kids in the vegetable garden and planting things in the greenhouse."

"We'll need to start getting some wood collected for the winter soon. They can help out with that as well. We'll need a lot if we don't have central heating."

"Don't forget to get that windmill working."

"I know," John sighed. "I was talking to Neil while we were on watch today and he said he would come and take a look at it." John took a sip of his tea. "Oh, that reminds me. Somebody came up to the village this afternoon and said they'd walked all the way from London."

"London? How long did that take them?"

"Two weeks he said. It was just one man on his own. Nice chap actually. I asked him what was happening there and he said it was the same as everywhere else. No electricity, no petrol, no food, people fighting each other for food. That's why he left. He said he was walking to the Brecon Beacons to be away from everyone else."

"That sounds like a good idea."

"I was tempted to invite him to stay with us. He looked like the sort of person who could look after himself. Obviously he must be if he'd walked all that way on his own. I offered him a bit of food and we ate while we chatted about what was happening in London."

"Did you ask if there is still any sort of government in place?" Emilia asked. "Surely there are people in the Houses of Parliament and Downing Street?"

"He said that the Houses of Parliament were one of the first buildings to be destroyed. People were protesting outside for weeks and then on the night when the electricity was cut it escalated. People broke in and set fire to the place."

"That doesn't sound good. I can understand their feelings but we still need a government."

"There are still people in Downing Street though. There was a huge military presence, lots of soldiers with machine guns and he thinks that the Prime Minister must still be living there. I know they've got all sorts of underground bunkers underneath Downing Street in case of an attack so presumably he can live there for months or years if he needs to."

"What about the rest of London?"

"It sounds like it's the same as everywhere else: anarchy. Apparently a set of army vehicles drives round occasionally. Not to restore order, but they're just going from one place to another. This man said that he talked to one of them one day and asked what was happening. They were outside a building in the City and he recognised one of the soldiers. An old school friend or something. The soldier said that they'd been tasked with taking all the gold reserves out of the banks to various military bases around the country."

"What about getting the electricity back on?"

"The soldier didn't know. He said he'd heard from another soldier that they were having lots of discussions in Downing Street about how to do it, but they couldn't agree. Some people wanted the army to run the power stations and others wanted to force the electricity company staff back to work. At gunpoint if necessary. There's still some petrol being shipped around the country by the army, but only for their own needs and it's only whatever we've got in the country at the moment. Nothing's coming in or out of course."

"It doesn't sound very promising." Emilia shook her head. "How could this all have happened so quickly?"

"This man said he'd heard from someone else that the world economy had been sabotaged deliberately. Well, it was in a bad way anyway, but a disgruntled ex-employee from one of the banks had set up a network of inter-connected financial dealings across the world. Then he pulled the plug on one of them and they all collapsed. Because of all the other problems around the world, they weren't able to recover the situation."

"This was all done by one man?"

"I don't know if it's true, but that's what he'd heard from a friend who worked at a bank. The guy who did it was running things via the internet from a remote Scottish island. The army are looking for him so they can try and understand what happened and get it sorted out."

"It's too late for that."

"It is. Far too late. I'm even more convinced now that we need to look after ourselves. Even if the government fixes things, it'll take years and we need to make sure we're self-sufficient in the meantime."

"Hopefully we'll have enough food if everything grows properly," said Emilia. "If I haven't done something wrong. I haven't grown peas and beans before. Or half of the other vegetables, for that matter."

"I'm sure it'll be fine," John smiled. "You're doing a good job and I'm sure they'll grow beautifully. But there's so much more we need to do. It'll be hard in the winter without fresh food. We need to preserve things, pickle them, dry them, salt them, like they used to in the old days. We need to learn how to do those things again."

"I could ask Frances. I'm sure she's done pickling."

"What are we going to use for shampoo and toothpaste when they run out? We'll need to learn how to make glass, crockery, clothes, shoes, weapons."

"More weapons? We've got the bows now, John."

"We've got a couple of weapons, but that's not enough. What if we get attacked by an army of fifty people? We could do with a blacksmith who can make swords, but then we need to get iron or steel from somewhere."

"Surely it's not all about fighting. Not everybody wants to fight."

"We also need a doctor, a dentist, all sorts of things like that. If somebody is ill, what are we going to do?"

"I hadn't thought of that." Emilia considered John's comment, the implications slowly sinking in. "Actually I wish you hadn't said that. What would we do if the children are ill or get hurt?"

"That's what I mean. There's so much that we need to do. I've been thinking about finding a doctor and asking if they want to come and live here in the village, but where would I go? And would they want to come?"

"I suppose it depends on their situation, if they have family."

"I've been wondering who we could ask … I used to play football with a doctor but I don't know exactly where he lives. The other side of Gloucester somewhere."

Emilia thought for a moment. "What about Yvonne Sibbald?"

"Yvonne? Of course – I should have thought of her. And she lives near here, doesn't she?"

His wife nodded. "On the edge of Prinswick."

John thought for a moment. "We could walk there in a couple of hours. It would be a fairly safe route as well, just through a couple of small villages. Do you think she might come?"

"Well, she would want to bring her daughter, Amelie. She's about twenty four now I think, but last I heard she was back at home with her. She's a doctor as well, qualified a couple of years ago."

"Two doctors. Even better."

"Actually, Yvonne would be great," Emilia said. "She's a general surgeon, which would be better than someone who just specialises in ears or bones or something like that. She's one of the leading surgeons in the area. And she could teach Sophia as well."

"That's what I was thinking. Sophia could work alongside her and learn from her. It's not medical school, but she'll still be learning."

"It's probably better than medical school. People have told me that Yvonne is really well thought of and Sophia would be actually doing the work, not just learning the theory."

"Do you think she might want to move to Brenscombe though?"

"It's worth asking her."

"I think we should go tomorrow. The sooner the better. I'm working on Peter's farm tomorrow but you could go with Mark."

"I'm on watch tomorrow," Emilia said.

"I wonder if we can swap it?"

"Sophia could go. Yvonne knows her of course. She went there half a dozen times to practice interviews for the medical schools."

"It might be better to wait until you're free, Emilia. Don't you think that you'd be more able to persuade her?"

"I think if Mark and Sophia are free tomorrow then they should go. I think Rachel's free as well."

"You're right," said John, standing up. "We shouldn't delay. I'll go and ask them. I'll ask them to set off first thing in the morning."

John walked into the kitchen.

10. Fetching Yvonne

Sophia, Mark and Rachel set off to Prinswick after breakfast the next morning. Rain was falling as they walked out along the road past the Parlane Farm, rain so fine it was almost mist.

"Did Dad tell you he's going out to bury food today?" Sophia asked. She glanced around at the dark clouds, took her hat out of her pocket and pulled it on over her long brown hair.

"Bury food?" her brother replied, confused. "What do you mean?"

"He's worried that we're going to be attacked so he's going to bury a stash of food at the end of the garden, some more in the field behind our house and he's even going to bury some cans down in Climperwell Woods."

"That's taking it too far," said Mark, smiling and shaking his head.

"He said the stash in Climperwell Woods is in case we have to abandon the house."

Mark laughed. "Typical Dad."

"He's been right about stuff up to now."

"He's like a squirrel."

"Did he tell you he's also going to look at the local reservoir?" Sophia asked.

"I thought he was meant to be doing a shift on the farm today. That's why *we're* going to get Yvonne, isn't it?"

"He's doing all this after his shift finishes. Haven't you wondered why we've still got water in the taps?"

"No," Mark said and then thought for a moment. "You're right though. Why is there still water coming out of the taps?"

"Dad said there's a covered reservoir somewhere between Brenscombe and Briddip, about half the size of a football pitch. The water gets pumped up into the reservoir from the water treatment works down near Gloucester and it feeds all the villages round here. But he thinks the water probably isn't being pumped up anymore. He's going to see how much is left."

"I thought the water was running a bit slowly yesterday," Rachel said thoughtfully.

"Dad thinks the reservoir might be running out," Sophia said.

"What are we going to do if there's no water?" Rachel asked.

"We'll have to get water from the stream down by Brenscombe Farm."

"That's half a mile away!" exclaimed Mark. "And uphill on the way back."

"You'll get fit then," his sister smiled.

"And should we be drinking water out of a stream?"

"We don't have much choice apart from using the rain barrels. Either way, we're going to filter the water through something first, like a pair of tights and then boil it."

"Perhaps we could set up more rain barrels," suggested Rachel.

"Dad said that, but he doesn't know where we could get them from."

"Good point," Rachel nodded. "We can't just go out and buy stuff anymore, can we?"

They walked past the end of the track that led to Parlane Farm away to their left. They were so busy talking they didn't look down the lane and therefore didn't notice Lewis emerge from the farmhouse and start walking up towards them. He had been helping Annie with the early morning chores again and was now heading home.

He frowned when he saw Rachel and his brother and sister. He realised that they were probably on their way to Prinswick and he was still annoyed. His father had said that he wasn't allowed to go with them – and his mother had given him a long list of jobs for the day – but why should Mark have all the fun?

When he reached the top of the lane Mark, Rachel and Sophia had already gone past, their backs towards him, heading down the road towards Cranwold. He watched for a moment, but they didn't look back. *I could just follow them to Prinswick,* he thought to himself. *Why not?*

"How long do you think it will take to get there?" asked Rachel, a hundred yards ahead, not aware that Lewis was watching them.

"Maybe a couple of hours," Mark replied.

"It's a shame we can't go on horseback," Rachel mused, pointing to a field on their right where a dozen horses were grazing.

"That's Langdale polo farm," Sophia replied. "I used to work there a couple of years ago, mucking out the horses and exercising them."

"I used to ride a lot when I was young," Rachel said.

"I didn't know that," Mark said, turning to look at his girlfriend. "If I'd known you were a horsey person …"

"What?"

"Well, you know what horsey people are like."

She laughed. "I haven't been on a horse since I was about fourteen. I rode every week for about eight years and then one day I just decided to stop. I can't even remember why now, but I wish I'd kept it up …"

They continued chatting as they followed the single track road where it dipped through Climperwell Woods and up the other side between fields of new wheat just starting to push up through the earth. The drizzle stopped and the sun edged through the clouds. After thirty minutes of brisk walking they arrived at the edge of the neighbouring village of Cranwold.

Mark looked around as they passed the sign announcing they were entering the village. "There are no guards," he noted.

They looked at the houses as they walked along, but everything was quiet.

"Maybe they don't have someone like your Dad to get them organised," Rachel suggested.

"Perhaps we should help Cranwold to set up a watch system," Sophia said, thinking out loud, "and the other nearby villages. We could explain how we've been running things. It would benefit us as well."

"How would it help us?" Mark asked.

"If all four of the villages around us have guards then we almost wouldn't need our own. Or we could provide guards for them. We'd be sharing the work, which would allow us more time for farming and other things."

"Good point," her brother nodded.

"I was already thinking that we're too small on our own. We need to form an alliance in case we're attacked by a large army or something."

"A large army? It's every man for himself at the moment."

"Right now, yes," she nodded, "but it's simply a matter of time until a feudal system springs up."

"A feudal system?" he exclaimed in surprise. "You mean kings and lords?"

"It might take a few years but it's bound to happen," Sophia said. "At the moment we're in a vacuum, but over the coming months little fiefdoms are going to be created all over the country. Wherever somebody has a way of gaining power, through force or a defensible position or maybe just because they've got food, then he's going to declare himself the lord of an area and pull together a bunch of people to help him – an army of friends or just people who have to do what he says in order to stay alive. That's how it was thousands of years ago and it'll happen again."

"You really think that could happen? In this day and age?"

"Absolutely. It's human nature. Isn't it obvious?" She looked at her brother. "And some leaders will be good, some will be bad. There will be battles over territory and ultimately one day there'll be a feudal system across the whole country again. They might not call themselves lords and kings, but in effect that's what they'll be."

"Aren't we still hoping that the government will get things going again?" Rachel said.

"Perhaps I could be a king," Mark joked.

By now, they were halfway through the sprawling village of Cranwold and Rachel realised they hadn't seen a single person. The village was scattered across a small valley, clusters of houses here and there.

"Mark," she said. "This place is quiet – where do you think everybody is?"

"It's strange, isn't it?" her boyfriend replied. "We haven't seen a single person, but I just have this weird feeling that we're being watched."

"They're all hiding in their homes," replied Sophia. "A couple of times I've seen a small movement at a window when somebody peeks out through the curtains to look at us."

"I think it's spooky," Rachel replied. "I'll be glad when we're out of this place."

They continued on through the village without seeing any other people and breathed a sigh of relief when they walked past the last house. The small road through Cranwold led up to the A46, the main Prinswick road.

"I think we're making good time," said Mark. "We should be there by midday."

"You're not cruel enough to be a king," his sister replied.

"What?"

"You said you wanted to be a king. It's easier to set yourself up as a ruler if you're prepared to be nasty and seize power through force. "

"I could be nasty if I wanted to be."

Sophia ignored his reply. "Instead you need a skill or trade that's worth keeping you alive. That's what Dad said. That's why he was so keen that Reid started his apprenticeship with Neville and one of the reasons why we're going to get Yvonne – so that she can train me up. It's all part of his master plan to provide some safety for his family. If a lord or king takes over our village then he'll be more likely to look after the people who are useful to him, those with a trade."

"Nobody's taking over our village. My trade's going to be swordsman." He grinned.

"You'll need a sword first," teased Sophia. "Actually you could become a smith and make swords. That would be a good trade."

"A smith … ?" Mark considered the suggestion for a moment. "No," he decided. "I'll use the swords, not make them."

"When we get back I'm going to suggest to Dad or Peter Parlane that we set up an alliance with Cranwold," Sophia said.

"You know," said Mark slowly, as they turned onto the main road. "I've still got this feeling that somebody's watching us."

"I can't see anyone," Sophia said, looking behind them. "Anyway there are no houses here."

"It's just a feeling. Like when we were back in Cranwold."

Rachel looked back along the road, but shook her head. "I can't see anyone either."

"When we go round this bend," Mark said. "I'll nip into the trees, circle back and see if anyone's there. You two keep walking."

They continued along the road and Mark quietly slipped into the woods. Sophia and Rachel tried to maintain the same pace and not look behind them.

Mark took up a position behind the trunk of a large beech tree near to the road and presently he saw a figure creeping furtively along.

It looked like a young man, moving cautiously, and he was definitely following them. In the darkness of the woods he couldn't make out the man's face, but saw that he was glancing around, obviously confused by the fact that he was now only following two people.

As the young man passed him, Mark jumped out and grabbed him from behind, putting his kitchen knife to the person's throat.

"Don't move," he demanded.

"Mark? Is that you?" the person replied. "Get off me, you idiot."

"Lewis?" Mark let go, pushing the figure away from him so that he could see who it was, but holding the knife ready, still not completely sure that it was his younger brother.

Rachel and Sophia heard the exchange and ran back up the road.

"Lewis?" Sophia said in surprise. "What on earth are you doing here?"

"Nothing."

"What do you mean: 'nothing'?" shouted Mark, clipping him around the back of the head. "Dad told you that you couldn't come with us."

"I don't see why you get to have all the fun," Lewis argued.

"Mum needs you to do jobs round the house," his sister said.

"Why should I do all the work while you're out on an adventure?"

"You're not coming with us," Mark said determinedly. "You have to go back."

"You can't tell me what to do."

"He can't go back on his own," Sophia interjected.

"Why not? He came here on his own. The turning to Cranwold is just back there and they're all hiding in their houses so he'll be safe. Then it's just a couple of miles back to Brenscombe."

"He's only sixteen and it's not safe to be on your own outside of the village. We should always travel in pairs at least."

"Well, he's not coming with us," Mark said defiantly.

"Why not?" Lewis asked petulantly.

"It might be dangerous," his elder brother offered weakly. "And I'm not going to get into trouble with Mum by letting you get hurt."

"I'll go back with him," Rachel offered.

Mark looked at her in surprise. "No, we might need you," he said. In reality he didn't want his girlfriend walking back through the countryside without being able to protect her.

"Sophia's right though," Rachel argued. "Lewis shouldn't travel alone."

The four of them debated the merits of the different options. Mark briefly considered allowing Lewis to accompany them to Prinswick, but finally decided he should stick with his original statement that Lewis should return home. Otherwise his brother would follow them again next time they went on a similar expedition. However, in the end, Mark conceded that Rachel and Lewis should head back together.

"You'd better look after Rachel, you idiot," Mark said to his younger brother sternly, poking him in the chest with his finger. "And don't muck about. Get home as fast as possible."

Rachel and Lewis started walking back up the road, while Mark watched them go. He still wasn't completely sure about splitting up the group.

"He's a bloody idiot," he muttered to Sophia as they watched them walk away. "I hope we're not going to regret letting them go back alone."

Mark and Sophia walked briskly down the deserted A46 for the next hour They reached their destination just before midday, the sun high above them, any remaining clouds having been burned away. It was a beautiful spring day in the picturesque Cotswold village of Prinswick. Except for the eerie silence.

"No guards again," Mark noted as they walked past the first few houses.

"It's as quiet as Cranwold," his sister replied softly.

Mark gestured to their left. "I thought I just saw someone in the window of that house."

Sophia followed his gaze. "I can't see anyone."

"He's gone now. It's all a bit unnerving again, isn't it?" He shook his head as if to dispel the feeling. "Anyway where does Yvonne live?"

"Just there," she pointed ahead of them. "The driveway on the left just after that lamppost."

They stopped at the end of the drive to look at the house, a large Cotswold stone building with an impressive, black-studded oak front door set inside a stone porch. The mullioned windows on the ground floor were dark. Upstairs the curtains were closed.

"Looks empty," Mark said.

"Did you see that?" Sophia asked suddenly. "I thought I saw a movement in the upstairs window. The one on the right."

"Let's just knock on the door, shall we?" Mark walked down the drive. Sophia followed him.

Mark pressed the doorbell beside the large oak front door. There was the faint sound of a chime inside but otherwise there was silence.

They waited.

Mark pressed the doorbell again.

Once more no response. He rapped on the thick wooden door as hard as he could. Nothing.

"Do you think she's gone out?" Sophia wondered. "Maybe I imagined the curtain moving upstairs. Or maybe it was the wind."

"Where would she go? She wouldn't be going to work anymore and any shops would surely be closed."

"To a friend's house perhaps?"

"Maybe she's scared to answer the door?" Mark suggested. "Why don't you shout through the letterbox and let her know it's you."

She shrugged and bent down to the letterbox. She called through: "Hi Yvonne, it's me Sophia. Sophia Strachan."

She stood up again and waited a short while. No reply, but after a couple of seconds Sophia thought she heard a small sound.

"Did you hear that?" she asked her brother.

"What?"

"A small scuffing sound."

"I didn't hear anything."

Sophia looked at the windows of the house. All quiet. "Maybe I imagined it," she shrugged.

Mark looked around at the nearby houses. "Why don't we ask the neighbours if they know where she is? If they'll answer the door, that is."

They walked back up the drive and along to the house which was to the right of Yvonne's home.

Mark knocked on the door. No answer. He knocked harder. Eventually a face appeared at the lounge window and looked out at them, an elderly man with white hair, a worried look on his face. The man assessed them carefully and then opened the window slightly.

"Can I help you?"

"We're looking for Yvonne Sibbald, your neighbour," Mark said, "but she's not answering the door. Do you know if she's still living there?"

"Why yes," the old man nodded. "I saw her yesterday. She was in her back garden and we had a brief chat."

"Can you think of anywhere that she might have gone? Friends in the village perhaps?"

"She certainly has plenty of friends in Prinswick. I suppose she could have called round to see somebody, but I think it's unlikely. Most people are staying at home. We spoke about that yesterday. Unfortunately we live on the main road here and over the last week there have been a few unsavoury incidents."

"What sort of incidents?"

"Some people passing through have been asking for food or a place to stay for the night and getting quite heated about it. There were a couple of rough looking men walking through this morning actually. They knocked on my door, but I didn't answer."

"Do you think they might have knocked on Yvonne's door?"

"I've no idea. But if they did, I'm sure she wouldn't have opened it. We also talked about this yesterday, how it's important to check who it is before you open the door."

"Perhaps we should just try knocking again." Mark wondered out loud. "Thanks for your help." He started to turn away.

"You don't have any food, do you?" the old man asked. "I can pay you."

"I wish I could help," Mark shrugged. "Sorry but I'm not sure there's much call for money anymore."

"I can give you some jewellery as payment. Either gold or silver."

"No, sorry. We only have a little food ourselves. Just enough for the day."

The man looked disappointed, but nodded and closed his window. Mark and Sophia walked back up to the road to consider their next move. They looked down the drive at Yvonne's house.

"We can't just go home," Mark stated.

"There are half a dozen shops in the village," his sister replied. "Shall we go and see if she's there?"

"That's pointless. They won't be open."

"What else can we do? Just sit and wait?"

"I'm going to knock on the door again," Mark said and moved to start walking down the drive.

"Hold on," Sophia said suddenly, grabbing hold of his arm. She pointed up at the bedroom windows. "A man just looked out through the curtains. Did you see him?"

"No." He shook his head. "Are you sure?"

"Yes, definitely. A man, unshaven, probably in his twenties. He pulled back the curtain slightly, looked out for a second, but then saw me looking at him."

"Perhaps it's those two men the old man was talking about."

"It could be a friend who's popped round …"

Mark looked at her. "A man in his twenties in one of the bedrooms?"

Sophia nodded. "What shall we do?"

"There's at least one man in the house and he's not answering the door so I think we need to assume that Yvonne is in trouble. I think we should get in there and find out what's going on."

"How?"

"Let's break in. I've got my knife and you've got your bow. Time to see if your practice has paid off. We'll get in there and ask these guys some questions."

Sophia thought for a second and then nodded slowly.

"Don't worry, little sister. You might know about feudal systems and doctoring, but I know about stuff like this." Mark smiled and started walking away from the house. "Let's go."

"Where are you going? I thought we were going into the house?"

"Yes, but round the back. Through the neighbour's garden. Meanwhile the bloke upstairs will think we've left." He smiled. "The element of surprise."

Sophia followed him back down to the old man's house where Mark knocked on the door again.

The man looked through his lounge window once more and his eyes widened slightly in surprise.

Opening the window, he said: "You've come back."

Mark nodded. "We think that the two men you mentioned are in Yvonne's house. My sister saw one of them at an upstairs window."

"Oh my God."

"We'd like to get in through the back where they won't be expecting us. Can we go through your garden?"

The man studied them closely for a moment, as if debating the authenticity of their story. Then he nodded, closed the window and a moment later the front door opened.

"Come around the side of the house," he said, closing the front door behind him and leading the way to a gate between the house and a high wall.

The man opened the side gate and led them through to the long back garden. There was a tall Cotswold stone wall running the length of the garden, but as they walked further down the wall become lower.

Near the bottom of the garden, Mark looked over the wall at the back of Yvonne's property. The mature garden contained a good number of bushes and a couple of small trees, all of which would provide cover. At the back of the house were some French windows facing the garden, but they were closed.

"We'll sneak up the garden," Mark said to Sophia, "then smash through the French doors and charge in before they have time to move."

"Okay," shrugged Sophia. She still wasn't sure this was the right approach but she took her bowstring out of her bag and looped it on to either end of her bow.

"Once we're inside we'll try and talk to them but if they make a move then put an arrow in them. I'll do the talking."

Sophia nodded.

Mark turned to the neighbour. "Have you got anything that I can use to break down the French windows?"

"You can't do that," the man replied aghast.

"Well, I'm not going to tap politely on the door. We tried that at the front and they didn't seem inclined to let us in."

The neighbour thought for a moment and then nodded. "I've got an old sledgehammer in the shed – I suppose you could use that."

He walked over to the other side of the garden and a moment later returned, struggling with the heavy hammer.

Mark hefted it, nodded in satisfaction and turned to his sister. "Ready?"

She took a deep breath and nodded.

They slipped over the wall and moved quickly to a position behind a tall buddleia bush on the side of the garden. Mark re-assessed the situation ahead. Nothing had changed. No movement from the windows.

They moved forward to another bush, paused for a second and then ran up to the French windows. Mark swung the sledgehammer at the huge six foot plate of glass which ran from the top of the window to the bottom. It smashed through so easily that it took Mark by surprise and the hammer slid through his hands and flew into the house.

The shattering glass fell around his feet, leaving a huge gaping hole, just the odd shard still in the frame. With hardly a pause, he stepped through and his sister followed immediately behind him.

In front of them, two young men whirled around at the far end of the large living room, as did a middle-aged woman sitting on a dining chair beside them. They had all been looking through an archway into another room which was obviously the kitchen at the front of the house.

The dark-haired man nearest to Yvonne grabbed hold of her arm. His friend, who had a closely shaved head and a tattoo of a swallow on the side of his neck, picked up a knife which had been lying on the dining table.

Mark stepped forward, picked up the sledgehammer again and announced: "I'm Mark Strachan of Brenscombe."

The two men glanced at each other and, looking back at Mark, the dark-haired man said: "So?"

"I wanted you to know who you're dealing with. You have one chance to leave Yvonne alone and get out of the house."

"Or else what?"

"That's your chance gone. Shoot them, Sophia."

An arrow already nocked on the string, Sophia quickly raised her bow slowly and drew the string back. She aimed at the man standing beside Yvonne and then, worried about hitting the wrong target, aimed at the other man with the knife.

For perhaps five seconds she stood there, bow drawn, looking at the man's fearful expression.

Then suddenly she lowered the bow. "I can't do it, Mark."

Her brother looked at her aghast and silence filled the room.

11. Josh And The Samurai Swords

Rachel and Lewis walked back up the road in the direction of Cranwold, the spring sun occasionally slithering through the canopy of ash, beech and sycamore above them. Every so often there was a break in the trees, unveiling the Severn plain stretching away to their left.

However Lewis wasn't interested in the view. "It's not fair," he muttered.

"You sound like a teenager," Rachel replied.

Lewis looked at her sharply, saw she was smiling and realised she was right.

"I am a teenager," he said, returning her smile, "but it still isn't fair."

They continued along the road until they reached the Cranwold signpost.

"Rachel?" he said.

"Yes," she replied suspiciously.

"My friend Josh lives a little way down the main road. I'd like to see if he's alright. Would you mind if we went down to see him?"

"Mark said we should go back home …"

"It's just a little way down the road. Just a few minutes."

"Your father didn't want you coming out in the first place ..."

"He's my best friend though. Couldn't we just have a quick look?"

Rachel sighed. "How far is it?"

"I don't know. Just half a mile I think. We can nip down there, see if he's okay and then come back. It won't take long."

"Where does he live exactly? It's not near a town, is it?"

"No, no. He lives up a little lane and there are just three other houses."

Rachel glanced along the road that forked off to the right in the direction of Cranwold and then Brenscombe. Then she looked down the main road that stretched out for half a mile through the trees until it curved to the left in the distance.

"It's just round that bend down there," Lewis said.

"Okay, I suppose." She sighed again. "If it's just round that bend."

-o-o-o-

Reid was in the workshop in Dowley under the tutelage of Neville Forrester.

He was now nearing the end of the third week of his trial and he couldn't wait for the end of the fourth week. He had decided that enough was enough. It had crossed his mind to quit immediately, but he still hadn't been allowed to actually fire an arrow in the lunchtime practice sessions and he wanted at least one opportunity to do so.

He must have slaved over the creation of at least fifty arrows during the last three weeks, but most of them had been snapped in half by his tutor.

Of the arrow shafts which had initially reached Forrester's high standards, the majority still hadn't been of sufficient quality in the subsequent stages of production and the old man had thrown them out in the end. Forrester had shown Reid how to attach arrow heads – or simply sharpen the point – and he had instructed him in the art of attaching three feathers, known as fletchings, to the other end, and finally Reid had been shown how to carve a nock in the end.

For something which sounded simple, this was unexpectedly the most difficult part of the process.

"A nock," Forrester had explained, "is the groove where the arrow clips onto the string. Did you notice I used the word 'clip'?"

"Yes."

Forrester had then picked up his bow and one of his own arrows, which he had clipped on to the bowstring. Holding the bow out horizontally in front of him, he had allowed the arrow to dangle from the string. Then he had flicked the string causing the arrow to drop onto his workbench.

"The arrow should attach itself to the string, but not too tightly. When you release the string, you obviously want the arrow to fly off easily. Modern manufacturers will attach pre-fabricated plastic nocks to the end of their arrows, but that's cheating."

Of course it is, Reid had thought.

"I have five hundred plastic nocks, but when they're gone, what are we going to do? I'm going to teach you how to carve a nock in the end so that you won't be dependent on our limited supplies. But I warn you it's not an easy task."

That had turned out to be an understatement. The first ten nocks he had tried to create had ended in disaster: the arrows had been consigned to the bin. In fact he had snapped one arrow himself in frustration, but his master had told him never to do that again. Only Forrester himself had the authority to break an arrow.

Finally on the eleventh attempt he had managed to create an arrow which would dangle from the string and then drop when flicked. Thereafter he was able to replicate the process with some consistency, but his rate of production was painfully slow.

Six arrows from three weeks work is pitiful, he thought as he glanced at them on the bench beside him. He returned his attention to the arrow he was working on now. The nock looked just right. He picked up his bow, clipped the arrow onto the string, flicked it and it fell onto the workbench.

"Thank God," Reid sighed. He looked up to see Forrester watching him.

"Good work," the man said.

"More by luck than judgement," Barnaby sneered across the table from him. The other boy and his brother Dominic had been working there all week and the only small consolation for Reid had been that Barnaby seemed less successful than him at making arrows.

"Barnaby," Forrester said, "please find Caitlin and tell her that we're breaking for lunch now. We'll be joining her for practice in fifteen minutes."

"Can I go with him?" Dominic asked chirpily.

"Yes, go on."

"Enjoy your lunch," Barnaby smiled mischievously at Reid and the two brothers ran off.

Reid reached down to his backpack at the end of the bench and pulled out his sandwich box. It was only when he pulled the lid off that he realised it had felt strangely light as he lifted it out of the bag. It was empty.

He looked around the workroom and then shook his head. Why was he looking for his sandwich around the room? He hadn't taken it out of the box. Perhaps his mother had forgotten to make him lunch today, but no, he remembered her saying that it was tuna again.

"Barnaby!" he declared as he recalled the other boy's grin.

"What's he done now?" Forrester asked him as he tidied his tools.

"Stolen my lunch."

"Are you sure?"

"My sandwich box is empty and did you see the look on his face when he said 'enjoy your lunch'?"

"I don't know what we're going to do with that boy," Forrester said, shaking his head. "Come with me to the kitchen and I'll find you something to eat."

"Really?" Reid said in surprise at a show of kindness from his taskmaster.

"I've got some more good news for you. I'm going to let you use some arrows this lunchtime."

-o-o-o-

Lewis and Rachel walked around the bend in the A46 and emerged from the woodlands which had been all around them since leaving Mark and Sophia.

As the trees cleared on the left of the road, a wide panorama was revealed stretching out across the Severn plain to the Malvern Hills in the distance. Sun glinted off the river snaking southwards out of Gloucester, the cathedral tower standing tall in the midst of the city's buildings.

Rachel looked down the road ahead of them. "I don't see any houses," she said, more to herself at first, and then turned to Lewis. "I thought you said he lived round this bend?"

"It must be the next one then …"

Rachel sighed as Lewis continued walking. She might have known. However, they had come this far so they might as well carry on. She set off after Lewis, occasionally glancing at the view to their left. All was serenely quiet in the valley below. The motorway, which cut across the gentle landscape like a scar, was now devoid of activity and she smiled.

She wondered if the return to a bygone age was such a bad thing – if felt as if the volume of the world had been turned down to disclose the sound of the breeze rustling through the trees and the calls of the birds in the skies above.

They turned the next bend in the road and she saw some houses in the distance.

"Can I ask you a question, Rachel?" Lewis said.

"Sure."

"Do you know Annie?"

"Peter Parlane's daughter?"

"Yes, that's right," he nodded. "We're going for a walk down to Climperwell Woods tonight."

"You and Annie? That sounds nice."

"The bluebells are out at the moment."

"Bluebells," Rachel laughed. "I never thought I'd hear you talking about flowers. Swords and bows maybe, but not flowers."

"I thought she might like to see them."

She nodded. "That sounds nice."

"I wondered though …"

"Yes?"

"What should I talk about when we're on the walk?" He scratched his head and ran his fingers through his hair. "Er, what do girls find interesting?"

Rachel smiled again. "Well, you can just talk about the flowers a little I suppose but why don't you just ask her a few questions about herself."

"Like what?"

As they talked they walked up to the two houses that she had noticed earlier.

"Nothing important, just what she's been doing during the day, what she likes doing when she's not working around the farm, what she wants to do in the future. Anything really."

"Okay," he nodded. "I like her, you know."

"I don't blame you. She's lovely."

"Do you think she likes me?"

"You asked her to go for a walk this afternoon and she said yes?"

"Yes."

"Then she must like you."

"Good," he nodded.

Rachel realised the two houses were behind them now. "Why have we walked past those houses? Doesn't your friend Josh live there?"

"Oh no, he doesn't live there. Maybe his house is round the next bend," he shrugged. "I didn't think it was this far."

Rachel sighed again and looked to their left. They had lost some height and were descending towards the valley floor, heading towards the outskirts of Gloucester. She hoped that it wouldn't be too much farther to Josh's house.

-o-o-o-

Reid was sitting at Neville Forrester's kitchen table eating some food which his tutor had given him, bread and dried rabbit meat. After some initial uncertainty about the meat, he found that he quite liked it and before too long his plate was empty.

"Okay, let's go and fire some arrows," Forrester said, standing up from the dining table. "Reid, can I just ask you not to judge yourself against the others on your first day? To start with,

Caitlin won a bronze medal at the Junior World Championships three years ago."

"Wow! Did she?" Reid was impressed.

"And don't let Barnaby get to you either. He's an annoying kid, but he's probably the most gifted archer I've ever seen. He just seems to correctly gauge the correct elevation on even his first arrow and feels how much he should allow for the slightest breeze."

"Is Dom good as well?"

"Not bad. He has some of his brother's skill, but it's difficult to say how good he'll become. He's a couple of years younger than you and if he came out from the shadow of his brother and put in some hard work then who knows?"

As they left the kitchen Forrester continued: "Remember you have the potential to be better than all of them in the long run if you work hard. Barnaby rarely practices and the only way I can get him to train is by setting up competitions against Caitlin."

They returned to the workshop to fetch their bows, but Forrester also picked up Reid's six arrows from his workbench. "I want you to use the arrows that you made yourself," he explained, as he led him out to the archery range.

Barnaby and Dominic were already there, wrestling on the ground while Caitlin simply stood watching, expressionless.

"Boys!" Forrester shouted and they jumped up quickly. "See if you can beat Caitlin then. The usual game on the eighty yard target. Reid and I will be on the short target over here, but might come over and join you later. Caitlin – you go first."

His daughter, who had been waiting patiently, simply stepped up to the line, turned sideways, placed an arrow on her string and loosed it towards the target. It hit the gold and, without a word, she drew her next arrow.

"Okay, we'll leave them to it," Forrester said as his daughter's next arrow sailed towards the target. "Come over here, Reid." They stepped over a six foot long, white wooden baton which was held in place by metal loops banged into the turf. "One foot either side of this line, sideways on to the target. Same as the drills we've been doing."

Reid did as he was told.

"Everything exactly as before," his tutor continued. "In fact I don't want you to think about the fact that you have an arrow on the string. It's a short target so just aim straight at the gold, don't allow any extra elevation. And repeat everything precisely on each arrow and let's see how you get on. Go."

Reid picked up one of his arrows, noticing that his fingers shaking slightly as he started to slip it onto the string. Why was he nervous? He glanced over and saw Barnaby watching him. He tried to relax but suddenly the arrow squirmed from between his fingers and dropped onto the wooden baton with a clatter.

"That one didn't go far," Barnaby called over. Dominic giggled. Caitlin didn't even glance over. She simply fired another arrow.

"Carry on," Forrester said gruffly.

Reid picked up his arrow from the grass, this time carefully nocking it on the string. He breathed out and went through the drill he had performed hundreds of times over the previous weeks, murmuring the steps to himself.

"Draw the string … left arm slightly bent … don't grip too tightly … thumb to the cheek … elbow up … aim … release."

As he said 'release', he loosed the arrow and it flew towards the target, thudding into the red circle around the gold centre, slightly up and to the right.

"Yes," he muttered to himself. Admittedly the target was only thirty yards away but it was immensely satisfying to see his arrow – the arrow that he had crafted himself – embed itself into the target.

"Next one," Forrester said. "Keep your head still. Aim for the same spot again."

Reid fired again, the arrow embedding itself into the red circle an inch from the first arrow.

The third, fourth and fifth arrows were the same, all grouped around the first arrow, slightly up and to the right of the gold. However when he released his sixth and final arrow it arced violently downwards as soon as it left his bow and punched itself into the ground a yard short of the target.

Reid looked sharply at Forrester and back at the arrow. His tutor shook his head and sighed.

"What happened?" Reid asked. "Did I do something wrong?"

"Yes, you did." Forrester replied, starting to walk towards the target. Reid ran a couple of steps to catch up.

"What was it?"

"You tell me." The bow-maker stooped to pull the arrow from the grass and handed it to his student. Reid looked at the piece of wood in his hand and noticed that it only had two fletchings.

"Oh," he said.

"That could have injured somebody. Next time make sure you attach them properly."

Reid nodded.

"That," said Forrester, shaking his head, "is why I wanted you to use your own arrows. It's vital that you create a shaft that is completely straight otherwise you'll never be able to hit the target. The fletchings must be positioned perfectly – and attached properly."

"I'm sorry, Neville."

"Put that arrow aside and use the other one that you finished this morning. We always shoot in groups of six arrows when we're training."

"Okay."

They took the five arrows out of the target, returned to the stand and collected the spare arrow.

"Your first five arrows were well grouped which is an important first step," Forrester said as Reid beamed proudly, "but they missed the target."

Reid stopped smiling. "But they were in the red," he said.

"Red is nowhere. I want every arrow in the gold." Forrester motioned with his hand. "Go again. And this time keep your elbow up."

For the next hour, Reid shot at the target repeatedly with Neville barking at him each time he did something wrong:

"Elbow up."

"Don't grip the bow so tightly."

"Draw the string back to exactly the same point each time. Exactly, I said."

"Keep your head still."

"Elbow up. How many times do I have to tell you?"

Occasionally Reid glanced over at the others and saw Barnaby and Dominic laughing and joking. Barnaby would crack a joke with his brother and quickly fire an arrow, without really seeming to even look where it was going, and it would land in the centre of the far target.

"Concentrate," Forrester said, when he saw him looking over at the others. "Just worry about your own technique."

By the end of the hour, Reid's shoulders were aching, but with his final set of six arrows he hit the gold three times.

"Yes," he said in satisfaction as the third slammed into the target. Maybe he would continue after the trial month after all. This was fun.

"Don't get too excited. We're only on the baby target," Forrester said and turned to his daughter and the other boys, he shouted: "Right, we'll stop there. Back to work, boys. See you later, Caitlin. Good luck."

His daughter retrieved her arrows from the eighty yard target and, without speaking, simply walked past it up to the far end of the field.

"Where's she going?" Reid asked as she wandered off.

"Who do you think caught the rabbit you had for lunch?" Forrester replied.

Reid looked back at Caitlin, just in time to see her disappear into the woods at the end of the field.

-o-o-o-

"Here it is," Lewis said, turning up a small lane.

"Thank goodness for that," Rachel replied. She glanced around. There was nobody to be seen, but just a few hundred yards further down the main road she could see some houses that marked the outskirts of Gloucester. "We shouldn't hang around too long."

Lewis walked up the lane past a couple of cottages and entered the gateway of a white house that was perched above them, dug into the side of the hill.

They climbed the steep driveway and knocked on the door. No answer. Lewis banged again, harder. Still no answer.

He stepped back and looked up at one of the bedroom windows.

"JOSH," he shouted. "JOSH."

He bent down picked up some small stones and threw them up at the window. Still no answer.

"I know where they keep a spare key," Lewis said, disappearing around the corner of the house. A moment later he was back with the key in his hand.

"You can't just go into someone's house," Rachel said, but too late, Lewis had opened the door and marched in.

"I've been here loads of times," he shouted over his shoulder as he walked through the kitchen. "His mum and dad won't mind."

Rachel stepped into the kitchen as he disappeared through a door at the other end. She looked around the room at the Aga, the old Welsh dresser full of cookery books, the fridge with magnets scattered haphazardly across the door. It was a large kitchen in a traditional style, but modern equipment and every cooking utensil you could possibly imagine hanging from a rack suspended from the ceiling.

Lewis came back in carrying two samurai swords and a crossbow. "Nobody's here," he said, "But I got these from Josh's room."

"You can't take those."

"Why not?"

"They don't belong to you. Your friend Josh might just have popped out for a while and he might need them himself."

Lewis looked at her dubiously. "Let's just have a quick go of the crossbow though. As we're here."

He smiled and walked out into the garden. Rachel sighed and followed him out.

"Where do you think Josh and his parents are?" she wondered.

"I don't know," he shrugged. "They have family on the Isle of Wight. Perhaps they've gone there?"

Lewis laid the two swords on a garden table, rested the crossbow on the floor, ratcheted the cord back and slid in the bolt. Aiming at a tree a dozen yards away on the other side of the drive, he pulled the trigger. With a loud kerchunk, the crossbow fired and the bolt embedded itself into the tree with a thud.

"That's a dangerous device," she said with a shake of her head.

"I think that's the idea," Lewis grinned. He cocked and loaded the crossbow once more and lifted it to his shoulder.

"Why on earth have they got a crossbow and two samurai swords?"

"They're not real swords. The blades are quite blunt. His dad just has them on the wall because he thinks they look nice."

"What about the crossbow?"

"I think Josh said his dad got it in France."

Reid lifted the crossbow and aimed at the tree again. Just as he was about to pull the trigger, they both heard a shout from down the lane: "Quick. He's slowing down. Get him."

Lewis looked down the lane and saw his friend Josh cycling up the lane, his face red with exertion as three boys chased him on foot. The road steepened as it neared the gateway to Josh's house and Lewis could see that the boys were gaining on him.

"Come on, Josh!" Lewis shouted, running towards him. He didn't know what was happening, but he could see that his friend was in trouble. Josh glanced up, recognised him and pedalled harder.

"Grab one of the swords, Rachel," he shouted.

One of the boys – Lewis estimated they were a similar age to him, around sixteen years old – had nearly caught up with Josh as he burst through the gateway, but fortunately the boy stumbled and fell heavily to the ground.

Josh sped past Lewis and collapsed to the floor. Rachel stepped in front of him, drawing one of the swords from its scabbard and standing alongside Lewis.

The other two chasing boys stopped by their friend who was lying on the ground and looked at the weapons being brandished at them. The first boy stood up and brushed himself down. He was breathing hard like his friends.

The boy was tall and gangly with closely cropped light brown hair. He was obviously the leader from the way the other two deferred to him. He looked at Lewis and at his weapon, trying to work out what it was.

"It's a crossbow," Lewis said, guessing at the boy's confusion. "It fires the bolt at around two hundred miles an hour and it has a range of around fifty to a hundred yards before it loses accuracy."

"Who are you?" the boy said. "This is nothing to do with you."

"I'm his friend so it *is* something to do with me."

"Shoot the bastard!" Josh shouted from behind him. "Just shoot him, Lewis!" He was sitting on the floor beside his bike, trying to recover his breath.

"Who are they?" Lewis asked, without taking his eyes from the three boys in front of him.

"I've no idea. They just started chasing me."

"He was on our patch," the leader of the boys said. "Nobody comes on our patch."

"Well, you're on our patch now," Lewis said, "so you can go home."

The boy looked into his eyes, without speaking, assessing his adversary. He came to a conclusion. "We're going," the boy said, "but we'll see you again one day. And you'd better hope that you have your crossbow handy." He turned to his friends. "Come on, lads."

Lewis kept his crossbow aimed at the boys as they walked down the lane and turned onto the main road. When they had disappeared from sight, he lowered the weapon, turned to his friend who was now standing up and brushing himself down.

"What happened, Josh?"

"I was out looking for my mum and dad."

"What do you mean? Where are they?"

"I don't know. I haven't seen them for a week. They went out looking for food and made me stay at home. And they never came back."

"Where did they go?"

"I don't know. I thought they were going to the nearest shops, but I've been out searching every day and haven't found anything of them. Something must have happened to them."

"Like what?"

Josh shook his head. "I don't know, but I've seen bodies everywhere. In fact I've twice seen somebody killed. Yesterday I saw a fight break out by a shop. It was stupid – there was absolutely nothing in the shop. But one bloke pulled out a knife and attacked the other one."

"I'm sure your mum and dad will be okay," Rachel said.

"No, they won't." Josh shook his head. "They wouldn't have left me, would they? For the last couple of days I've really just been looking for their bodies so I can know for sure. Obviously I picked the wrong area today though."

"Do you want to come and stay with us?" Reid said.

His friend didn't reply for a few seconds as he thought it through before replying. "I can't. What about my mum and dad? What if they come home and I'm not here?"

"We can leave a note or we could come back in a few days to look for them again, but it's not safe at the moment with those lads about."

"I think Lewis is right," Rachel said. "In fact I think we'd better go soon. They might come back with some of their friends."

That decided it for Josh. He quickly packed a bag and ten minutes later the three of them set off up the road to Cranwold. Rachel wanted to put some distance between themselves and the outskirts of Gloucester as quickly as possible.

12. Fetching Yvonne.

"What do you mean, you can't do it?" Mark said, as their two adversaries relaxed visibly.

"I can't shoot them in cold blood," Sophia repeated, pointing the arrow down to the floor and slowly releasing the tension on the string.

"It's not cold blood," Mark insisted. "That guy's holding Yvonne and the other bloke's got a knife in his hand."

"We should take them to the police or something."

"The police? You're living in a dream world. There are no police anymore." He drew a deep breath. "Sophia, when I say you have one chance, then we have to follow through. Otherwise they won't respect you." He turned to the men. "Isn't that right?"

The man with the tattoo smiled and nodded. "Yeah, why don't you two get out of the house now?"

The man moved over to where Yvonne was sitting, took his friend's place and put the knife at her throat.

The tattooed man continued: "Get out now or – "

He never finished his sentence, because, in one rapid, fluid movement Sophia raised her bow, drew the string back and released.

The aluminium arrow flew too fast to be visible across the twenty foot length of Yvonne's lounge but suddenly it was embedded in the shoulder of the tattooed man, sending him staggering backwards. He screamed, dropped the knife and fell to his knees. He twisted as he dropped and Sophia could see the arrow protruding three inches out of the man's back.

However she paid it no attention as she drew a second arrow, nocked it on the string, drew back and aimed at the dark-haired man. He was staring at his friend, but when he glanced back at Sophia, his eyes widened and he slowly raised his hands and shouted: "Don't shoot."

"That's more like it!" Mark shouted. "What a shot. Maybe I should take up archery after all. I thought you said you couldn't do it?"

"He put the knife to Yvonne's neck and I decided you were right," she replied shakily. "Are you okay, Yvonne?" Their friend nodded her head and gasped: "Where did you two come from?"

"Your neighbour let us in through the back," Mark answered.

"But why are you here in Prinswick?"

"We'll explain in a minute," he replied. "Let me sort these two out first. I don't suppose you have something I could tie them up with, do you?"

Yvonne explained where he could find some cord and duct tape. A few minutes later, he had tied the un-injured man's hands behind his back and secured him to a chair.

"Now, are you okay, Yvonne?" Mark asked when he had finished.

"Oh, I was so stupid," she replied. "I was just popping out to see a friend when they walked past. They asked me if I had any food and I should have just run back inside. When I said I didn't have any to spare they grabbed me and came in to search the house."

The tattooed man had stopped writhing in agony but was still on his knees, moaning quietly, holding his arm.

"What shall we do with him?" Mark wondered out loud.

"I'll see if I can patch him up," Yvonne said, now starting to recover her composure.

"Are you sure?" Mark asked. "He just had a knife at your throat."

"We can't leave him with an arrow in his shoulder."

"Couldn't we?" Mark looked at Sophia.

"She's right."

"If you say so," Mark shrugged.

"It might be best if you do it."

"Me?"

"You're stronger than me," his sister said. "Just pull it out like drawing it out of a target. Put your other hand on his shoulder with your thumb and fingers either side of the shaft. It's just a smooth shaft, no arrow head or barbs."

Mark shrugged and moved towards the man.

"No way," the man shouted, his voice trembling with the pain. He leaned away from Mark.

"You don't want to have it in your shoulder forever. Keep still."

Roughly, completely ignoring the man's pain, in fact enjoying it slightly, Mark put his left hand on the man's shoulder, grabbed the arrow and yanked it out. The man screamed in pain and fell over onto his good side, clutching his injury.

Yvonne stepped forward, knelt down, unbuttoned the man's shirt and pulled it off his shoulder.

She inspected the wound briefly and turned to Mark. "Can we get him onto a chair?"

He helped the man onto one of the dining chairs and Yvonne probed gently around the injury, as he winced occasionally.

"It looks like you've been lucky," she announced finally.

"Lucky?" the man groaned.

"It looks like the arrow missed your clavicle – that's the collar bone – but it went through the trapezius – that's the muscle across the top which goes to your neck."

The man groaned but didn't reply.

"So basically you've just got a hole in the muscle," Yvonne continued, "which should simply repair itself over a few weeks. There's no point in cutting you open to sew it up – we'll leave nature to do the work. However you'll need to keep the shoulder completely still while it starts knitting back together again. Any movement could create a tear in the muscle and that's obviously not good. We'll put your arm in a sling."

"Okay," the man grunted.

"Keep it in the sling for a couple of weeks and then don't do anything stupid for another couple of weeks after that."

Mark snorted. "I doubt that's possible for him."

Yvonne went to the kitchen and returned with material for a sling.

"You're lucky you broke into a doctor's house," Mark said to the man.

As she fitted the sling, she took the opportunity to talk to her rescuers. "So why are you here in Prinswick, Sophia?"

"We came to see you."

"Me?"

"Mum and Dad asked us to come. They want you to come and live in Brenscombe with us."

"Live in Brenscombe?" Yvonne finished tying the sling and looked at Sophia. "But I can't leave my home."

"We've formed a village council which has stationed guards on the boundaries of the village and set up a rota for work in the fields. You'll be safer in Brenscombe than here and we have food."

"Which is more than can be said for Prinswick," Mark added. "And people like these two are going to become more commonplace – it's only going to get worse as people start to leave the towns and cities."

"I have to admit," Sophia added, "that we're suggesting this for selfish reasons: we don't have a doctor in the community and we'd like you to come and help us. But Mum also thought you and Amelie might be safer living with us – if you want to come."

"Amelie has been working up at a hospital in Newcastle for a few months," Yvonne replied. "So I can't leave. What if she comes back home? I need to be here."

"Let me ask you a question," Mark said. "How much food do you have? It's been about a month since any shops were open."

She nodded in acknowledgement of his point. "I have a couple of tins of soup and then I'm down to things that are useless on their own like jam, flour, spices, salt and pepper. That's what I told these two fools." She pointed at the two men sitting on the chairs.

"So you can only stay here for another couple of days anyway," Mark pointed out.

"But what if Amelie comes back looking for me?"

"We're not too far away in Brenscombe," Mark said. "You could come back occasionally to see if she's here."

"And you could leave a note telling her where you are," Sophia added.

"Hmmm …" Yvonne wasn't sure.

"That's a good idea. We'll leave a note," said Mark, trying to make the decision for her. "But somebody else could break in again." He looked around the room. "You know what I would do? I would paint a message on the wall."

"On the wall?" Yvonne was aghast.

"It'll be more permanent." Mark knew he would have to leave that suggestion to sink in. "What are we going to do with these two?"

"That's a good question," Sophia said.

"We can't leave them here to terrorise Prinswick. We could kill them?"

"Mark!"

"I'm only joking." He turned to the tattooed man. "Tempting though it is. Where are you from?"

"Stroud. But we were heading to Gloucester where my brother lives."

"Let's escort them up the road," Mark suggested to his sister. "We're heading that way to start with. At least they'll be a few miles out of Prinswick and then they might as well keep going to Gloucester."

They decided it was time to head off and finally Yvonne agreed to join them. She wrote a note which she left on the kitchen table, but while she went upstairs to pack a bag, Mark found a marker pen in the kitchen drawers and took the opportunity to write "Gone to Brenscombe to live with the Strachans" in large letters on the lounge wall.

Sophia went next door to retrieve their backpacks from the neighbour and Mark ushered Yvonne out of the door without allowing her to see what he'd done to her lovely lounge.

With the two Stroud men in front of them, they left Prinswick behind.

13. Harry Goes To Baxley

Harry saw the signpost for Baxley in the distance and breathed a sigh of relief. Nearly there. He was looking forward to leaving this road. The wide, open highway made him feel utterly exposed.

That morning he had been escorted to the edge of Gloucester by Uros' friend Brett and two other men – and he hadn't felt safe since he leaving them. He smiled to himself as this thought went through his head. Who would have imagined that he would miss those thugs?

It was now nearing five o'clock in the afternoon. All day he had been walking along the A38, which had once been the main arterial road between Birmingham and Bristol before being replaced by the M5 in the late sixties. Whilst it was the most direct route to Baxley it was probably the most risky with its sections of wide dual carriageway and stretches which were raised above the surrounding fields.

Around midday he had spotted a group of people walking towards him in the distance and he had quickly jumped over a gate and run along behind a hedge to the cover of some woods. From his vantage point in the trees, a few hundred yards from the road, he had watched until the strangers had disappeared from view.

Harry had then returned warily to the highway and for the rest of the afternoon had not seen another soul – but he had been on edge the whole time.

As he walked towards the turning to Baxley, Harry realised that a figure was sitting at the base of the signpost. He swore under his breath and stopped. He looked over to his right, wondering if he could cut across the open countryside, but a wide stream ran down the middle of the nearest field and at the other end was a tall hedge. Not impossible, but difficult.

He looked down the road again and saw the figure stand up. Was it a woman? he wondered, straining his eyes to see. She stretched and sauntered back and forth across the road. It was definitely a young woman and she seemed to be on her own, perhaps waiting for someone or something.

He decided to risk continuing down the road. A young, single woman shouldn't be any threat, he decided.

As he approached the woman, she happened to glance in his direction. A look of fear appeared on her face and she began to back away. She looked like she was just about to start running.

"It's okay," he called. "I'm not going to do anything to you."

Harry raised his hands and slowed his pace. She looked doubtful, but waited for him to approach.

When he was twenty yards away, she said: "Stop there."

"I'm just on my way to Baxley," he said, waving a hand in the direction of the side road. "Do you live round here?"

"No."

He was surprised by her curt response. "Which way are you travelling?" he asked.

"Do you have anything to eat?" she asked, ignoring his question.

"Yeah, I've got a couple of things," he replied, taking his bag off his shoulder.

He was just about to unzip his backpack when he heard footsteps behind him, but, before he could turn around, he felt a hefty crack on the side of his head.

The last thing he heard before he fell unconscious was a man's voice saying: "Nice one, Kerry."

-o-o-o-

Harry opened his eyes and looked around. He was lying in a bed – a comfortable bed – and it was dark all around him.

A little light filtered under the door, enough for him to see the outline of the curtains, a bedside cabinet and a wardrobe. On the other side of the door he could hear voices.

He started to sit up, but immediately lay back down as a sharp jab of pain went through his head. He tried again, this time ready for the sensation that speared through his temple, and managed to get his feet over the side of the bed and lever himself into a sitting position.

Sitting for a moment to let the pain subside, he once again heard men talking through the door, but couldn't make out what they were saying.

He looked around for his bag, but couldn't see it in the faint light. His shoes had been taken off. He could just about make them out on the floor beside the bed.

He briefly considered putting them on, but decided that was a bridge too far. He put his hand to the side of his head, where it hurt the most. There was something dried in his hair, which he presumed was blood.

Harry forced himself to stand up. He walked unsteadily to the door and tried to open it. It was locked.

The voices on the other side of the door stopped. He heard footsteps coming towards him, the sound of a key in the lock and then the door opened.

Blinking in the light, he saw the shape of a large man silhouetted in the doorway.

"You're awake then," the man said.

"Where am I?"

"Baxley Castle. One of our patrols found you unconscious on the A38 and they must have been feeling soft because they brought you back here."

"Can I – "

"What happened to you?" the man interrupted. Harry's eyes were becoming accustomed to the light now and he could see that the man almost filled the doorway. He must have been around six foot two and sixteen stone. And the man was wide. Not fat, but solid. Short, dark hair and a long goatee beard. The man's eyes drilled into him. "Why were you lying there unconscious on the A38?"

"Somebody hit me on the head."

"Obviously," the man snorted. "Who did it?"

"I don't know. I was chatting to this girl and then everything went black. Somebody hit me from behind." Harry groaned. "I think they were after my food."

The big man nodded. "Where are you from?"

"I'm from Gloucester but I was coming to Baxley."

"Why?" the man asked suspiciously.

"Look, am I being held prisoner?" Harry realised he was feeling woozy from the bang on his head and he stepped backwards, felt for the edge of the bed and sat down. "Why are you asking me all these questions?"

"You're our guest for the night, but you'll forgive me if I don't give a stranger the run of the place. Why did you come to Baxley?"

"I heard you were raising an army," Harry said, thinking quickly, "and I thought I'd come and join up."

"That's a good one!" The man laughed gruffly and his face quickly went serious again. "What's the real reason you're here?"

"That's the truth. That's what I heard anyway. Aren't you building an army?"

The man simply looked at him for a few seconds.

"In the morning," the man said eventually, "we'll decide what we're going to do with you."

"But – "

Before Harry could say another word, the man closed the door and he heard the key turn in the lock. As another jolt of pain travelled through his head, he decided to lie back down on the bed. Almost immediately he fell asleep.

14. Reid's Last Day Of Probation

One early morning on the last Friday in April, Reid cycled to Dowley for his day of work. The first part of his journey, along a country lane lined with trees bursting into leaf, was accompanied by a patch of clear, blue sky, but, as he emerged from the woods, dark clouds had appeared. As the rain poured down, he cycled between the rolling meadows and corn fields.

In just a few minutes he was soaked to the skin. Reid briefly considered looking for shelter but decided it would be closing the stable door after the horse had bolted.

Just as he pulled in through the gate of Forrester's place, the rain stopped as suddenly as it had begun and by the time he had leaned his bike against the dry stone wall, the sun was shining again.

Forrester happened to be looking out of his kitchen window and opened the door when he saw his young apprentice. "Come in for a minute, Reid. You can dry yourself by the fire while we have a chat."

This is it, thought Reid, as he walked into the snug, warm kitchen. For the first three weeks of his probationary month, he had been looking forward to the day when it would end, but over the last week he had decided that he wanted to continue. He had really enjoyed the training sessions over the last few days – it was hugely satisfying when his arrows thumped into the bullseye on the large straw wheels and in just a few days he had progressed to regular success on the fifty yard target.

He even drew some satisfaction from his labours in the workshop now that he truly saw the point of the exacting nature of the craft. Firing his own arrows on the longer range had shown up the slightest imperfections and he now strove to create shafts that were perfectly straight and symmetrical.

"Sit here," Forrester said, putting a kitchen chair in front of the fire for him and then sitting down himself.

Now that he wanted to stay on, Reid realised he was nervous. Did Forrester want him? Had he come up to scratch?

"So what have you thought of the last month?" the bow-maker asked him.

"Good," Reid nodded enthusiastically. "I've really enjoyed it."

"Really?"

"Yes."

"All of it?" Forrester smiled. "Tell me the truth."

Reid paused a moment and decided honesty was the best policy. "The first few weeks were hard work and it was like a nightmare to work all day on an arrow shaft which was just thrown in the bin."

"And now?"

"I can see why I'm doing it. I want to hit the centre of the target and I don't want an arrow that will veer off line because of a small flaw."

"I wondered at one point whether you would even last the month."

"Me too," Reid admitted.

"Okay," Forrester smiled, sitting back in his chair. "What do we do now? That's the question."

Reid waited for the man to continue. What was he going to say?

"A few hundred years ago," Forrester said, "a traditional bowyer would have three or four apprentices, each boy learning the trade for five years."

"Five years?"

"You think that's a long time?"

"To be honest, I was surprised when the probation was a month. I thought the whole apprenticeship might be a month when you first started talking about it."

"A month!" Forrester laughed.

"Yes, I realise now that I was under-estimating it a bit."

"A bit? We've hardly scratched the surface, lad. You've done one type of arrow, there are dozens of others we need to cover. Different cultures around the world have used arrows of different lengths and they all have their pros and cons. And we haven't even started on bows yet. Short, manageable bows for firing from horseback through to the full longbow."

Reid realised he had touched a nerve. "I didn't mean – "

"The bow you've been using has a 25 pound draw. The longbow I have is 75 pounds, but an archer at Agincourt would consider that a training bow for a youngster. Their bows were 100 pounds and some longbows were discovered on the Mary Rose had a much higher draw weight – you've heard of the Mary Rose?"

"Yes," Reid lied.

"The Mary Rose was Henry VIII's warship which sank near the Isle of Wight in 1545 and was raised in 1982 in one of the most complex and expensive projects in maritime archaeology. 172 longbows were discovered in the ship and some are estimated to have had a 170 pound draw weight. You wouldn't have been able to move the string more than a few inches and the precision that would have been required in the manufacture of that bow would have been phenomenal. Do you know how far you can fire an arrow with that kind of bow?"

"No."

"Five hundred yards."

"Wow."

Forrester paused for a moment. "In those times an apprentice would stay with a master bowyer for five years and then, if he was lucky, would join the business and start earning a small fee for each bow that he made. The majority of the fee would of course remain with the man whose name was above the door."

"Yes," Reid nodded.

"I've been impressed with your work," continued Forrester, "and your application during the training sessions. You've turned up on time every day and always leave your workbench tidy. I'm happy to offer you an apprenticeship if you would like to continue. However, instead of specifying an amount of time, I was thinking that we should just take it as it comes. The world is changing rapidly at the moment and neither of us can commit to five years, or even one for that matter. Who knows what will happen tomorrow, let alone in five years' time."

"Okay," Reid nodded.

"So would you like to continue?"

"Yes please." Reid wanted to say more, but was just relieved that the man wanted to keep him on.

"Good." Forrester held out his hand, to Reid's surprise, but he regained his composure quickly and shook his tutor's hand.

"Er, thanks, Neville," he said.

"If we're still here in a year from now then let's have another discussion like this. Around the end of April. We'll see if we both want to continue." Forrester stood up. "Right let's get back to work. Make me a couple more arrows today and we'll start on a bow next week. I was thinking you should make your own bow."

"That would be great, thanks." Reid smiled proudly and stood up as well. The two of them went over to the workshop to start work.

Reid attacked his work with enthusiasm and laboured hard over some arrow shafts for the next few hours. Shortly before lunchtime, as the two of them were working quietly, the door was suddenly thrust open and Barnaby and his brother Dominic entered.

"Good morning, Neville," Barnaby said in a loud voice. "Sorry we're late."

Forrester looked over at him and put down the plane he was using.

"We're here in time for practice though," Barnaby continued, with a grin. "That's the important thing."

Forrester walked slowly round to the front of his workbench and leaned back against it, folding his arms and looking at Barnaby. Watching from the corner of his eye, Reid felt the weight of the silence as an almost physical thing in the room.

Barnaby was just about to speak again when Forrester held up his hand to cut him off. And then he said: "You can leave, Barnaby, and don't bother coming back."

"What?"

"I've had enough."

"But, Neville, I had to help my Dad. It wasn't my fault I was late."

"There's always something with you, Barnaby. For a week or two you might arrive on time, but then you won't turn up at all for a few days. Or you stroll in halfway through the morning like today."

"But my Dad needed me and Dom to help him with a fence around one of our fields."

"It's just one excuse after another and I've had enough now."

"My Dad won't be pleased."

"I never cared how rich your father was and I care even less now."

Barnaby looked from Forrester to Dominic to Reid.

"It's because of him, isn't it?" he said pointing at Reid. "You've got a new golden boy so you don't need me anymore."

Forrester sighed. "It's true that I like someone who turns up on time every day. It's also true that Reid applies himself to his work, but this isn't about him. It's about you."

Barnaby looked at Reid. "I'm going to get you for this."

Reid was taken aback and wanted to say something in return, but didn't know what. Forrester simply said: "Please leave Barnaby."

Looking back at the bow-maker, Barnaby retorted: "I will, Neville, and I'm never coming back. I hated it here anyway. Come on, Dom."

He turned to leave and his brother started to follow, bewildered at the turn of events.

"Dominic?" Forrester said, as the younger boy was about to go through the doorway. Dominic turned around with a worried expression on his face, but the old man said: "Why don't you head off with your brother now, but have a think about things over the next few days. If you're interested in continuing here then I'm prepared to give you a try on your own. You're a good lad and maybe without Barnaby around, we could turn you into a decent bow-maker and a good archer."

"Okay," the young boy replied unsurely.

"Don't listen to him, Dom," his elder brother sneered from the doorway. "He's an idiot. Let's go."

Barnaby grabbed Dominic's arm and pulled him out of the door.

There was a sudden silence in the workshop and, sighing, Forrester dropped his head onto his chest. Two seconds later he looked up and, seeing Reid looking at him, barked: "What are you looking at? Get on with your work."

-o-o-o-

At five o'clock Forrester declared the day's work at an end and Reid tidied up his workbench and headed out to his bike.

To his relief the sun was shining and he cycled along the road, thinking about the day's events. He was pleased to have made the grade and be offered the apprenticeship, but he felt uncomfortable about what had transpired with Barnaby.

The other boy obviously blamed him, but Reid didn't feel that it was his fault. All he had done was work as hard as he could and surely Barnaby couldn't fault him for that?

Reid cycled along the small country road through the fields of maize and the meadows where the cows were grazing until he reached the incline where the lane started to wind its way up through the woods.

He always had to pedal hard to climb the steepest part of the slope and, with his head down, he didn't notice a log lying across the road – until he was almost upon it. It was just a few inches thick but it was enough to make him stop on this steep section of road.

Climbing off his bike, he looked around, but there was nobody to be seen. A small brook ran down the side of the road and all he could hear was the gurgling of the water as it ran over the stones.

He started to lift his bike over the branch when suddenly he heard a shout of "Now!" and four figures ran out from behind the trees on either side of the road. Three of them ran straight towards him carrying something in their arms.

Two of the boys were unfamiliar to him and they charged past throwing bundles of nettles over him. He recognised the third figure as Dominic as he went by, but his nettles missed him by a few inches.

The fourth boy, who he now realised was Barnaby, had bent to scoop up a huge pile of mud from beside the bank of the stream and then ran forward to throw it over him. Reid had finally regained his wits in the few seconds since the attack had started and he tried to dodge out of the way, but Barnaby anticipated his move and Reid only succeeded in ducking into the shower of wet earth and stones.

"Not so golden now, are you?" Barnaby shouted as he ran off. He caught up with his younger brother and the other two boys and all four ran off down the road shouting and laughing.

"Enjoy your ride home, golden boy!" was the last thing Reid heard before they disappeared out of sight.

15. Lady Baxley

Harry woke the next morning with a groan. His head still hurt. Perhaps even more than the night before.

He sat up slowly, expecting the pain to lance through his head again, but it didn't happen. Instead the intermittent, searing pain had been replaced by a constant, strong ache. After a few moments he wondered which was worse.

Daylight was seeping through the curtains and he walked over to the window, but before he could open them, he heard footsteps and a key in the lock.

The door opened showing a young man, a couple of years older than himself.

"Lady Baxley wants to see you," the man said. He smiled a little, his expression inviting more than demanding.

The young man led him out through a small kitchen area, where another guard was waiting. The man fell in behind Harry as they walked down the stairs and out of the building.

"We're just going over to the castle," the young man said, gesturing ahead.

"I thought I *was* in the castle," Harry replied, looking behind him at a long, single-storey, stone building.

"We're inside the castle walls, but you were in the stable block. Half a dozen of us stay there each night just in case."

Harry nodded, but then said "Just in case what?"

"In case we get attacked I suppose." He shrugged. "I'm Chris Woodgate, but they call me Woody. Me and Dean were the ones that carried you back last night."

"And you were bloody heavy," Dean said from behind him. "Two miles we carried you."

"Sorry," Harry said, not really knowing what else to say.

"And we got a load of stick for bringing you back," Woody said, as they entered the castle.

"From the man I met last night?" Harry asked, looking around at the beautiful main hall that they were walking through. Long pennants hung down the walls above a cavernous fireplace, shields and pikes on either side.

"That's Warwick. Warwick Yorath. You don't want to get on the wrong side of him. He's worked here for about ten years, running falconry shows and weaponry exhibitions for the tourists. You should see him with a sword – he's amazing. I think he's one of the few people who are actually quite glad the world doesn't have electricity anymore. He runs the place now."

"Where are you taking me?"

"To Lady Baxley. They were trying to work out what to do with you and she wanted to speak to you herself."

They walked through one stunning medieval room after another and then Woody led him up a narrow winding stone staircase, the treads worn down over hundreds of years.

"People actually live in this huge place still?" Harry said.

"The Baxley family have lived here since the 12th century, but most of the castle is just for visitors these days. Or was. Elizabeth – that's Lady Baxley – and her daughter live in a few small rooms at the back."

"What's she like?" Harry asked as they reached the top of the spiral staircase.

"She's okay. She's in her late seventies, but she's a nice old girl. It's Deborah you want to watch out for."

"Deborah?"

"That's her daughter. She must be about fifty now I think." He paused and dropped his voice to a murmur. "She never says a word, just stares at you through her snake-like eyes."

"Shut up, Woody!" Dean hissed from behind them. "The room's just up there for Christ's sake."

Woody led Harry across the landing and opened the door.

Harry didn't know quite what he'd been expecting, but it certainly hadn't been this after the ornate splendour of the rest of the castle. The room reminded him of the lounge in his parents' house: it was around the same size with a mantelpiece and sideboard laden with ornaments. Either side of the window were long floral curtains, both ends of the room contained shelves full of books and, in the centre of the room, a sofa and two armchairs positioned around a wooden coffee table.

The man he now knew as Warwick was sitting in one of the chairs, a dainty teacup incongruously in his large fist. The Chesterfield sofa contained two women, one of whom rose from her seat as he entered.

"I'm Elizabeth Baxley," the lady said, shaking his hand. "Why don't you take a seat?"

Harry sat down in the unoccupied armchair as he watched Elizabeth lower herself back onto her seat. He thought that she moved well for someone in her late seventies, with a grace that matched her clothes and perfectly presented hair.

"This is my daughter, Deborah and I believe you've met Warwick." She indicated the tray on the table between them. "Would you like a cup of tea?"

"Er, yes, that would be very nice, thank you."

"And your name is …?" Elizabeth asked as she poured the tea and put the cup on the table in front of him.

"Sorry. Harry. Harry Barkley."

"I understand you live in Gloucester, Harry? Please help yourself to milk and sugar."

"Yes, I live with my parents in Kingsholm."

"Oh, that's a nice part of Gloucester. I wonder if I might have met your father? May I ask his name?"

"Er, his name is Nigel. Nigel Barkley."

Warwick leaned forward and was just about to speak, but Elizabeth raised her hand slightly.

"No," she shook her head pensively, "I don't believe I've made his acquaintance. In what field does he work – or rather did he work before all of this." She waved her hand in a gesture which seemed to embrace all the recent troubles.

"Er, he, er …" Harry wasn't sure if he should be divulging any information would which give away his father's current role. "He ran an accountancy firm."

"That's always a good business to be in," she nodded, "And yourself?"

"I'd just finished university and was starting to look for a job."

"What did you read at university?"

"Maths. At Leeds."

"Ah, a numbers man as well?"

Harry nodded and smiled. He was a little surprised by this meeting. He had been expecting an inquisition but this was like being invited to tea with a long lost great aunt.

"We're always keen to hear how things are going elsewhere," Elizabeth continued. "We're a little bit off the beaten track here, which has its advantages of course. Could you tell me what's happening in Gloucester at present? How are things there?"

"Er, well, it's not great. There's no food left, which is why I decided to leave."

"Is there much trouble?"

"Trouble? Yes, it's terrible. Riots, fighting, everything. It's not safe anywhere really."

"We've heard that the Mayor of Gloucester is trying to instil some discipline back into the town …"

"Have you?" said Harry, surprised. "Yes, he's appointed some guards."

"And what do you think of these guards?"

"They're just a bunch of thugs really." Harry felt he was simply telling the truth.

"Did you see many people out and about while you were travelling here?"

"Not really, everybody seemed to be hiding away in their houses."

"In Gloucester as well?"

"More so there. Everywhere in the city is so dangerous that you don't feel safe outside your front door."

Lady Baxley nodded and took another sip of her tea.

"We've heard that the Mayor has announced that the government is distributing food in Birmingham …"

"Have you? But that announcement was just made a couple of days ago."

"People know that I like information," smiled Elizabeth.

She didn't say any more and the silence stretched out uncomfortably. Harry looked down at his tea and then up at his hostess again. Elizabeth simply smiled at him once more.

She seemed to know everything already. Harry wondered if she knew that his father was the Mayor. He wished he hadn't said his name now.

Elizabeth finally broke the silence. "Why did you come to Baxley, Harry?"

"I heard you were setting up an army and I thought I might join up," he replied, sticking to his story of the previous evening.

Warwick snorted derisively.

"An army?" Elizabeth smiled. "I'm interested to know what people are saying about us."

"Maybe army is too big a word. Somebody told me that they had heard you were recruiting people to help as soldiers here at the castle."

"And what else?"

"That's it really."

"And you thought you might just come along and join up?"

"Have I got it wrong?"

"Well, I certainly wouldn't call it an army," she smiled. "Would you, Warwick?"

"It might be a good image to project," he suggested.

"I feel it could work both ways," Elizabeth replied. "It could put people off coming here, but at the same time it could attract others who rise to a challenge or feel threatened."

She turned back to Harry and asked another question: "Weren't you tempted to go to Birmingham? Surely the offer of food would be appealing?"

"I didn't believe them." Harry felt he was less likely to make a mistake if he kept his answers short.

"Why ever not? What motive would the Mayor have for giving out misinformation?"

"Er, well, it just seemed a bit far-fetched to me. And I didn't want to go all the way on the off-chance."

"That's understandable," she nodded and he quietly breathed a sigh of relief that she seemed to believe him. "What about other people?"

"Oh, they all believed it. Quite a few people left that day."

"Yet, you were the only person to head south rather than north?"

He nodded and kept his mouth shut.

"You said earlier," Elizabeth continued, "that Gloucester is a dangerous place to walk about?"

"Yes ..."

"Would it be sensible to go through the city on your own at this time?"

"No, but – "

She didn't let him finish. "Yet you have travelled here from Kingsholm, which is on the northern side of the city, so you must have walked through the centre and all the way down the Bristol Road. How is it that you were able to do that alone?"

"I was just lucky, I guess ..." Harry said weakly.

"He's lying," Warwick blurted out. "Look Elizabeth, we should either lock him up or kick him out. I say we lock him up."

"No," said Deborah, speaking for the first time. "He'll just use up valuable food."

"We can't let him go," argued Warwick. "He'll run straight back to whoever sent him and tell them all about our setup here."

"I'm not saying we should let him go," Deborah replied.

"What are you – " He stopped and looked at her, realisation dawning.

"Times are different now," Deborah said. "It's a state of war and he's a spy. You know what the penalty is for that."

"We don't know that he's a spy," interrupted her mother. "We cannot mete out draconian punishments based on suspicions, Deborah." Her daughter was about to argue, but Elizabeth raised her hand and continued: "I think we should give him the benefit of the doubt."

"What!" exclaimed Warwick. "You can't do that. He's already admitted that – "

"Warwick," she interjected sharply. "Don't say anything that you'll regret. Or that I'll regret."

The man closed his mouth but didn't look happy about it.

Elizabeth turned to Harry, whose head with spinning. "Harry," she said softly. "You'd like to join our so-called army?"

"Yes. Yes, I would." He continued as though he was arguing for his life, which maybe he was. "I came to join a community that treats people fairly, not the dictatorship that I left behind. I'm prepared to work hard and fight to protect the village. I won't let you down, Elizabeth."

"Our village and the surrounding farms contain around three hundred people and of those perhaps a hundred would be able to fight. Currently our numbers are growing by half a dozen each week as friends and relatives flee the towns and cities to join families here. Admittedly we wish to have a strong defensive force, but this immigration can't continue for much longer – we can only support so many."

Harry nodded.

"However, for the moment," she continued, "we are pleased to accept those who are able to fight or work in the fields. We need them. Warwick trains the volunteers for a day each week, in two groups of fifty on different days. Effectively he's our Master-at-Arms. He's also responsible for a core of twenty or so full-time guards and they train every day. Woody and Dean are part of this group."

Harry looked over his shoulder at the two men who were waiting patiently by the door.

"You can join this core group and in exchange you'll be provided with board and lodging. We're fortunate to have a stronghold here, which has an abundant supply of weapons. When you're not training, you can help clean and repair these weapons. Unfortunately some are obviously very old and in need of some attention." She nodded in conclusion. "How does this arrangement sound to you?"

"That sounds great. I won't let you down."

She nodded thoughtfully and looked at him earnestly. "I hope you don't, Harry. I'm taking a chance on you."

"Thank you. I won't – "

She held up a hand. "No more words. Show me in your actions over the coming weeks and months."

Looking up at the two men standing by the door, she said: "Woody, Dean, would you mind taking Harry to the stable block please? Perhaps he could be allocated the room in which he slept last night?" She looked back at him. "Thank you, Harry," she said, with a small nod. He realised he was being dismissed and stood to follow the two guards out.

As soon as the door had closed, Warwick blurted out: "Are you mad, Elizabeth? He admitted he was Nigel Barkley's son."

"Thank you for not questioning my sanity in front of Woody and Dean. Or our new friend Harry."

"I'm not questioning your sanity. I didn't mean it like that."

"But you did question my opinions when they were in the room. I believe that we should present a unified front at all times."

"You're right, I just wanted to – "

"I'm grateful to you for everything you have done over the years, Warwick, and especially now. I know I can't order you to do anything, because we are all free to do as we choose, but I feel it would be best if we gather information and then retreat to discuss it between the three of us. Information is our most important resource. Don't you agree?"

"Yes," he nodded. "I'm sorry, Elizabeth."

"No, please don't apologise. We're all in this together."

"Now that we're alone," Warwick said pointedly, "can I ask a question?"

"Please do."

"Why do you want to let him stay here?"

"Firstly, we don't know for sure that the Mayor of Gloucester does not have good intentions. Perhaps he's a good man, just doing his best to drag the city out of the anarchic chaos into which it has plummeted."

"I doubt that very much."

"So do I, but I'm keeping an open mind. Secondly, we may have to forge an alliance with Gloucester one day."

"From what we've heard I don't think that would be a good idea."

"They may be too strong for us," Elizabeth suggested. "It's a large city, after all. And having Harry here gives us two options: we can either use him as a bargaining tool, a hostage if you will, but that's a distasteful approach. I would prefer the other alternative: if we treat him well then he might be favourably disposed to us."

"I'm not going to treat him nicely."

Elizabeth smiled. "I didn't think for a moment that you would, Warwick."

Warwick nodded. "You still want me to train him?"

"Yes, absolutely, it's the best way of keeping an eye on him. Keep your friends close and your enemies closer."

"And if he tries to escape?"

"That's a good question," Elizabeth said thoughtfully. She gazed out of the window for a second and then replied: "If he is indeed a spy then we certainly don't want him returning to Gloucester with valuable information about our strength and our defences. I would suggest that you drop everything in order to track him down and bring him back."

"And then?"

"And then Deborah might have the evidence which she requires …"

16. Reid The Bowyer

For the week after Barnaby and his friends attacked him, Reid had taken a different route home. There was a track that ran through the woods, a few hundred yards up the hill, parallel to the road. His mountain bike easily coped with the rough path and it didn't take him too much longer to arrive home.

On the second day he had seen Barnaby and another boy waiting at the same ambush point where they had attacked him before, hiding behind trees and looking down the road for him. They were unlikely to hear him up on the track, but all the same, he dismounted and pushed his bike along as quietly as possible.

The path re-joined the road after another half mile at which point he jumped back on his bike. Happy in the knowledge that his adversaries were well behind, he cycled back to Brenscombe. Just as he arrived home it began to rain heavily and he smiled to himself, hoping that the boys were still waiting for him in the woods.

He didn't see Barnaby again for a few days, so towards the end of the week he returned to cycling along the road, always listening carefully and keeping a keen eye on the road ahead. If he ever heard anything suspicious, he quickly put the bike over his shoulder and carried it up through the trees to the track on the ridge.

Over the next few weeks Reid was able to relax and concentrate on his apprenticeship work and his archery sessions. He always went to bed exhausted after a full day's work along with archery practice, evening exercises and cycling to Dowley and back, but he was already becoming stronger and fitter.

His time in the workshop under Forrester's tutelage had turned to the fashioning of a bow and he felt as though he had achieved a promotion of sorts.

"Your first bow will inevitably not be your finest," Forrester had said to him, "but it will be a decent one which you can pass to one of your friends or brothers. You should make fewer mistakes in your second bow, which I hope will be a good everyday workhorse for you for many years to come. Then, if you're interested, we can make you a longbow. It's probably best that we work on it together, because we want to get it right and it's not a quick process. I have a batch of yew timber that I've been drying for two years and it'll take quite a few months to fashion the wood into a good bow."

Reid started on his first bow and came to realise that arrows were simple in comparison. Some days Forrester asked him to return to arrow manufacture, which actually provided him with some light relief – even though he now started to work on tapered or barrelled shafts and even arrows with heavy wood at the front, spliced with lighter wood at the rear to reduce weight.

In the lunchtime practice, his tutor moved him up to the seventy yard range and towards mid-May he began competing occasionally with Caitlin. The competitive sessions focussed his attention and he progressed from simply hitting the long-range target – which initially provided him with some satisfaction in itself – to regular arrows in the red with occasional golds.

However he never came close to beating Caitlin. Forrester's daughter was disappointed if one of her six arrows wasn't in the gold. She spoke little but her face darkened when she occasionally missed by half an inch.

"I'll be impressed if you ever beat Caitlin at this range," the bow-maker said to him one lunchtime, "but wait until you have your longbow. You'll probably have greater accuracy over a hundred yards and certainly over a hundred and fifty and Caitlin's bow won't even be able to reach some of your longer targets."

Forrester was extremely passionate about archery and couldn't resist throwing in facts and figures about medieval wartime and bow manufacture during their practice sessions:

"In battle the longbow archer's primary function was to rain arrows down on the enemy. They fired and immediately picked up the next arrow without waiting for the first to hit its target. A good archer could have three arrows in the air at any one time."

"For many decades during the Hundred Years War it was mandatory for every adult male in the country to train with a longbow."

"An English archer didn't keep his left hand steady and draw his bow with his right; but keeping his right in place, he pressed the whole weight of his body into the horns of his bow. In that way they were able to use bows that no other archers were strong enough to pull. Archers used to talk of "laying the body into the bow" or "bending the bow" and the French used to talk of "drawing" a bow."

"A bowyer made bows and a fletcher made arrows. They were completely separate skills in those times but of course you and I need to learn both."

After a few weeks Reid had completed his first bow and, as Forrester had forecast, it was decent but not perfect. Reid practiced with it every day, but it somehow didn't have the accuracy of one of his tutor's bows.

Nevertheless it was his bow and he took to carrying it across his back every day as he cycled between Dowley and Brenscombe. Not only was it useful for protection, but occasionally he saw a rabbit or pheasant on the way home and stopped to loose an arrow at it.

He missed more frequently than he hit, but a few times he was able to take home some food for the dinner table, much to his pleasure of his family.

And then one day, he came to be even more thankful that he always carried his bow:

Cycling home in the late afternoon sunshine, he reached the stretch of road that ran through the woods and heard voices ahead, around a bend. He stopped and listened, wondering if Barnaby was lying in wait for him again.

Loud voices tumbled through the trees towards him and he thought that one of them sounded like Barnaby. The other was a man whose voice was raised, presumably at the boy.

Reid put his bike over his shoulder, left the road and climbed up through the woods to the footpath at the top of the slope. He walked quietly along the track, pushing his bike, looking back down to the road, through the trees on his right, to see if he could see the source of the shouting.

He rounded the bend and saw Barnaby in the road a few hundred yards below, looking to a man who was shouting at him, jabbing a finger towards his face. Reid didn't recognise the man. He stopped to peer down through the weak light in the woods and was shocked to see the man grab Barnaby's arm, pull out a knife and brandish it at him.

The boy tried to backed away, holding his free arm up to protect himself.

Reid decided to move closer to see if he could hear the conversation. He slowly laid his bike on the ground and started to creep down the slope, moving from the shelter of one bush to another. Fortunately the man was concentrating his attention on Barnaby and didn't look in Reid's direction.

The man seemed to be in his mid-thirties with long, dark hair and a beard. His clothes were ripped and dirty.

Moving to the cover of a large, leafy wild rhododendron bush, Reid started to hear fragments of conversation. He crept a little nearer through the centre of the bush.

"I don't know what you're talking about," Barnaby said plaintively.

"Don't play dumb with me, boy," the man snarled. "I saw you comin' out of Dowley House."

"I didn't."

The man sighed in exasperation. Reid smiled to hear somebody else irritated by the boy.

"Let's start again, shall we?" the man said, still waving the knife. "I was chattin' to my next door neighbour last week and she told me a story. Before the crash she used to work for a rich bloke who used to run an estate agents. He had five shops around the area, she said. She was his secretary or personal assistant or somethin'. Anyway he saw what was 'appenin' to the economy and he decided to turn some of his money into gold. Apparently that's what rich people do when things are lookin' dodgy. Makes sense, don't it?"

"I suppose so."

"The thing is he asked my neighbour – his secretary – to buy them for him, which was a mistake. If you're goin' to buy fifty thousand quid's worth of krugerrands you should keep it quiet really. I'd heard of krugerrands, but I didn't know that's what rich people buy when they want to invest in gold in a handy shape. Do you know what a krugerrand is?"

"No," Barnaby replied, shaking his head.

"I'm an expert on gold now thanks to Rosie – that's my neighbour – yeah, I thought you'd recognise the name."

"I don't. I've never heard of her."

"I saw it in your eyes, boy. Anyway she told me that a krugerrand is a South African coin which has one ounce of gold in it and one of these things is worth nearly a thousand quid. And this rich bloke has fifty of them. So I said to Rosie, like I was just makin' conversation, who's this bloke then? What's his name? And what do you think she said?"

"I don't know."

"Jonathan Deane, she said, and he lives in Dowley. The biggest house in the village, Dowley House. And you know what else she told me?"

"She said he has a sixteen year old son called Barnaby with blonde curly hair. His dad sometimes brings him into the office. Annoying kid, she said. Walks around like he owns the world. And I think that's you."

"I've never heard of any of these people," Barnaby protested. "I don't know what you're talking about."

"So what I want to know is: where does your dad keep these krugerrands?"

"I don't know," the boy replied plaintively. "I've never even heard of krugerrands."

"Maybe you don't know about this box of gold coins, but you know where he would keep somethin' valuable, don't you?"

"No, no, I don't know anything."

"Well, maybe I should just tcll him that I've got his son and ask him how much you're worth. Perhaps I could take him an ear as proof?" The man moved the knife towards the side of Barnaby's head.

"Aaargh, help!" the boy shouted as loud as he could.

"There's nobody around to help you, boy. It's just me 'n' you. So are you goin' to tell me where I can find these coins or shall I take your ear?"

Reid realised that he had to do something. He had never liked Barnaby, but he couldn't simply allow him to be seriously hurt. He stood up behind the bush and strung his bow. He took an arrow and nocked it on the string.

Taking a deep breath, he stepped out from behind the bush. He was still fifty yards from the road and he started walking slowly downwards, always keeping his eyes on the man but moving his feet carefully over rocks and fallen branches.

"Tell me!" the man shouted, shaking Barnaby's arm.

He was shouting so loudly that he didn't notice Reid creeping through the trees until he was twenty yards away and then, catching sight of him out of the corner of his eye, he whirled round and pulled Barnaby in front of him as a shield, the point of the knife at the boy's throat.

"Who are you?" the man shouted.

Reid hadn't expected the man to pull Barnaby in front of him. What was he going to do now? He didn't want to risk firing an arrow with such a small part of the man's body visible.

"Put that bow 'n' arrow down, boy. Now. Or I'll stick this knife in your friend."

Reid actually laughed out loud at the man's words. "He's not my friend," he smiled.

The man was slightly taken aback. "What are you doin' then?"

"I don't know," Reid replied. "I must be an idiot."

"I think you – " There was a thunk and the man's words were cut short. He gurgled and blood started bubbling from the side of his mouth. Reid wondered what was happening.

The man's body sagged and dropped the knife. Glancing dizzily down at the ground, the man stooped to pick up the knife again, but never completed the movement. He slowly toppled forward and crumpled to the floor, an arrow protruding from his back.

Reid stared at him for a few seconds, keeping his own arrow trained on the man, but he lay completely still.

Lowering his bow, Reid looked around to see who had killed Barnaby's aggressor. On the other side of the road, fifty yards up the other slope, he saw Caitlin step from behind a tree.

She picked her way down to where he and Barnaby were standing dumbfounded. Upon reaching them, she put her fingers on the man's neck for a few seconds to feel for a pulse, then pulled the arrow out of his back and wiped the blood on the back of the man's jacket.

"Thanks, Caitlin," Barnaby said weakly. "Is he … is he dead?"

"He is," she replied in a matter-of-fact manner. "And you should thank Reid too."

"He didn't do anything. Apart from stand there opening and closing his mouth like a goldfish."

"He got the man to present me with a nice target."

"Huh," Barnaby shrugged, obviously not impressed.

"What are we going to do now?" Reid wondered.

"Can you ride back on your bike to get my Dad?" Caitlin asked. "He'll know what to do."

Reid nodded and turned to scramble back up the hill as quickly as he could. That was the first time he had seen a man killed and he was eager to leave as quickly as possible. He hoped that it would be the last time he saw a person die. That might be wishful thinking, he thought to himself, as he pedalled back towards Dowley.

Death is a friend who visits too frequently, but it sharpens our senses for life like a plunge into an ice-cold river. Death and life are two sides of the same coin. Bitter and sweet, dark and light, death and life.

We Brenscombe people have seen much of death, but it strengthens our resolve and spurs us onwards. I see death in the eyes of each of you gathered around the fireplace tonight, but this is the flint which creates the spark in you. Your eyes are alive, your senses are heightened, you feel the world around you, because of what you have seen.

As we embrace life, so too must we embrace death.

17. Nigel and Uros

"And one final thing," Nigel Barkley proclaimed loudly, glancing around at the assembled faces.

His midday announcements outside Shire Hall were starting to draw large crowds. He estimated that there were perhaps a couple of hundred people in the square today. *Not bad*, he thought, especially considering thousands had left for Birmingham a few weeks before.

"I'm pleased that things have been progressing well with the distribution of food," he said, "and I thank you for your patience and good spirits in the queues. I believe it's vital that we begin to re-build a community that can support itself in the long term, not just survive on handouts from a diminishing reserve. Therefore I'm pleased to announce that from next Friday we will deliver the first phase of this re-generation: there will be a weekly market here in the square."

Nods from the crowd, he noticed, even some oohs and aahs.

"We have started visiting some of the surrounding villages, talking to local farmers and persuading them to support the return of Gloucester's market day. We have promised their safety in exchange for a small contribution to the city's food supply. I know that none of you here today have been responsible for the looting that has occurred in recent times and you join me in condemning such mindless acts of violence."

He paused to look at their faces and saw some guilty looks.

"I assure you that nothing of that kind will be accepted in future. I have asked Mr Viduka – " he indicated Uros on his right " – to deal severely with any transgressions. It is of the utmost importance that we provide a safe environment for farmers to trade. It benefits them and it benefits all of us here in Gloucester."

Nigel paused again. A man tentatively put up his hand, to Nigel's surprise. On all of his previous midday announcements, nobody had been brave enough to raise any questions. He assumed that people didn't want to draw attention to themselves - especially with Uros and his men around.

"Yes?" he said.

"How will we pay for things at the market?" the man asked. "We can't use money anymore."

"Initially you will simply have to trade for goods," Nigel replied.

"What if we don't have anything to trade?" a woman shouted.

"Everybody must have something to trade, jewellery perhaps, items from your house, perhaps even your time."

"But – " the woman started, but Nigel held up a hand.

"I know it's not perfect, but we must all take responsibility ourselves for doing the best we can. I'm working on re-introducing some kind of monetary system, but it's complicated. We obviously can't use the old system because it was all on credit cards and computers in banks – and all of us just had a few notes and coins in our pockets. We need to devise some new physical form of money that can't be forged and then we all need to have the ability to earn a wage. There are many things to consider but I promise you that my team and I are working on it."

"But at the market next week – " the woman started again.

"That's enough for today. There will be no more midday announcements until Monday as I will be visiting other farms and villages around Gloucester," Nigel said and nodded to Uros, who waved at the teams of guards positioned strategically around the crowd. His men started roughly pushing people out of the square. Nigel had long ago decided that the populace of Gloucester needed a firm hand.

He and Uros retired to the office inside Shire Hall and Nigel slumped into his chair. Uros sat down opposite him.

"Nice speech, Mr Mayor," Uros smiled.

"These bloody people want it on a plate, don't they?" Nigel sighed.

"It's a good point though. We need money."

"You think I don't know that? But what do we use? I still haven't come up with a good idea."

"What's wrong with using normal money?"

"People just had fifty quid in their pockets when cashpoints stopped working and then they spent most of it."

"The farmers won't come back if people at the market just pay them with junk out of their houses. It'll be like a car boot sale."

"I know."

"Why did you tell them to trade their belongings then?"

"I don't know." Nigel shook his head, exasperated with himself. "We have no other option though."

"Jewellery wasn't a bad idea," Uros mused. "Gold and silver would be even better though."

"Actually you're right," Nigel said, sitting up. "We need gold and silver that we can turn into money. Can you get your men to go round all the empty houses looking for valuable items? Tell them to look for cutlery, candlesticks, anything like that. If it's silver or gold then maybe we can melt it down and make new coins. How many men have you got now?"

"Maybe two hundred. Perhaps two hundred and fifty. It's difficult keeping them organised so I don't know exactly."

"You don't know? I've told you that you should create platoons with captains leading them. Just like the real army," Nigel said, and, when he saw Uros' expression, decided not to continue with an old discussion again. "That's not the point though. How many people do you think are left in the city?"

"Can't be more than a few thousand. They left in droves when you made that Birmingham announcement."

"So there must be thousands of houses that are empty and they can't have taken everything with them. Get your men to look round them all."

"You're going to start making coins? How are you going to do that?"

"I don't know," Nigel shook his head. "Let's just collect this stuff and see how much we get. If it looks enough then we'll try and work out how to mint coins. One step at a time."

"When do you want to do this?"

"Straight away. This afternoon."

"And how many men do you want for visiting these villages tomorrow?"

Nigel thought for a moment. "I guess I don't need as many as last time. It just slowed things down. I'll just take a couple of dozen this time."

"Is that enough? I thought you said we need to make a show of strength."

"We need to strike a balance. We need them to realise they don't have any realistic alternative, but we don't want to frighten them completely."

"Are we taking your farming bloke? What's his name again?"

"Geoff Horsfield. He used to be the chairman of the Gloucestershire branch of the National Farmers Union and he seems to know all the farmers in the county. I thought he would be a friendly face that they could trust."

"Where are we heading this time?"

"I think we need to visit the villages to the south of Gloucester. That reminds me, there was something I was wanting to ask you: we haven't heard from Harry for nearly two weeks now. While Geoff and I are visiting the villages near Gloucester, would you mind going down to Baxley to see if you can find Harry?"

"I'm not your babysitter, Barkley."

"It's not just my son I'm worried about. We also need some information about what they're doing down there. I still keep hearing reports about them training soldiers."

"You never should have sent Harry. He's probably got himself caught or killed."

"That's what my wife is worried about," Nigel admitted. "However, what's done is done. We now need our best man to go down there and find out what's happening. And that's you. We need to find out how many men they have and what they're planning."

"I'll send Brett."

"Brett's an idiot."

"You said that last time and then you sent your own idiot instead. Anyway Brett can handle himself in a fight."

"Maybe but we need someone with a bit of common sense who can look round without drawing attention to himself. Someone who can ask a few gentle questions about their plans. And about Harry. Do you think Brett would be okay doing that?"

"Hmm. Maybe not actually."

Nigel decided not to push it. He waited for his colleague to make up his own mind.

Uros sighed and was silent for a few seconds. "Okay," he nodded finally. "But I'm only going because someone needs to find out what they're up to there. I'm not risking my neck for your stupid son. If he's been captured that's his look out."

Uros knew that Nigel was right, which was the most galling thing about the whole conversation. He stood up and walked out, slamming the door behind him.

18. Village Meeting In Brenscombe

"I'm going to get you for that." Mark nursed his hand whilst staring malevolently at his brother Lewis.

"It was an accident." Lewis shuffled nervously from one foot to another. His brother was a lot bigger than him. He shouldn't have made him angry.

"It's a good job you weren't practicing with the real swords," Josh said, pushing himself backwards on the swing.

The three of them were in the back garden of the Strachan family home. Mark had suggested that they practice with the swords which Lewis had brought back from his friend's house. Lewis had agreed to the suggestion keenly, but fortunately Josh had suggested that they start with wooden sticks. He had just rapped Mark on the hand.

"You're going to pay for that," Mark said, launching a furious attack on his younger brother, fuelled more by an instinctive need to lash out as a result of the pain rather than a desire to hurt his sibling. With his significant advantage of weight, strength and a couple of inches in height, he drove his brother back across the lawn.

Lewis had surprised himself in the first ten minutes of their mock swordplay: he seemed to be quite proficient at blocking and parrying. And it was fortunate that he had some natural talent: Mark now swung his stick violently in an attempt to inflict a similarly painful strike on some part of his brother's anatomy, but Lewis managed to deflect all of his advances, backpedalling quickly.

"Mark," he breathed, in between parries, "I didn't mean to hit you."

"I bet."

Mark jabbed his stick forward towards his brother's belly, but Lewis deftly knocked it aside and jumped sideways. Unfortunately he didn't notice the garden bench behind him and he stumbled backwards. Mark saw his chance and struck his younger brother's leg sharply.

"Aaargh," Lewis cried in pain, lurching further backwards in surprise and then losing his footing entirely. He fell over onto the grass in a heap and Mark pounced forwards, bringing the point of his stick to his brother's chest.

"I win," he shouted triumphantly. He jabbed Lewis playfully in the stomach, his anger having evaporated with his victory.

"Mark!"

He turned around to see his father walking down the garden. "Leave Lewis alone," John shouted.

"I wasn't going to hurt him."

"He smacked me on the leg, Dad," Lewis complained, still lying on the grass. "Hard."

"Well, don't fall over next time," his father replied. "If we get attacked, do you think they'll let you get up if you fall over? You'll be dead."

This response surprised both brothers but before they could say anything John continued: "Come inside, boys. You as well, Josh. We have guests." He smiled and beckoned them towards the house.

"Guests?" said Mark, giving his brother one last jab with his stick.

"Who is it?" Lewis asked as he stood up and brushed himself down.

"Come and see," his father replied, turning back towards the house. "Tim came over about ten minutes ago. He was on watch at the Briddip side of the village and he said there was somebody there asking for me and your mother. Of course Tim didn't want to let them enter the village without checking with us first." John opened the back door and went into the kitchen. "And when I got there who do you think I found?"

Mark and Lewis came into the kitchen. "Aunt Sarah!" Lewis exclaimed in surprise. "And Rose and Elizabeth!"

He and his brother stepped forward and hugged their aunt and two teenage cousins.

"How did you get here?" Mark asked.

"We just walked," Sarah replied succinctly.

"All the way from Oxford? How long did that take?"

"About four days," his aunt replied, with a sigh.

"We slept in a wood one night," Rose added, "and it poured with rain all night. It was horrible."

"But we couldn't stay in Oxford anymore," Sarah said, with a shudder. "It was becoming a nightmare."

"I imagine any town will be the same," John nodded.

"Well you did the right thing coming here," Emilia said, hugging her sister again.

"Are you sure?" Sarah asked. "Do you have enough room?"

"We seem to have run out of beds, but I'm sure we can sort something out."

"Just a floor will be luxury after the nights we've had on the way here," Sarah said, her daughters nodding. "I'm so glad we're here."

-o-o-o-

"They can't stay," Melissa Dacourt announced. It was the monthly village meeting that evening in the village hall and Melissa had heard that Emilia's sister Sarah and her two daughters had arrived that day.

The six members of the village council were sitting at a table at the front, with Peter Parlane in the centre, Sandy Woodall on his right hand side, Hamish on his left and John Strachan beside him. Tim Butterworth and Jane O'Leary were the final members. Tim was in charge of the work on the fort and Jane was another local farmer and landowner.

During the last two hours of discussions the most vociferous people had of course been the Dacourts and, when Peter had asked if there was Any Other Business, once again Melissa had raised her hand.

"What do you mean?" Peter asked, in response to Melissa's statement.

"Just as I said a moment ago," Melissa pronounced, standing in the middle of the rows of seats. "I have nothing against the Strachan family, but there must be a dozen mouths to feed in their house now. And it's not just them. Many other people have welcomed family members into the village."

"What do you expect us to do?" called a woman from the back. "We can't turn them away. My brother and his family came all the way from Bristol because there was no food there."

"We can only support so many people though," Melissa replied. "We only have Hamish, myself and our son in our house – "

"I wonder why?" shouted the woman at the back, to a chorus of laughter.

"And," Melissa stated loudly above the hilarity, "And I believe that to be a sensible number. We have members of the community working hard in the fields – "

"Unlike you," shouted another man.

Hamish stood up and pointed at the man. "We are organising the farm rota," he said haughtily, "but we are still doing our fair share of the work."

"Only when Peter threatened to kick you out if you didn't," the man shouted.

Hamish barked a reply at the man, just as another member of the gathering made a further rude comment causing Melissa to shout a heated response. Within seconds the whole meeting was in turmoil with everyone talking at once.

John and Peter looked at each other across the top table and shook their heads.

With a sigh, the village leader stood up and banged the table. "Quiet!" he shouted. "Quiet!"

The uproar subsided slowly. Hamish sat down beside him but Melissa remained on her feet.

"Thank you, Peter," she said. "As I was saying before I was rudely interrupted – "

"Melissa," Peter interjected.

"Yes?"

"I believe we've heard your point of view and I thank you for it. Perhaps it's time we heard from somebody else?"

"But – "

"Thank you, Melissa. That really is very kind of you. Would anyone else like to contribute on this point?"

Melissa slowly sat down.

There were a few seconds of silence and John raised his hand.

"Go ahead, John," Peter said, taking his seat.

"We all know what he's going to say," Melissa muttered loudly.

"I really just wanted to say," John started quietly, and then remembered to raise his voice. "I just wanted to say that I agree with Melissa."

"You do?" exclaimed his wife Emilia from the front row. She looked like she thought her husband had taken leave of his senses.

"You do?" queried Melissa in surprise.

"Yes," John replied. "We can't keep increasing the size of our community indefinitely. Melissa is right. There is a point beyond which the village will become unsustainable and unmanageable."

"So what do you propose?" his wife asked from her position just opposite him. "If *your* sister arrives at the village tomorrow with her children that we turn them away?"

"I agree it's difficult and I don't have the complete solution, but perhaps each house should have a quota, a maximum number of occupants. Obviously all the new people still need to take a turn on the watch and in the fields."

"Exactly," Melissa agreed emphatically.

"And what do you think the quota should be?" Emilia asked, still amazed that her husband was taking this stance.

"I don't know, but I wanted to make another point as well. These meetings were intended as a forum for people to raise issues such as these, but we can't run the community in this manner. I believe this topic should be discussed by the village council, that is the six people here at the front with Peter as chair and then they will issue a statement when the decision has been reached."

"What?" said Hamish, standing up. "You can't make decisions behind closed doors without consulting everyone."

"And you can't run things with all two hundred people, well probably two hundred and fifty now, being involved in every tiny decision. Peter was voted in as village leader and he appointed his council. They should run things on our behalf. Melissa has raised her point and now she should leave it to the council to decide."

"But – "

"We all voted and Peter was given a three month trial term and if people don't like the council's decisions then they can vote in somebody else in a couple of months. In any case, Hamish, you have a position on the council so you'll be able to make your voice heard."

"Not with the other people on the council being Peter's mates. Anyway I'm not thinking of myself. What if other people don't like the decision?"

"That's how a democracy works, Hamish. You of all people should know that." There was some quiet laughter at this point.

"Well perhaps we don't want Peter to continue as village leader," Hamish said loudly. "Perhaps we should have another vote tonight. I would like to put myself forward as his replacement."

"Hamish," John said, shaking his head. "We don't want to have a vote every month or every week. A leader needs time to make things work and three months is a short time as it is."

"But – "

"Thank you, John, for your contribution on this point," Peter said, standing up again and cutting Hamish off. "I look forward to standing against you at the end of the three months, Hamish, but in the meantime we will continue this discussion at the next council meeting. Thank you for raising it, Melissa."

Hamish sat down, still fuming.

"Now," continued Peter, "does anyone have any other matters they wish to raise?" The expression on his face indicated that he sincerely hoped they could all go home now.

"Yes," a quiet voice said from the side of the room. All eyes looked in her direction. It was Sophia. John looked at his daughter in surprise.

"Go ahead," Peter said, taking his seat once more.

Sophia stood up and addressed the room nervously. "It's just that … I was thinking that we should … we should form an alliance with other villages around us. Cranwold, Crundle Green and Dowley. And of course Briddip."

She paused, half-expecting somebody to interrupt, but the room was silent.

"I walked through Cranwold a few days ago with my brother Mark and his girlfriend Rachel," she continued, "and we didn't see anybody. All of the people in the village were hiding in their houses. I believe that we need to show them what we have done here in Brenscombe, how we've formed work groups for the fields and how we're taking it in turns to guard our community. They would benefit from some support and guidance from us – and we would benefit as well. Together we would be stronger."

Sophia paused again and glanced around nervously. She wasn't used to speaking in front of a large audience, but there were nods of approval which gave her the encouragement to continue:

"I'm sure they're currently wasting their resources – the produce growing in the fields around them – and they're leaving themselves open to attack. All around the country there will be communities, armies and fiefdoms springing up. Some will be benign like ourselves and some will be aggressive."

"What makes you think that?" asked Peter. "Perhaps we're the only ones getting organised."

"If we're doing it here then other people will be as well. Wherever there's a source of power, be it food or a stronghold or just someone who is bigger or nastier than those around him. And some of these communities will become larger and stronger. At some point we'll be attacked by a hostile force much larger than ourselves. It may be next month or next year or in five years from now, but we'll definitely be attacked. Our only hope is to form an alliance with the villages around us so that we can protect each other."

The room was quiet as Sophia's words sank in.

Unfortunately these words came too late. Everybody saw the wisdom of the suggestion and the council acted but there was too much to be done in too short a time. The surrounding communities were a timid child that needed to be coaxed from its hiding place and the resulting alliance – when it eventually was formed – did not have time to develop before the predicted attack occurred.

The attack came earlier than any of us expected and that is why I tell you – all of you here at this gathering tonight – to speak out when there is something to be said, sooner rather than later.

As John said that evening, the tribe is run by the council but we can all make our contribution. Speak and our leader will listen.

19. Harry Trains Hard

"Move, boy!" Warwick shouted.

Harry tried to increase his speed but his legs wouldn't respond. The rain was pouring down but he couldn't be any wetter than he already was. Ahead of him the other members of Warwick's core unit were running – just about – through ankle-deep mud around the edge of a field.

They had run for three miles to this large field planted with wheat and were now on their fifth lap around the fringes of the crops on the churned-up earth beside the hedges.

Harry was exhausted before they even started. That morning he had carried piles of Cotswold stone back and forth, helping a farmer build a dry stone wall, before reporting for training with Warwick. This was his second week as part of the unit of twenty men stationed in the castle and every day had been as tiring as this one. There was work on the farms and at least five hours of exercises every single day, including the weekends.

But it wasn't just Harry. Warwick was determined that his squad would be extremely fit and well-drilled, but he lavished special attention on his new recruit.

"Catch up with the others," Warwick shouted in his ear, but, if anything, the group was pulling away from him.

Harry tried to accclerate but slipped in the deep mud and fell to one knee.

"Get up!" Warwick bellowed at him furiously. "We're a unit and we stay together."

Harry struggled back to his feet. "I'm trying to catch them," he gasped, setting off again.

"Try harder. If we're attacked, I may need to move you into position a few miles away and I need someone who can get there quickly. Not someone who'll flounder around in the mud."

Harry ran as hard as he could and fortunately the men ahead of him slowed down to filter through the gate at the end of the field. He caught up with them as they turned out onto the road.

"You were lucky there," Warwick grunted, running alongside him. "Don't drop back again. Stay with them this time."

"Okay," Harry panted.

"I'm twice your age, boy, and I can run twice as fast as you."

Harry didn't respond, but wondered how the older man was able to run this hard *and* shout a constant stream of abuse at him.

They covered the three miles back to Baxley Castle and ran through the gateway into the grounds. Harry rested his hands on his knees and breathed in deeply.

"Swords!" Warwick commanded. "Pair up and fight. Woody, take the new boy and don't go easy on him or you'll be fighting me next."

Each of the men had been carrying wooden training swords and now they drew them from the belts. Harry looked up just as Woody swung his sword in his direction. Fortunately it was a half-hearted swing and he was able to stumble back out of the way.

"What was that?" Warwick shouted at Woody. He drew his own sword and cracked Harry smartly on the leg. "Draw your sword and defend yourself, boy." He struck Harry on the arm, as he started to pull his sword out.

"Two against one isn't fair," Woody said.

"Fair?" Warwick turned to face Woody. "Fair? Do you think the enemy will wait in line to fight you one by one?" He swung at Woody, who quickly moved his sword to parry the blow. "If we're under attack," continued Warwick, "then I might need you to run five miles and immediately begin fighting – and we may be out-numbered two or three to one."

Warwick turned back to Harry, who was standing ready.

"Finally, you've drawn your sword, boy," he shouted as he lunged at Harry. However, to his astonishment, the younger man smoothly deflected the attack and shuffled back a step.

Warwick looked momentarily surprised and then swung his wooden sword in a chopping motion at Harry's side. The blow was parried again and this time Harry stepped forward to make a counter-thrust. His tired legs moved slowly and the older man just moved his sword in time to stop a blow to the side of his torso. He stepped backwards smartly to take stock of his opponent. Woody had moved out of the way, leaving the other two to their duel.

"So, boy," Warwick smiled. "We've finally found something you're half-decent at. Or were you just lucky?"

"I – "

Warwick launched a furious assault on Harry just as he began speaking. The younger man managed to block the initial swings, but one blow struck him on the shoulder. Warwick didn't let up, constantly swinging his sword, first one side, then the other, then a thrust at Harry's midriff.

Harry couldn't cope with the blistering onslaught from the larger, more experienced man and soon every second or third strike was hitting home. Harry backpedalled as quickly as he could until he found himself pinned against the castle wall.

"Warwick!" shouted Woody, trying to intervene.

The other men had either stopped or were half-heartedly going through the motions while they watched. Warwick didn't appear to have heard the shout and he swung at Harry again, too fast for the younger man, resulting in a loud thwack on his arm.

Harry cried out in pain and this seemed to bring Warwick back to his senses. He paused and looked at the younger man.

"You take over again," he said to Woody, lowering his sword. "And the rest of you: keep going."

"I think Harry needs a rest," Woody suggested.

"A rest? Do you think the enemy would let him have a rest? Attack him again. Or would you like me to have another go?"

"No, it's okay," Woody replied, readying himself. "I'll do it."

Warwick nodded and moved away, ostensibly to look at another group.

Woody swung his sword slowly and Harry blocked it easily. They continued to joust at half-pace while Harry recovered his breath.

"You did pretty well against Warwick there," Woody said quietly, glancing over his shoulder to see how far away their commander was.

"It didn't feel like it."

"I've never seen him attack anyone like that, but you managed to block most of his blows."

"Plenty of them landed."

"You look like you've done this before."

"I have," Harry admitted, deflecting a blow. "I was in the fencing club at university."

"I should have guessed."

"There was this girl I liked," he smiled. "She dropped out after a few weeks, but I carried on."

"Stop yapping you two!" Warwick shouted as he came near them. "Everybody swap partners. Now!"

They all duelled with a different opposite number and then swapped again – and again. After that Warwick organised combat in pairs and then groups of three and four.

An hour later he finally called a halt. "Okay, that's it for today," he announced to everyone's relief.

The men started heading slowly back towards their quarters but Warwick wasn't finished with Harry.

"Not you, Barkley," he said. "Come with me."

Harry's heart sank but he followed Warwick around the side of the stables and into a large wood store.

"You're not fit enough," Warwick announced, "but, luckily for you, these logs need splitting." He pointed at a huge pile of wood on the floor.

Harry sighed.

"What are you sighing for, boy? You can leave any time you want. You want to go back to Gloucester?"

"No."

"Well, get chopping. The axe is over there."

He indicated the corner of the room and Harry picked up the axe.

"I want you to drop out, boy," Warwick continued while Harry started splitting the logs. "I don't trust you. Lady Baxley asked me to take you on, but I don't want you. Nothing would give me greater pleasure than to have you decide to drop out."

"I'm not going to drop out," Harry said vehemently, swinging the axe.

"You will. Or you'll decide you don't want to follow my orders which will amount to the same thing. You're soft and I only want fighters in the core unit. Men who never give up. The enemy – whoever they are – won't go easy on you. They'll try to kill you. You're soft so you might as well stop now."

Harry kept on splitting the logs and Warwick kept on shouting and needling.

After a little while, Warwick announced: "I'm going for a cup of tea and a little sit down. If you'd like to give up then there's a nice cup of tea waiting for you inside. Otherwise continue until you've finished this pile and then I want them all stacked over there. Neatly."

The old man stalked off and Harry slowed his pace, but continued to swing the axe. He wasn't going to let Warwick beat him and, he realised, he didn't like the thought of leaving Baxley.

It was dark outside when he finally finished. He looked at the stack of logs with both resentment and satisfaction and put the axe back in the corner. He stumbled back to his room and lay on his bed.

I'll just have a few minutes rest, he thought to himself, *and then I'll get something to eat.*

Within a few seconds he was fast asleep.

-o-o-o-

"Wake up! We're under attack!"

Harry jerked upright in his bed and looked around. It was dark apart from the light coming past Warwick. The man seemed to be almost filling the doorway, his head nearly touching the lintel.

"Didn't you hear me, boy? Get up."

Harry jumped out of bed and pulled on some clothes. "What time is it?" he mumbled, still not properly awake.

"Two o'clock," Warwick shouted. "Move faster, boy. I'll see you out on the grounds. Bring your training sword."

Harry nodded and then wondered why he just needed his wooden sword if they were being attacked. He pulled on some shoes and stumbled out of his room, down the stairs and outside.

"About time. Woody, Dean and the others are under attack. Help them."

Harry saw that twenty men were in combat in the centre of the castle grounds. He ran over to take his position next to Woody, his wooden sword in his hand, and wondered how that was going to save him.

Then he noticed that the men they were fighting were also part of the core unit of guards. He half-heartedly blocked a cut from one of the men attacking Woody and said to his colleague: "What's going on? These are our guys aren't they?"

"Yes, of course," Woody replied, "it's just a drill."

"In the middle of the night?"

"Yeah, he does it every couple of weeks. He says this is the time we're most likely to be attacked so we should practice."

Harry shook his head, but begrudgingly saw the sense of it and entered into the skirmish with a little more energy. Woody's group started to dominate and pushed the others back farther and farther. Warwick called a halt and then organised exercises in pairs, threes and fours, just as he had in the afternoon.

He drilled the men for an hour before finally announcing: "Okay, that's it. Back to bed."

The group stopped and trudged back to their quarters, but once again Warwick had more in store for Harry.

"Come here, Barkley," he barked. "I've got other plans for you."

Harry sighed internally but tried not to let it show this time. He followed the Master-At-Arms to the stables.

They entered the stables and Warwick said: "Toby, the young stable hand, fell ill earlier in the night and I want you to keep an eye on the horses."

"Keep an eye on the horses?" Harry repeated. "What do you mean?"

"Toby's in bed in the castle so I want you to sleep in here."

"In here? Where do I sleep?"

"Where Toby normally does." Warwick pointed at a small cot with a straw-filled mattress at the end of the corridor that ran along the front of the stalls. "If there's a problem with one of the horses come and get me."

"Right," Harry said, looking at the lumpy mattress and the rough blankets.

"These horses are very important to us," Warwick said. "Not just for getting around but potentially in combat when we've trained them up. Look after them."

"Okay," Harry nodded.

"I still want you on parade at the usual hour," Warwick commanded as he walked out of the stable door.

Harry shrugged and looked around the stables. A couple of the horses were looking out of their stable doors. "Hi guys," Harry said to them as he walked past on his way to the small bed at the end of the corridor. He lay down on the old mattress, which felt luxurious after his tiring day and the night-time drill. Once again, within a few seconds he was fast asleep.

20. Alliance

"You're back later than I expected," Emilia said.

"What a day," John sighed, slumping onto one of the kitchen chairs.

It was nearly nine o'clock in the evening and John and his daughter had just returned from Cranwold where they had been putting forward the idea of an alliance.

Sophia sat down heavily at the kitchen table next to her father. "I'm exhausted," she said.

"We knocked at the first few houses we came to, but nobody would answer the door," John said.

"They were scared," Sophia explained to her mother.

"Finally we found someone who was prepared to talk to us," John continued, "and we asked if they had a village leader. He just looked at me blankly like I was speaking a foreign language. Everybody has been doing their own thing, hiding in their houses, no attempt at any kind of organisation. We had to knock on all the doors in the village to get them together for a meeting."

"You thought that would be the case, Dad," Emilia said.

"True, but I didn't think it would take that long to get everyone along to the village hall. It took forever. Most of them didn't want to leave their houses. They thought we were going to … I don't know … break in or something …"

"They've had a couple of incidents there recently," Sophia interjected. "Outsiders coming to the village, stealing things, breaking in. One woman said she was even attacked in her garden."

"We only managed to get half of the community to the village hall, about a hundred people. I gave them the same speech I did here at our first meeting, but the outcome was even worse in a way."

"What do you mean?" Emilia asked. "A big argument?"

John shook his head. "I'd have quite liked it if they'd argued with me, but there was just apathy or, rather, a sort of docile acceptance of the situation. And nobody wanted to volunteer to be village leader – in the end I had to make someone do it."

"One of the guys who helped knock on doors," Sophia said.

"His name is Imre Varadi," John added.

"Imre?"

John stood up and poured himself a glass of water.

"He's Hungarian, but he's lived over here for twenty years. He's a dentist. Anyway he didn't want to be the village leader, but I told him it was just for three months and he could organise another village meeting to vote someone else in after that time. We then appointed others to do the guard rota and start liaising with the farmers around Cranwold."

"So, do we have an alliance with them?" his wife asked.

"Yes," John nodded, sitting back down at the kitchen table. "Of a kind. We told them that Brenscombe and Cranwold would be stronger if we worked in partnership and they just nodded. The whole room. I don't think it's a marriage of equals."

"They just need to follow someone else's lead for a short while," his daughter said, "until they find their feet."

"Yes," John sighed, "but it'll take more of our time. I think I'll need to go back in a few days to make sure they're actually doing stuff. I might need to be on their village council and attend their meetings. I'm not sure if anything will get done otherwise."

"Maybe they'll get themselves organised now that we've started the ball rolling," Sophia said.

"You're an optimist, aren't you?" John smiled at this daughter and then turned to his wife. "We're going to talk to Crundle Green and Dowley over the next few days as well. I hope they're not as bad. It's hard enough running one village let alone four."

"It will be what it will be," his wife said, "and you'll deal with it."

"You know, I'm glad it was just Sophia and I who went over to Cranwold. It's a good job we didn't have a large group of armed guards. They would never have opened their doors. Imagine if they'd seen Mark with his sword." He smiled at his daughter.

"Mark and Rachel were given archery lessons by Reid earlier this evening," Emilia said. "I watched for a little while and was quite proud of our baby boy."

"Reid's the tallest in the family now," John pointed out with a laugh.

"But he's still my baby," Emilia smiled. "He was a good teacher, confident and authoritative. He seemed to be quite pleased with his new skills and being better than Mark at something. Rachel was better than Mark as well – she picked it up quite quickly."

"She's a good girl," John nodded.

"Oh, by the way," his wife added. "She's planning to visit Langdale polo farm tomorrow and see if she can borrow one of their horses."

"Borrow a horse?" her husband muttered in confusion.

"For her job as watch commander. She thinks it'll be the best way to travel between the guard posts."

"Oh, I see," John nodded. "I wonder if the people in Cranwold will ever be that proactive," he mused. He sat up, a pensive look on his face. "That's a good idea, you know. We should have a whole unit of our people trained up in riding horses – if the polo farm will let us. They would be the perfect horses for a battle I'd have thought. I imagine they're able to turn quickly and used to a melee with people swinging sticks. We would have a formidable defence for the village if we had a cavalry unit."

"Stop coming up with new ideas," his wife smiled. "You were just complaining about all the work you have to do."

"We might need something like that one day."

Emilia shook her head fondly at her husband, little realising how soon he would be proven right.

21. Horse Feathers

Harry was awakened by the sound of the stable doors opening. This was his third night on the small bed in the stables, but he had slept well on each occasion. The pale morning light trickled through the doorway and Warwick marched in. "What do you know about saddling a horse?" he asked, looking along the corridor at Harry.

"Nothing," Harry answered matter-of-factly, sitting up and looking at his watch. "I thought I wasn't meant to be on parade for another half an hour?"

"Lady Baxley and her daughter want to visit some of the nearby farms this morning so we need to get four horses ready. Myself and Joe will be accompanying them. Get up and watch me do the first one."

Warwick marched up to one of the stalls while Harry quickly pulled on his clothes. He entered just as the older man was placing a saddle on the horse's back.

"This is Hermes," Warwick said, patting the animal's flank. "He's Lady Baxley's horse, aren't you boy?" Harry watched as the Master-At-Arms saddled the young stallion and gently pulled on the bridle, talking to him and stroking him all the time. Harry was surprised at the gentle tones coming out of the burly man's mouth.

"Right," Warwick said, turning to look down at Harry when he had finished, his tone changing abruptly. "Do the same for the horse in the next stall. The saddle will be on a stand on the wall."

The younger man nodded uncertainly, turned to go but then had a thought: "What's the horse's name?"

"Polly."

"Polly?"

"Yes."

"Not a Greek god?"

"Are you still here?"

Harry quickly left the stall and entered the neighbouring compartment where a pair of baleful eyes looked at him inquisitively.

"Hello, Polly," he said as he rounded the horse apprehensively and lifted the saddle off the frame on the wall. "Don't worry, girl, this won't hurt a bit. I hope."

He gently placed the saddle on her back, half-expecting the horse to buck wildly, but Polly simply stood quietly. She was obviously quite experienced at this. Harry nervously cinched the strap and then pulled on the bridle. This took a little longer, but eventually it was done and he thanked Polly for her help, stroking the side of her neck.

"What's taking you so long?" Warwick shouted from outside. "Bring her out into the yard when you're finished."

The Master-At-Arms was just tying a second horse's reins onto a rail alongside Hermes and he checked over Harry's handiwork. "Not bad," he muttered gruffly, to Harry's amazement.

Warwick went back into the stables, saddled another horse and brought it out, just as Lady Baxley and Deborah were approaching.

"Ah, thank you, Warwick," Lady Baxley said. "That was very kind of you."

"I'll just fetch Joe."

"Actually, Warwick, would you mind if Harry came along with us today?"

"Him?" he replied, looking at Harry almost in disgust.

"I would like to catch up with Harry and this seems like a good opportunity. Have you ever ridden a horse, Harry?"

"No, I haven't, I'm afraid," he answered, glancing apprehensively at the horses.

"Well, now might be a good time to learn. Why don't you take Polly? Perhaps Warwick could quickly run through the basics with you."

The Master-At-Arms sighed and brusquely gave Harry some brief instructions while the two women climbed onto their horses using the stone mounting steps alongside the stables. Warwick jumped effortlessly onto his horse while Harry struggled to mount Polly. Finally they set off through the castle gate in the direction of Baxley village.

"It's been over a week since we last spoke, Harry," Elizabeth Baxley said, as they rode along the lane through the castle grounds. "Has Warwick been looking after you?"

"Er, yes," he replied, glancing at the large, gruff Master-At-Arms who was riding just behind.

"And how are you settling in?"

"Fine, thank you." Harry didn't know how best to respond. Should he say that Warwick Yorath was a slave-driver who was constantly bullying him?

"Is it what you expected?" Lady Baxley asked.

"I didn't know what to expect really."

"You came here looking to join our army, as you called it, and as you've seen we're simply a group of like-minded folk doing our best to make a life for ourselves. I wondered if you were of a mind to remain with us?"

"Oh, well, yes, if I may," stumbled Harry, "I certainly don't want to go back to Gloucester."

"Well, we would be pleased to have you stay here."

Harry heard a small noise from behind him and glanced back at Warwick's scowling face.

They rode through the village, which took quite a time as Elizabeth stopped to speak to everybody she saw, asking about their families and whether they had enough to eat. Harry was impressed by her recall of their names, not only of the people she met, but their children, their brothers and sisters – and even their cats and dogs.

On leaving the village, they travelled out along a country road lined with tall ash trees. Harry noticed that Elizabeth looked firstly at the trees and then keenly studied the crops in the fields, her eyes examining every aspect of the world around them.

After a few minutes, she nodded to herself, seemingly satisfied, and turned her attention back to Harry.

"You ride well," she said, observing him, "Polly's a good girl, she knows her job, but when you ride other horses you must let them know who is in charge. You should care for them, let them know you love them, but they must be aware that you are top dog, so to speak. It's like that with all animals, even chickens have their pecking order."

Harry nodded.

"The ash trees are coming into leaf," she continued and Harry followed her eyes to the branches above them. "Ash are always a little behind the rest so you know spring is well and truly here when their black buds start to appear."

Harry nodded again.

"I like spring," she mused out loud, looking at the countryside around them. "I suppose that's not very original, but it always fills me with hope for the months ahead. It's good to know that the days are lengthening and we can all emerge from our winter hibernation. However this year, for the first time, spring makes me nervous as well."

"Really?"

"For many reasons," she nodded. "I have never looked at our crops so keenly before. It is so important this year that we have good weather and achieve a good harvest. A poor year could almost wipe out our community or at least give us great hardship over the winter."

"I suppose so," Harry agreed, looking at the fields around him.

"And as the weather improves, all sorts of animals become more confident about venturing out further. Especially humans. In the past generals would wait for spring or summer to make a move, they would never launch an attack during winter. It's obviously more difficult to live off the land and to keep your soldiers warm and dry at night."

"True," Harry nodded, wondering where this was going.

"Now that spring is upon us, the world is starting to stir, Harry. Over the last week the Mayor of Gloucester has been visiting villages around the city and asking them to join forces with him."

"Has he?" Harry asked in surprise, not noticing that Elizabeth was studying him as intensely as she had the fields a few moments before.

She nodded. "He is offering them protection in exchange for a small contribution from their harvest. A laudable offer on the face of it, but he makes this suggestion with seventy five men standing behind him."

"That doesn't surprise me," snorted Harry and looked sharply at Lady Baxley, wondering if he had said too much.

"What do you know of the Mayor's motives, Harry?"

"Me? Nothing."

"I wonder if he's really interested in protecting these villages or if he simply wants their food."

Harry was silent for a few seconds. He wasn't entirely sure of his father's intentions himself.

"Perhaps he's simply being pragmatic," Harry offered eventually.

"Hmmm, maybe," nodded Elizabeth thoughtfully. "Perhaps it's similar to my earlier statement about handling horses."

"Pardon?"

"He's showing them a firm hand, but perhaps he really does care for the people and wants to create a safe community for all."

Harry snorted again, almost a laugh, but short and sharp.

Elizabeth smiled. "Your reaction suggests that this view is unlikely."

Harry wondered if he had given too much away. And surely his father wasn't an evil man? Uros and his men were the problem really. "The guards certainly don't care about the people. They're a vicious bunch of thugs."

"So you said at our previous meeting," Elizabeth nodded. "And disturbingly they are only a few miles away today."

"Pardon?"

"There is a unit of roughly twenty five men halfway between here and Gloucester. Not seventy five on this occasion so maybe he is softening his approach. The Mayor visited some villages yesterday and then camped just off the main highway. We heard about this late last night and Warwick has sent some men to observe their movements."

"They're near here?" Harry said worriedly.

"About ten miles away, but we don't think they'll be coming any further south on this expedition. They seem to be visiting the villages nearest to Gloucester first, which is only natural."

"Good."

"However," continued Elizabeth, "it's only a matter of time until we receive a visit. It may be next week, next month, next year, but we need to decide what our response will be."

"It's got to be no," Harry blurted out. "They're not nice people. That's why I left."

"My preference would be to maintain our independence, but if they succeed in building an alliance of all the villages in a ten mile radius around the city then they'll be a powerful force. At twenty miles from Gloucester we are a little distant but perhaps not remote enough to escape their attentions. The castle itself is obviously a formidable stronghold – and I'm proud to say the walls have never been breached in a thousand years – but we cannot protect the village and the farms around us. The whole community could hide in the castle for weeks, but meanwhile an attacking force could strip the land of all crops and animals."

"You said you have a hundred men who can fight."

"Currently that would probably be enough, but Gloucester may be able to increase their numbers over the coming months." Elizabeth paused for a moment. "There are also other considerations."

"Like what?"

"Trade. We don't want to fall out with a close neighbour. It is not imperative currently, but our farmers will want to trade at some point in the future. We have also heard that there will be a market in Gloucester every Friday and the Mayor has promised to ensure the security of everyone who attends."

"Really?" Harry thought there must be a catch.

"So, whilst I would prefer not to become part of the protectorate of the city of Gloucester, I do want to ensure that we have a relationship which allows trade. We need to strike a balance. And I was thinking that maybe our best chance of resisting the overtures of Gloucester is to form an alliance with another party, ideally with a more equal partner."

"Who? You mean somebody other than Gloucester?"

"That's the question, Harry. At present I don't see any other suitors. It's quiet to the south for now and the west is difficult due to the width of the river Severn as it opens out into the estuary, but we've heard vague murmurings about a cluster of villages to the east that are forming an alliance. However they are twenty miles away and at the top of the Cotswold escarpment, not down here on the Severn plain. Perhaps not the best-placed allies, but something to consider."

"What are you going to do?"

"What would you do in my shoes, Harry?"

"I certainly wouldn't have anything to do with Gloucester."

"I understand your feelings, but, as I said, we need to keep our trade options open. Not so much now, but in the near future. Well, that is my opinion. Warwick and Deborah are a little more hard-line, I think it is fair to say. So that is why we're out on horseback this morning."

Elizabeth turned Hermes down a farm track and Polly followed suit without any guidance from Harry.

"We're visiting some of our farmers today to ask for their opinion, Harry. Warwick wonders if they are even interested in trade and maybe there's something in what he says. Perhaps a market in Gloucester doesn't offer them much."

"What are people doing for money at this market?" Harry asked.

"That's a good question and, from what I've heard, I don't think the answer has been found yet. Initially I think the plan is simply for an exchange of goods, which limits the potential somewhat." She pointed at the farmhouse ahead of them. "The first person we're visiting is an old friend by the name of Alessio Palmer."

"Alessio Palmer?" Harry repeated dumbly.

Elizabeth smiled. "There are many Palmers around Gloucestershire and Alessio's father was fortunate enough to marry an Italian lady by the name of Gina. Alessio now owns the fields which are around us and has a milk herd of around two hundred and fifty cows. His father passed away ten years ago, but his mother Gina still lives with him on the farm. However she's over eighty now, more's the pity. She's an old friend of mine, but she's not able to visit me in the castle as frequently these days due to her hips."

As they approached the farmhouse, Harry happened to glance across the field to his left and saw a figure standing beside a tree on the far side of the meadow. The distant figure held up a hand and then stepped behind the tree. Harry hadn't been able to tell who it was, but there was a familiarity about his shape and the way he moved. He looked at Warwick and Lady Baxley but they were looking ahead at the farmhouse. Then he realised where he'd seen that tall, lithe figure before.

"Uros?" Harry murmured quietly, continuing to stare at the tree in the distance.

"Pardon?" Elizabeth said, following his gaze.

"Nothing," said Harry, coming back to his senses. "I was just thinking that, er … that, er, two hundred and fifty cows is quite a lot."

"That's very true. As there is no electricity Alessio has had to return to manual milking, but his farm is part of the rota that we've devised for people in the village to help out in exchange for food. We have a dozen willing helpers here each morning and evening."

As they approached the farmhouse, the door opened and a large, white-haired lady hobbled out with the assistance of two walking sticks. Harry guessed that this was Gina.

Elizabeth gracefully dismounted from her horse and looped the reins around a fencepost.

"Vecchia amica!" Lady Baxley exclaimed loudly as she approached Gina with her arms open wide. A huge smile was spread across the face of the Italian woman as the two old friends hugged. They chattered rapidly in Italian as Deborah dismounted and joined them. The sounds of the new arrivals had obviously travelled as far as the barns, because a burly, middle-aged man emerged. This was obviously the incongruously named Alessio Palmer, olive-skinned with black hair.

"Good morning, Elizabeth," he said, surprising Harry with the thick Gloucestershire twang in his voice.

Warwick had not dismounted from his horse and Elizabeth turned back to him. "Why don't you join us, Warwick?" she said.

He looked surprised and glanced at Harry. "I can't leave him alone with the horses out here."

Elizabeth stepped back over. "I think it would be useful if you could join the discussion with Alessio and Gina. You, Deborah and I need to make a joint decision about the way forward and therefore you should hear what all the farmers have to say today."

"What about him? I don't trust him."

"I believe we can rely on Harry," she said earnestly to Warwick and then turned to the younger man. "I can trust you, can't I, Harry?"

"Absolutely," he assured her quickly, wanting her to believe him, wanting her to believe *in* him. "I'll look after the horses. I won't let anything happen to them."

"There you are, Warwick," Elizabeth said. "Why don't we take a chance on Harry and see if he is as good as his word?"

Warwick took one last, surly glance as Harry, dismounted and walked over to the farmhouse with Lady Baxley.

After they had gone inside, Harry looked across the field to his left, towards the tree on the far side where he thought he had seen Uros. Had it been him? His father's men were on patrol in the area so it was possible.

He stared at the tree in the distance and then scanned along the over-grown hedge that ran around the field. Nothing.

Just as he started to relax, he heard a voice: "Hello, Harry." The Serbian stepped out from behind the hedge, but stayed close to it so that he couldn't be seen from the farmhouse.

"Uros," Harry said with a start.

"Out for a ride with the locals?" Uros smiled at him.

"What are you doing here?"

"Your father asked me to come and find you. He thought you might be in trouble. Little does he know."

"You have to leave, Uros. Before they see you."

"Surely you'd put in a good word for me?" Uros smirked. "Who's the woman? The one who did all the talking."

Harry wondered what to say. He didn't want to divulge anything which could be used against the people of Baxley. "I don't know."

"What's happening here, Harry? Have you sold us out?"

"What do you mean?"

"Have you changed sides?"

"I was never on your side, Uros. Why would I want to be with a thug like you?"

"Careful, little boy," Uros said, taking a step forward. His eyes were a few inches from Harry's, looking down at him, staring malevolently.

"You should go," Harry re-iterated nervously. "They'll see you."

"Maybe that would be a good thing. Do they know you're the son of the Mayor of Gloucester?"

Harry said nothing.

"They don't know?" Uros smiled.

"Just go. You can tell my father that you've seen me and that I'm okay."

"Why don't tell him yourself."

Harry shook his head. "I'm not coming back."

"So you have changed sides," Uros smiled. "I told him you weren't to be trusted."

"I'm not taking any sides. I just want to stay where there are normal people who aren't trying to kill each other. They don't fight each other for food, they work together."

"They're posh people with too much land. If they lived in the city where there wasn't enough food then you can be sure they would be fighting to stay alive like the rest of us." Uros paused. "You were meant to assess the strength of their force. Are they building an army here? It doesn't look like it to me."

Harry didn't reply for a few seconds. He didn't want to give anything away, but perhaps the quickest way of getting rid of him was to give the man something.

"Well?" Uros said impatiently. "It doesn't look like they have an army here. It's just a bunch of farmers, isn't it?"

"You should stay away from here, Uros. They have hundreds of men."

"Hundreds?" Uros scoffed.

"Lady Baxley told me that there are about five hundred people living in this area and I've seen fifty men each day come up to the castle for training. Warwick – that's the man who's in the farmhouse over there – he's a trained fighter and he's their sergeant-major. You wouldn't want to mess with him."

"He looked like an old man. Big, but old and slow."

"Warwick is far from slow," Harry contended. "And the castle is impregnable. Lady Baxley's family have lived here for a thousand years and she told me that the castle has never been taken. And they have loads of swords and other weapons."

"Antiques from the castle?"

"They may be old, but they're better than that kitchen knife you're carrying around."

Uros studied him for a moment. "So you're staying here?" he asked finally.

"Yes," Harry nodded defiantly.

"Well, it may be useful to have a spy in their midst."

"I'm not spying for you."

"We'll see," Uros smiled. "Anyway I'm already looking forward to seeing your father's face when I tell him. If only I could tell your mother as well – that would be amusing."

Harry sighed deeply. "Please ask my dad to tell my mum that I love her and that I'm okay."

Uros laughed loudly. "I'm not here to pass messages to your mummy, little boy. Thank you for the information." He glanced at Harry and smiled again. "I know you were exaggerating and I know what the real numbers are. I've been here for two days waiting to speak to you and I've seen you training in the castle grounds. There are twenty men and only half a dozen know what they're doing."

"You didn't see them all. There are hundreds of men."

Uros laughed again. "I'll be back when I need something from you, boy." With that, he slipped around the corner of the hedge.

Harry was still for a moment, staring at the space where Uros had been standing a moment before. He realised that he was pleased that his father would now know that he was staying in Baxley. This was the right place for him.

He patted Polly's neck. "Good girl," he murmured, patting her flank. "I'm glad to be here with you."

Harry didn't see Warwick at the farmhouse window, observing him through steely eyes.

22. Medicine And Seed

"I don't know why you asked me to be on the village council if you never listen to me," whined Hamish.

The weekly council meeting was taking place at Peter Parlane's house and they were gathered around his large kitchen table eating a carrot cake baked that afternoon by his wife, Clare.

"We spend half the meeting listening to you," Tim Butterworth muttered. Tim was in charge of the work on the fort.

"Calm down, Hamish," said Peter. "We value your input. It's just that surely the fixing of your fence is a personal matter for you and not for discussion during the council meeting."

"But my fence was blown down by the strong winds last night."

"So were some of my fences," replied Peter.

"Exactly," said Hamish firmly, "and people on the farm rota helped fix your fences this afternoon."

"That's because Peter is sharing his crops," interjected Tim. "What are you sharing from inside your fence? The cabbages or runner beans which are growing in your vegetable patch?"

"No, those are my – "

"If somebody else needed their garden fence fixed would you offer to help them? Say Fran and Anthony round the corner from me. Would you help them?"

"Well, I'm not sure if that's quite the same."

"Why on earth not?"

"My fence borders one of Neil Westlake's fields."

"Nothing is in that field!" blurted Tim. "Not since you asked him to take his cows out two years ago, because Melissa found them too noisy and smelly. If I was Neil, and Melissa had said that to me, I'd have just put more cows in there. And pigs."

"I've had enough of this," Hamish said, standing up. "That's typical of your attitude, Tim. All of you in fact."

"Calm down, Hamish," Peter said. "Why don't we – "

"I will not calm down until Tim has apologised for insulting my wife."

"I didn't insult your wife, you fool. I just thought she might like some pigs for company," Tim smiled. "I'm sure they'd make her feel right at home."

"Right, that's it. I'm not going to be part of this stupid council a minute longer. These meetings are a complete waste of time anyway."

Hamish pushed his chair back, stalked to the kitchen door and walked out, slamming the door behind him.

There was silence as the remaining council members looked at each other. Peter sighed.

"He's a fucking idiot," proclaimed Tim. "Good riddance, I say."

"I had hoped to keep him on side," Peter said. "I thought he would be less divisive within the community if he had a voice here with us."

"I think we're better off without him," Jane O'Leary said. She was another of the local farmers. "All he did was argue."

"Maybe I'll talk to him tomorrow." Peter said and took a large swig of his tea. "Oh well. Shall we continue? What's first on the agenda?"

"Food and security are the only two things that really matter," John said. "Shall we cover the crops first?"

"Sure," Peter replied. "It shouldn't take long. Everything is going well at present here on my farm and I spoke to Neil Westlake today and he said the same. How are things with you, Jane?"

"No real problems," she replied. "Just the usual stuff. The rota is working well. All our helpers are very enthusiastic and they're a little more experienced now. We seem to be on top of everything and I was going to suggest that we get some more crops planted actually."

"What do you mean?" asked John, looking at each of the farmers. "Are we able to plant more?"

"In the last few years," Jane replied, "most farmers never really planted to their maximum capacity. We used to get EU subsidies for leaving a field fallow – and besides most of us had other jobs. My husband Pat and I used to teach at the local agricultural college so we only had so much time around the farm."

"It might be a good idea to get a few more things on the go," mused Peter. "A bit of variety would be nice. As you know we've mainly got wheat, maize and beans because that's what we'd got in the ground last autumn before this all happened, but it would be nice to set out small areas of a wider range of crops like cabbages, potatoes, carrots and so on. The only trouble is … "

"… where are we going to get the seed?" Jane finished for him.

"Where do you normally get it from?" Sandy asked.

"You would ring up a supplier who would deliver it from one of their depots around the country," Peter replied.

There was silence for a moment.

"Do you know where any of these depots are?" John asked.

Peter turned to Jane. "Is there one in Gloucester?" he mused out loud. "By the old cattle market?"

"I don't know," she replied, shrugging her shoulders.

"I'm pretty sure it's there," Peter nodded to himself. "I wouldn't be surprised if it's been ransacked though."

"It might not have been," said John. "How many people know this place exists?"

"Who knows?"

"Well, even you're not sure. And if anybody broke in they'd just find a load of seed, would they?"

"Yes, but the seed for crops like potatoes and beans are obviously potatoes and beans."

"Well it's worth a look I think," John replied.

"I agree," said Sandy.

"Do we really want to go into Gloucester?" asked Jane. "It's a risk, isn't it?"

"Well actually I was going to mention something else later," John announced. "Yvonne wants to go to Gloucester hospital to get some medical equipment and as many medicines and dressings as she can find. I was going to ask if we could spare half a dozen people to go with her for protection."

"We could cover both objectives together," Sandy nodded, "but I'd suggest a team of a dozen. And we should go in at night when there will be fewer people around. Late night, something like 3am."

"And you're going to need a truck," Jane chipped in. "We're talking about a few dozen tonnes of seed."

"I hadn't thought of that," Sandy said, rubbing his chin.

"I've still got some diesel," John offered. "It's only enough for one trip so I was saving it for something important. I think this qualifies."

"We could take my tractor down with a big trailer," Peter offered.

"I'm not sure if I've got enough diesel to get there and back," John said doubtfully. "What about this: we walk down carrying my diesel canister between us and find a truck down there in Gloucester so we only need enough fuel for one trip. When I was last down there I saw loads of abandoned vehicles – some with the keys still in the ignition. Maybe we can grab one, put our diesel in it, load it up and drive it back."

"So when do you want to go?"

"Why not tonight? No point in hanging around."

"Shouldn't we check that there actually is a depot there first," Jane suggested. "Before we go storming in with a dozen men."

John and Peter looked at each other. They turned to Sandy. "What do you think, Sandy?" Peter asked.

"If you're more than fifty per cent sure there is a depot by the old cattle market…?"

"I am," Peter nodded.

"Then I don't think we need to go in advance. However there are some preparations we need to make so I think we should do it tomorrow night. We could take a dozen men, check the place out and if there's nothing there then just come back quietly. No harm done and we've taken a big enough team to ensure each other's safety. And we need to get the medical supplies anyway."

Peter nodded. "Are you happy with that, Tim?"

"Wasn't John going to Dowley tomorrow to set up an alliance with them?"

"I can do that during the day," said John. "And then go to Gloucester in the evening. No problem."

"Right," said Peter. "That's settled then. We go to Gloucester tomorrow night."

23. A Conversation About Harry

Warwick Yorath wearily climbed the stone castle steps up to Lady Baxley's living chambers. He had worked his men hard today and it was getting more difficult to stay ahead of them – whilst still shouting, chivvying, goading and trying to appear as though it was effortless for him.

His Achilles tendons were always sore at the end of the day and stiff in the mornings. His back ached and he was starting to feel his left hip. He needed a day off, but the men were nowhere near ready. What if an attack came tomorrow?

He walked slowly across the landing, knocked on the door and stepped through when he heard Lady Baxley calling him in. Deborah was sitting silently next to her mother, a sullen look on her face and he shivered inwardly. She spoke little but when she did it was negative at best and often vicious, spiteful or malevolent. He turned to Elizabeth and she indicated the chair opposite.

"Thank you for coming, Warwick," Elizabeth said. "Please sit down. Would you care for a drink?"

"No thanks," the Master-At-Arms replied succinctly, lowering his large, tired frame into an armchair.

"How was training today?"

"Not bad."

Elizabeth left a deliberate silence for Warwick to elaborate. She sipped her tea.

Warwick simply looked around the room with a hint of a smile on his lips. He was used to her subtle ways and occasionally realised what was happening before he stepped into the trap. He knew it was petty, but he decided enjoy the silence on this occasion. However her daughter gave way before Lady Baxley did.

"Can you tell us any more than that?" Deborah asked, her eyes glaring at Warwick.

"What do you want to know?" he responded with a smile. Deborah didn't have her mother's patience and it was nice to achieve the occasional small victory over her.

"How are the two new men?" Elizabeth asked softly before her daughter was able to snap a reply. "Steven's friends from Cam."

"You can tell they're mates from his rugby team. They fight well enough with their fists but they don't know one end of a sword from the other. They won't last long if we're in a real battle."

"I'm sure you'll be able to make something of them," she nodded. "However you'll be pleased to hear that I have decided that you are right. We should stop accepting new arrivals into the community now."

"It's about time."

"I know your feelings on the matter, Warwick, and that was one of the factors in my decision. I always rely on your advice."

"We don't have enough swords or bows. Or weapons of any kind for that matter. Your family's five hundred year old swords look threatening but half a dozen have snapped or shattered in training. We now have twenty five men in the core unit but only twenty or so useful weapons."

"Yes," Elizabeth nodded. "It's a problem. Which is why I've asked you here this evening to discuss a way forward. I've been wondering if we should venture out into the world looking for a solution to our lack of weapons."

"Venture out where?"

"We are a little isolated here and what little information we receive simply comes from passers-by. And we are more concerned with repelling visitors than talking to them."

"We agreed that our policy was just to accept people who know someone here, like these last two. A member of the community needs to vouch for them."

"I meant no complaint. In fact I believe your guards on the boundary are doing an excellent job of keeping us safe. My point is simply that we need to know what is going on in the country around us and there are items we require, most immediately weapons but many more other articles. And as you know I am keen to explore building relationships with other friendly communities."

"We certainly could do with a few things," Warwick nodded. "What are you proposing?"

"If you remember, we heard a rumour about a village near Briddip that was forming an alliance with other villages around them. And that they have weapons such as bows."

"Yes … what was the place called again?"

"Brenscombe," Elizabeth replied. "My suggestion is that we should visit the people of Brenscombe and hold out the hand of friendship, if we deem them to be of a similar mindset to ourselves."

"When you say 'we should visit them' …?"

"I'm not sure if I'm really up to travelling that far and, at my age, I don't think I would be happy camping out below the stars. Therefore I've asked Deborah if she would be willing to go."

"Deborah?"

"And I would be grateful if you could send some men with her of course. What would be your advice in that regard?"

Warwick stroked his chin. "The more the better really, but we don't want to leave the castle undermanned."

"And we don't want to appear heavy-handed when we visit a potential friend. What would be the minimum number that you would be happy to send?"

"Half a dozen, I suppose," he answered. "If they were good men."

"I had a similar thought. That number would not seem too aggressive, but six good men should be able to cope with an amateur force of two or three times the size. And if they were on horseback, they would be able to retreat swiftly if required. Do you think that you should go along with them?"

"Me?"

"There is a case for you to stay here in command of the castle of course, but I could manage for a few days and I would want my best man to protect Deborah. In addition you will want to assess their force and discuss weaponry and such, if the opportunity arises. What do you think?"

"I suppose you're right," Warwick mused. "We could pull in a few replacement guards to be stationed inside the castle."

"Who else would you take?" Elizabeth asked. "Who is the best swordsman beside yourself?"

Warwick looked up sharply. "No, I'm not taking him."

"Who do you mean, Warwick?"

"You know who I mean. Barkley. I don't trust him."

"Harry? Is he good with a sword?"

"You know he is," Warwick muttered. "I hate to admit it, but he's still improving rapidly. None of the other men can get near him."

"And how is he with a horse now?"

"He seems to have a real affinity for them, but I still don't want to take him."

"You think he should stay here in the castle while you're away?"

Warwick looked at her. It was obvious that he didn't like either option.

"We could get rid of him," Deborah volunteered.

"I like that idea," Warwick agreed enthusiastically.

"What are you proposing exactly?" asked Elizabeth.

Warwick looked at Deborah, who simply smiled enigmatically.

Elizabeth shook her head. "I don't think you're the kind of person who wants to kill people in cold blood, Warwick, and you don't want to simply release him, do you?"

"No," he said, shaking his head. "He'll just run back to his dad and tell him all about our setup here."

"He's been with us for a month now and has shown no sign of wanting to leave. In my opinion, he has fully embraced our little community here and wants to remain a part of it. I trust him, but I will defer to your decision with regard to this trip."

Warwick thought for a moment.

"What do you want out of this trip, Elizabeth?"

"I think it should simply be exploratory, we need to assess whether they would be a useful ally and then leave them to consider the proposal. It would simply be the first step in a courtship."

"And we need to find out what sort of weapons they have and if we can have some," Deborah added.

"To my mind," Lady Baxley said, "the perfect outcome for an initial visit would be identifying a way of improving our defensive capabilities and also a positive response in principle on the suggestion of an alliance. Always supposing you deem them to be worthy of a partnership."

Warwick nodded. "Can I ask a more sensitive question?"

"Certainly, Warwick. We are friends and we need to be open with each other."

"Who would be in charge on this trip?"

"I've suggested to Deborah that she be my eyes and ears, while you do the talking. And you are of course responsible for the safety of the group at all times."

"What does that mean? Me or her?"

"Brass tacks, as ever," Elizabeth smiled. "I would hope that you both could work in harmony."

"That's all very nice, but when the chips are down we might not have time for a harmonious discussion. You need to nominate one person."

"In that case I would suggest the person is you."

"Okay," he nodded. "The trip sounds like a good idea actually. Hopefully they'll be sensible people."

"And your decision regarding Harry?"

Warwick looked at Elizabeth and then at Deborah. He leaned back in his chair and ran his hands through his hair as he deliberated.

Eventually he made up his mind: "I'll take him with me where I can keep an eye on him. And if he does anything suspicious …"

24. A Visit From The Mayor

"I wish I was going to Gloucester with you tonight." Lewis asked. "I'm going to ask Dad when he gets back."

"You're not old enough, little brother," Mark replied.

It was early afternoon and Mark, Sophia and Rachel were in the garage making preparations for the trip to fetch seed and medical supplies from the nearby city.

That morning John had travelled to Dowley with Reid to talk to them about a possible alliance and he had left a list of tasks for Mark and the others. They had fixed a pair of canisters to one of the bikes so that they could transport the diesel down to the city that night and now they were gathering together their weapons and other items.

"I'm sixteen now and I'm as tall as Dad," Lewis said, "and anyway, that's my sword." He pointed at the samurai sword that Mark was tying on to his waist.

"I thought it belonged to Josh."

"Yes, but he lent it to me, not you."

"I need to have some kind of weapon."

"And why are Sophia and Rachel going?" Lewis moaned. "They're just girls."

"I'm older than Mark," said Rachel. "I'm twenty-seven, you know."

"They're going because they're archers," Mark said. "Sandy wants them at the back of the group to provide covering fire if required."

"Rachel's only been doing it for a week," Lewis contended.

"That's a week longer than you," Rachel replied.

"Anyway she's pretty good," Sophia interjected.

"You're lucky Reid's not going," Mark smiled. "Sandy asked him if he wanted to come."

"He didn't!"

"Yeah, he's the best archer, but he didn't want to go. That's why Rachel's using his bow tonight."

"Perhaps I should start doing archery," Lewis mused.

"You would never practice," Sophia said. "Anyway you and Mark are both good with a sword."

"I beat Mark yesterday, you know."

"You were lucky," Mark smiled.

"Lucky? I – "

They all stopped talking as they heard the sound of the church bells. They all looked at each other.

"The alarm," said Mark. They listened as a second and third peal of bells sounded. They listened for more but there was just silence.

"Three rings," Lewis said. "That's just level two, right?"

Mark nodded. "Between three and fifty people." He touched the sword was at his side and walked out onto the road. The others followed him.

"At which post?" Lewis asked, looking up and down the road. Their neighbours were also coming out of their houses and looking around.

"Let's find out," Mark said, starting to run down the street towards the church. On reaching the gate, they found a dozen other villagers armed with sticks and farming tools.

Tim came running down the footpath towards them from the church. "There are about twenty five men on the road from Briddip," he said breathlessly to the group. "Come on."

Everyone asked him questions as they ran up the road in the direction of the Briddip watch.

"I was on watch with Pat O'Leary," he explained, "when we saw a large group of men approaching from Briddip. We saw them in the distance and I came back to sound the alarm. Peter and Sandy are already up at the guard post. I saw them on the way to the church and they went straight up to help Pat."

As they hurried along the road to the Briddip watch, more people joined them from the surrounding houses and, by the time they reached the rise in the road where the guard post was stationed, a group of at least thirty villagers had gathered.

The small force of twenty five men that was approaching from Briddip halted in the dip in the road a hundred yards away. After a short discussion, four of the men detached from the group and started walking up towards them, led by a man in his fifties with a bald head, glasses and a moustache; alongside him was a tall, lithe man in his thirties.

They came to a halt just in front of Peter and the older man stepped forward and held out his hand.

"My name is Nigel Barkley," the man said. "I'm the Mayor of Gloucester."

"Can I help you?" Peter asked, ignoring the man's hand.

"What a large welcoming party," Nigel said, realising the handshake wasn't going to happen and gesturing towards the group of villagers instead.

"Your party is pretty big too," Peter said curtly, indicating the force of twenty five men that were standing a hundred yards down the road.

"I'm aware that our numbers might appear aggressive, but that's not my intention. These are difficult times and there is safety in numbers when you travel around. Shall I ask our men to withdraw a little further?"

"That's entirely up to you," Peter said with a shrug.

"May I introduce Uros Viduka," Nigel said. "He's the Captain of the City Guard." He turned to the tall Serbian. "Uros, would you mind if Lee went back and asked the men to wait at the top of the far rise by Briddip?"

Uros nodded at the man standing next to him, who immediately set off towards the other men.

"Can I also introduce Geoff Horsfield," Nigel said. "Geoff was formerly with the National Farmers Union and he's now advising us on the best approach to an agricultural alliance."

"We've met," Peter said succinctly.

"Oh?"

"Geoff and I had a difference of opinion about how the local NFU branch should be run. I thought it should be for the benefit of the farmers but Geoff wasn't so sure."

"That's not fair, Peter, my interests are always – " Horsfield began.

"Well, Geoff," interrupted Nigel, "I wish you'd mentioned that you knew … I'm sorry, but I didn't catch your name?"

"Peter Parlane."

"It's a pleasure to meet you, Peter. Is there somewhere we can go and talk?"

"We're talking here, aren't we?"

"Well, yes, I suppose we are." Nigel shrugged and decided to make the best of it. "I just wanted a few moments of your time to put forward a suggestion."

He looked at Peter, who didn't respond. He then looked at the other members of the village gathered behind him. He sensed hostility from most of the on-lookers, but he didn't mind, he had encountered difficult audiences before.

Switching on his smile, he spoke to Peter but loudly, so that all could hear: "We're attempting to restore a little order to life around Gloucestershire. I had the misfortune to be Mayor at the time when everything collapsed, but sometimes you need to step forward in order to do your bit for the community. I'm doing my best to ensure that things don't dissolve into anarchy. I have to say that it's been an uphill task: in Gloucester we've had looting, food shortages, riots, all sorts of things, but we've finally been able to return to a quieter way of life of late. This is of course what we all want – the vast majority of the population are law-abiding people who simply want to live their lives in peace and safety."

He looked at Peter who, once again, didn't respond.

"We're now travelling around the local communities to announce that the city of Gloucester is once again open for business and to offer our hand in friendship. I believe we need to work together in these troubled times and therefore I am here to offer a partnership."

"A partnership?"

"The people of Gloucester are still struggling for food and we hoped that you might be in a position to enter into a trade alliance. For our part, we would be grateful for any food that you might be able to spare."

"I'm not sure that we have any *spare* food."

"Obviously we would be willing to trade. Of course money has become obsolete, but perhaps there is something else that we can offer."

"What do you have that we might want?"

"I would hope there might be many items of interest. We can barter with gold, silver and jewellery. A fair number of the shops in the city were not looted and there might be hardware goods that you need, tools and so on. In addition, we might be able to help you with other agricultural supplies."

"Such as?"

"Do you need any seed or fertilisers?"

"No," Peter lied promptly.

"Then you're in a more fortunate position than the other farmers we've spoken to," nodded Barkley, "but the situation might change in the future and we have two depots in Gloucester that might be of use to you. As I said earlier, I have asked Geoff to be responsible for the country's agricultural policy and he has begun by assessing what we can offer our partners. One of our depots contains seed for a wide variety of crops and the other houses fertilisers, insecticides and other chemicals."

"We'll bear that in mind."

"In addition I have re-instated the weekly market in the centre of the city. I'm pleased to say that once again there is a market every Friday and we are guaranteeing the safety of anybody who attends."

"That's very magnanimous of you."

"We simply ask for a very small percentage of what you're selling – merely to help feed the guards who are there to protect you."

"To protect us?"

"Absolutely. And that's the final reason I'm here. We would like to offer you security." Nigel took a moment to glance at the crowd behind Peter and he spoke to them as much as to the village leader. "Working in partnership we are stronger, safer, more able to bring up our children in what could become a violent world. I would like to offer you the protection of the city of Gloucester and our guards."

"In exchange for what?" Peter asked.

"We ask nothing in return – simply that we work together and not against each other. If you are occasionally able to spare some supplies for the city guard then we would be extremely grateful." He looked around the faces again and was pleased to see occasional nodding, less outright hostility. He turned back to Peter. "So, what do you think? Can we work together?"

"Aren't we a little far from the city for you to worry about?"

"No, on the contrary, we're hoping to bring the whole county of Gloucestershire together under one umbrella. It will take time, but that's our objective."

"With you in charge?"

"Me? Well, I'm the current Mayor, but I would be happy to return to a system of elections once we have restored secure, safe government to the county."

"We'll think about it."

"Pardon?"

"We'll think about it," Peter repeated. "We'll discuss your suggestion."

"You'll discuss it? The whole village?"

"Yes, the whole village. We'll call a meeting in the next few days and debate your proposal."

"I assumed I was talking to the village leader," Nigel said.

"Just for another few weeks. We're planning to have a vote every three months. Perhaps that's a system you could try."

Nigel smiled. "It's something to consider," he nodded. "So when might we receive an answer from you?"

"I don't know."

"You don't know?" Nigel was starting to become frustrated, but he took a deep breath. "Can I call back in a week or two?"

"I can't stop you, but don't come with so many men next time." Peter stepped forward. "In fact, if you turn up here with what looks like an army again then I won't bother even talking to you.

I see what you're doing. It's a show of force. Well, if you come back next time then make sure you don't have more than a handful of people with you."

Nigel waited, considering his next move. There didn't seem much more that he could do.

Beside him, the whole time that Nigel had been speaking, Uros had been scanning the faces in the crowd. He too had seen the hostility but, in contrast to the other villages they had visited, no fear. These people were far more organised than any other community that they had encountered and the villagers had appeared extremely promptly to defend themselves.

Towards the end of Nigel's speech, he had seen a slight softening of the mood. Some were still defensive but a good number seemed interested in the offer. He wondered which way their decision would go. *Perhaps they'll need a nudge*, he thought to himself.

"Well," said Nigel finally, realising that he wasn't going to receive the immediate acceptance they had received elsewhere. "Thank you for your time. I hope we can do business together. I'll call back in a couple of weeks, but you can normally find me at Shire Hall in Gloucester. I look forward to seeing you again soon."

"One other thing," Peter said. "You don't need to bother calling at Cranwold or Dowley. They're the villages to the east and west. They're in an alliance with us. And I would expect Crundle Green to the south to be joining us soon."

Nigel looked at him in surprise, but there was nothing to be said. He made to leave.

As Uros turned to follow his colleague, he unexpectedly caught sight of someone in the crowd behind the village leader. A girl's face looking out from behind others. He looked back quickly but could no longer see her. She had ducked behind the people in front of her.

Where had he seen that face before? He searched through the crowd one more time, but couldn't see her. Perhaps he had imagined it. He turned again to follow Barkley, scanning his memory for any recollection of the person.

The three men walked down the road, heading back towards the rest of their force in the distance, waiting on the edge of Briddip village.

"You could have warned me about these people," Nigel muttered angrily to Geoff Horsfield as they walked quickly along. "Why do you think I bring you on these trips?"

"I'm sorry, Nigel. I forgot that Peter's farm was around here."

"Well, next time – "

"The girl from the hospital!" Uros said suddenly, slapping his forehead. "Of course."

"What are you talking about?" Nigel asked.

"There was a girl in the crowd back there. I just caught a glimpse of her at the end and I've been trying to think why I know her."

"Which girl?"

"You won't have seen her. She was at the back of the group, keeping out of sight, but she looked out from behind someone just as we were leaving. I met her at Gloucester Hospital a few weeks ago."

"Well, that's very interesting, Uros, but – "

"You don't understand, you old fool." He almost spat the words at Barkley, who was taken aback by their sudden vehemence. "She thinks I killed someone."

Geoff Horsfield stopped and stared at Uros, aghast. "You've killed someone?"

"Keep walking, you moron," the Serbian commanded angrily. "They'll be watching us still."

Horsfield trotted forward a couple of steps to fall in beside them again.

"I don't think I want to know what happened," said Nigel slowly, "but are you telling me that they might not think that we're the friendly people we just told them we are?"

"That's right," Uros affirmed. "We've got a problem with this village, Nigel. They're well-organised, armed with shotguns and bows and, what's more, they've formed an alliance with the villages around them. If they grow any bigger they could get out of hand. And once that girl tells them about me they're not going to want to enter into a partnership with us."

"That's a shame," Barkley nodded. "And we don't want them talking to all the other villages in Gloucestershire that we've been carefully cultivating. It's all precariously balanced at the moment."

"You know what I think?" Uros said. "We've got to do something about this village – and do it pretty quickly."

"Let's not be too hasty. There were a lot of people nodding towards the end so they might decide to work with us. Let's wait to hear the outcome of their village meeting."

-o-o-o-

An hour and a half later, aside from the two people on watch, the entire Brenscombe community was gathered in the village hall. Peter had decided that the visit from Nigel Barkley merited an immediate discussion.

As the people of Brenscombe were congregating on the village hall, John and Reid returned from their visit to Dowley, surprised to see so much commotion. They reached their house just as the rest of the family were coming out and Emilia explained the situation as they walked down to the hall.

When everybody had squeezed into the building, Peter opened the floor for discussion. "So what does everyone think?" he asked. "I have my own opinions but I'd like to know how you feel."

There was silence for a few seconds and then Hamish Dacourt stood up. "It sounds like a good idea to me," he said.

"What does?" Peter asked.

"Working with Gloucester, of course. It's a much better notion than the so-called alliance with these useless villages around us."

John was about to respond angrily, but he bit his tongue.

"Thank you, Hamish," Peter said, hoping that the man would sit down. "What does everyone else think?"

"I didn't like the look of him," Tim said from the other side of the room. "The Mayor, I mean."

"That's not the basis of a reasoned argument," Hamish retorted, still on his feet. "And besides, I've known Nigel Barkley for a long time. He's a very sensible man, who has done a lot of work for the county over the years."

"If you like him then I think even less of him," called Tim, to a chorus of laughter from the room.

Hamish spluttered with indignation and was about to respond angrily, but Peter spoke first: "I'm interested to hear that you know this man, Hamish. Could you tell us a bit more please?"

"Certainly," Hamish replied. "He used to run an accountancy firm in Gloucester and I first met him around twelve years ago when he helped me with some tax advice. He was extremely knowledgeable and saved me a lot of money. Then he worked for a few years as a county councillor and, of course, our paths frequently crossed when I became involved with Brenscombe parish council. He was a useful ally on many important matters."

"Do you trust him?" Peter asked.

"Absolutely. He's an honourable man who has sacrificed many years for the good of the community."

"That's useful to know, Hamish," Peter nodded. "Personally I didn't like his heavy-handed approach, coming to see us with twenty five armed men standing beside him, but I'm prepared to keep an open mind. Having said that I also don't care for the man who was with him: Geoff Horsfield. Do other people know him? Neil?"

"I never had a problem with Geoff myself," Neil Westlake replied. "But I know a few other farmers who didn't like him."

"Should we trust him?"

"I don't know," Neil said. "I have no reason to distrust him."

"Pat? Jane? What do you think?"

"I wouldn't touch him with a bargepole," Pat replied firmly. "His only interest is himself."

Peter smiled. "That's my feeling as well actually." He looked around the room. "Does anyone else know these people?"

He looked around the room, seeing lots of shrugs and shaking heads.

Then Sophia slowly raised her hand. Sitting alongside, John looked at her in surprise.

"I know the other man," she said. "The Captain Of The Guard."

"Do you?" her father said in surprise.

"I was waiting for an opportunity to tell you."

"Tell us what?" Peter asked.

"I saw him kill someone in Gloucester a few weeks ago." There were gasps around the room and small conversations broke out.

"You mean that man in the shop?" John said, with a sudden realisation. "When I picked you up from the hospital?"

"You know him as well?" Peter asked.

"If it's the man I'm thinking of. Was it him?" John asked his daughter.

"Definitely," she nodded. "The Mayor introduced him. Uros something."

John turned to Peter. "We don't want anything to do with this man," he said. "He's the scariest man I've ever met. I was pointing a shotgun at him, but I was still terrified."

"Tell us what happened," Peter asked.

Sophia told the story, explaining how she had met Uros in the hospital, initially liking the man. She then told how she and Jane had gone to the nearby shop to find the shopkeeper murdered and Uros alone in the building with the body.

"Did you actually see him kill the man?" Peter asked.

"No, but he definitely did it. He said he got rid of the shopkeeper because he had a store of food."

"I saw him attack Sophia's colleague," John added. "I arrived just as it happened and fortunately I had borrowed Anthony's shotgun in case of trouble. While I pointed the gun at this Uros guy, Sophia helped her colleague to my car. But he wasn't worried by the gun, he was just waiting for an opportunity to jump me if I took my eyes off him. He certainly gave the impression that he'd had a gun pointed at him many times before."

"It was terrible." Sophia shuddered as she remembered the incident.

"If this man is helping the Mayor of Gloucester then we shouldn't get involved with them," John said conclusively.

"Hold on," said Hamish. "Nigel is a good man. Perhaps he doesn't know what this man is like. These are difficult times and people can be thrown together by circumstance. And it sounds like you don't know for certain that he killed this shopkeeper."

"You weren't there, Hamish. If you'd seen the look in his eyes, you'd feel the same way as me."

"But Nigel is right, we need to trade. They have things we need. Or will need in the future. We can't shut ourselves away from the world."

"But we need to choose our partners carefully," John argued.

"What about the supplies he mentioned?" Hamish asked. "I thought you were going there tonight to get some seed from one of these depots?"

"That was the original plan," agreed John, "but obviously we should postpone it now. What do you think, Peter?"

"I was thinking the same thing," the village leader nodded. "Now that we know they're well-organised I'm sure they'll have the depots under guard. But I suppose we could send one or two people down tonight to check the place out."

"No," Sophia said quietly. "I don't think you should."

"Why not?" Peter queried.

"They'll be back tomorrow."

"Nigel Barkley? How do you know?"

"It's obvious. It's what I would do if I was him."

"What do you mean?" Peter asked.

"Uros saw me and therefore he knows that *we* know they're not to be trusted. He knows we're organised. You told him we're forming alliances with other villages, which will make us stronger. We're a problem that needs to be eliminated before it gets any worse."

"They won't attack us tomorrow," Hamish said dismissively. "Nigel isn't like that. Anyway he said he'd come back in a couple of weeks."

"He'll be back tomorrow," Sophia said quietly but firmly. "Nigel Barkley might not be like that, but Uros is. He won't hang about."

-o-o-o-

At the same moment, Nigel Barkley, Uros Viduka and their twenty five men were marching back through the outskirts of the city of Gloucester.

Geoff Horsfield had left to return to his home in a neighbouring suburb leaving Nigel and Uros walking on their own twenty yards ahead of the column.

"I've been thinking about Brenscombe," Nigel started.

"So have I," Uros interjected. "We need to go back tomorrow and sort them out."

"Tomorrow? I don't think they'll be ready to talk to us yet."

"I don't mean talking. Action is required with these people."

"I was thinking that maybe if I went back without you – with just a couple of men – then perhaps I could persuade them of the benefits of partnership."

"No, Nigel, this time you're going to do what I say. You're lucky to have me," Uros smiled. "This is no longer a world for talk and persuasion, the future will be made by people like me who are able to act while the sheep are bleating at each other."

"What do you mean?"

"I'm going to take their village away from them. Tomorrow. Before the problem gets any worse. Before they have a chance to improve their defences or increase the size of their force. We'll hit them hard with a hundred men and take their village. I learned this when I was fourteen years old growing up in the council estate in Matson. There was a boy who was bigger than me, but I hit *him* hard before he was ready and I made sure he stayed down."

"But they have shotguns."

"The boy in Matson had better weapons than me – his size and strength – but he didn't have time to use them. Yes, he hurt me a little, but I won the fight. Tomorrow we might lose some men, but we'll win the battle."

"And then what?" asked Nigel.

"Then we take their weapons and put our own man in charge."

"They won't like that."

Uros laughed. "I don't care if they like it or not. We'll remove anyone who complains and we'll put our own man in place of that village leader along with a team of a dozen men. Our men."

Nigel was quiet for a few moments. "Why don't you let me talk to them first?"

"No. You're very good at talking, Mr Mayor, but you're never going to persuade that group of people. I could see it in their eyes. They were hostile enough anyway, but once that girl tells them about me …"

"But we want them to keep working in the fields. We can't alienate them completely."

"I don't care about that. It's a problem and we're going to get rid of it. We're doing this and I don't care if you agree or not. Just remember: I control the men."

"We need food, Uros, and we're not farmers."

"There are plenty of other farms."

"What if there's a problem in another place?" Nigel asked. "Are you going to wipe them out as well? And another and another? You can't just destroy everything." He paused. "Look, I think I agree in principle with what you're suggesting, but – "

"It doesn't matter if you agree or if you disagree."

"If you're set on this course of action, why don't you let me try and re-build the community afterwards. With a dozen of our men there like you said, but let me choose the man that we install as the village leader. I'll try to get them working again afterwards, tending the crops, but sharing the harvests with us in a way that is beneficial for them as well."

Uros considered the other man's suggestion. "Okay. What you do afterwards is up to you. Who do you want to put in charge?"

"I know someone who lives there. I've never liked him, but I know he'll jump at the chance of being the boss. And he'll be a person that we can control."

Uros didn't reply, but Nigel took that as acquiescence. It was as much as he would have from the man. They marched the rest of the way in silence, each with their own thoughts about the next day.

25. A Difficult Decision

After the village meeting had ended, Sandy Woodall invited the other members of the council to his house to continue the discussions. All five were seated around his dining table: Peter, Sandy, John, Tim Butterworth and Jane O'Leary – Hamish Dacourt was of course no longer part of the committee.

"So what do you all think of the discussion at the village hall?" Peter asked.

"I'm amazed there wasn't a unanimous decision to avoid all dealings with them," John replied. "Especially after Sophia and I explained what Viduka had done."

"I can understand how they feel," Jane said. "Your story also made people realise that we could be attacked if we say no to Barkley – and they are potentially much stronger than us."

"We absolutely cannot go into partnership with them," John said forcefully. "I'll have no part of it."

"Don't worry, John," Peter said. "I think everybody in this room is in agreement on that. Sandy and I definitely feel the same way. Tim? Jane? What about you two?"

"There's no way I want to work with Barkley," Tim stated.

"I don't want to," Jane said, "but what's our alternative?"

"To continue to build alliances with the other villages around us," John replied.

"How did you get on at Dowley today?" Peter asked. "We haven't had a chance to discuss it yet."

"Dowley are with us. And they're really well organised. They only started a couple of weeks ago but they've already caught up with us. You know my son Reid is over there every day for his apprenticeship and he mentioned what we're doing here so they decided to do the same."

"Who's in charge? That chap that took Reid on as an apprentice?"

"Neville Forrester? No, he's not the kind of man who wants to be village leader, but they've made him responsible for security – the equivalent of Sandy, so to speak. A man called Jonathan Deane was voted in as leader."

"I know him," Peter said. "He's a good man. For an estate agent," he added with a smile.

"Neville Forrester has started training the whole village in archery, in groups of a dozen each morning and afternoon. I think they'll have a formidable defensive force soon."

"How many bows do they have?" Sandy asked.

"They're up to about twenty five now, half of which are training bows. Forrester explained at length how they don't have the range, but he and Reid are making additional bows."

"So, they could have a unit of twenty five archers then?" Sandy asked. "What about ammunition?"

"That's where they're a little short. They have around two hundred and fifty arrows – that's only ten for each man."

"That's not many, but it's more than we have by a long way. They could be a useful ally."

"There are a few people in Cranwold that would support us if required," John replied, "and I know one or two have shotguns. Every little bit would help."

"So what are you thinking?" Peter asked.

"That depends on the size of force that Gloucester bring. Unfortunately I believe it will be a lot more than fifty men and the fort is still not fully defensible. How did you get on today, Tim?"

"Not bad. We've completed the barricade on all but a forty yard stretch now. If we had another week then we could finish it off."

"What do you think, Sandy?" John asked. "Can we defend the fort as it stands?"

"Hmmm … I still think the biggest force we can hold out against indefinitely would be fifty men – and that's if we get some archers from Dowley to defend the open stretch. Obviously we could hold out against a larger force for a short time, but they would over-run us eventually."

"In my opinion Barkley will be knocking on our door with over a hundred men. Hopefully not tomorrow but at some point in the next few weeks. We've no idea really, but if he brought twenty five men just for a chat, then I think we need to plan for him returning with more than fifty."

"That makes sense," agreed Sandy. "If I was in his shoes I would be considering an immediate move – and you might as well bring as large a force as possible to do the job quickly."

"So we either need more men or more time," Tim said. "Neither of which we have."

"Any suggestions?" Peter asked, looking around the table.

"It's a difficult one," Sandy said. "We need to station somebody the other side of Briddip so we get advance notice of a large force coming in our direction. If they don't turn up then we continue to build the fort and by next week we should be ready. However if they attack sooner then we simply have to yield the village." He looked at each of his colleagues. "If we can't defeat them then we have to withdraw."

"You're right," nodded John, "But I don't want to give up my home for long."

"What do you mean?" Peter asked.

"If Barkley returns with a force greater than fifty men tomorrow, then we need to leave the village, but only for a couple of days. And then we take the village back again."

Everybody looked at John.

"How are we going to do that?" asked Peter.

"A couple of days will give us time to arrange support from both Dowley and Cranwold, but it will also give us time to organise our secret weapon, our hidden advantage, a sudden escalation in power that the enemy will not have expected."

"What are you talking about, John? What secret weapon?"

John smiled. "We're going to send for the cavalry…"

26. Pushing On An Open Door

At eleven o'clock the next morning, Nigel Barkley led a cohort of 110 men through the village of Briddip and out along the road to Brenscombe. The mists down in the Severn plain had given way to clear sunshine as they had marched up Briddip Hill with most of the men taking off layers of clothing as the temperature increased.

Nigel had been impressed by how quickly Uros and his men had rounded up such a large force. His friends had spent the previous evening knocking on doors and ordering people to turn up at Shire Hall at eight o'clock in the morning with whatever weapons they could find.

He knew of three handguns that Uros and his friends carried with them, but otherwise their army was poorly equipped, simply carrying sticks, knives and bats. The men obviously had no uniforms, but were merely dressed in a mixture of jeans, shorts, tracksuit trousers, t-shirts and sweat-shirts.

Some of the so-called soldiers had turned up at Shire Hall with unbelievably impractical clothing and poor footwear for a ten mile hike up the Cotswold escarpment. Nigel glanced at some of these men near him, hobbling along in fashionable loafers or deck shoes.

The group included teenagers, men in their twenties and thirties but also quite a few who were obviously considerably older. Some looked relatively fit, but others were visibly struggling after such a long walk; he noticed one man who was seriously overweight and now marching a lot more slowly.

It was not a very impressive army, but it would have to do. At least they had numbers on their side.

They reached the long, shallow dip in the road between the two villages and Nigel could see the rooftops of Brenscombe in the distance.

He heard a scuffling of feet behind him and turned to see Uros holding up his hand to bring the men to a halt. Nigel stopped and turned, not sure what his colleague was doing.

"Gather round, lads," Uros shouted. The men shuffled slowly into a semi-circle around him, the ones at the back standing on the grass bank that ran beside the road.

"That's Brenscombe over there," the Serbian announced. "The village is full of rich people who have been living in these big Cotswold stone houses for years while we've been slaving in the factories in the city."

Nigel wondered what he was talking about. There weren't many factories left in Gloucester – it was all offices and call centres these days.

"Yesterday we came up to ask them to work with us, to help us feed the people of Gloucester, to feed you and your children. They laughed in our faces as they have been doing for decades. All around us are fields of corn or cows, pigs and sheep. But they want to keep this food for themselves – even though there is far too much for a small group of people to eat."

Nigel looked at the faces in the crowd. Over half of the men had been press-ganged to join this mission and at first they didn't seem very interested in what Uros was saying, but there were plenty of others who seemed instantly re-invigorated by his words after the long walk.

"The reason we're here," the Serbian continued, "is to liberate this food for our families. We're starving in Gloucester while these rich country people are living in the lap of luxury. They have a village leader who doesn't want to share his food with the lower classes and we're going to replace him with a leader who believes in fairness, someone who is prepared to help his fellow man."

Nigel was surprised that Uros was making such a long speech. He didn't think he had it in him.

"If they don't give in quietly then we're going to take the village by force and imprison the village leader and his henchmen. And you all can have as much food as you can carry."

This final message seemed to make the difference with most of the doubters and the group seemed to shuffle forward slightly, keen to find whatever supplies the village could offer.

Uros smiled. "Let's go, lads," he said setting off at a brisk pace.

Nigel was slow to react and a dozen men had walked quickly past him before he moved, suddenly enthusiastic to arrive at their destination for the riches they had been promised. He attempted to push his way back to the front.

He had only regained his position at the head of the column as they arrived at the edge of the village and, breathing hard, he turned to Uros and said: "You didn't tell me you were going to let them grab food for themselves. We should have discussed this beforehand."

"The men need an incentive and anyway that's what we're here for. To get food."

"Just a second," said Nigel, as they passed the sign announcing they were entering Brenscombe, "there was nobody back there."

"Back where?"

"Yesterday they had two guards at the top of the rise before the village." Nigel looked at the first few houses. "Where is everyone?"

"They probably saw us coming and are hiding in their houses," Uros replied, still marching briskly. "But they're not going to be safe in there. We'll smash the doors down."

"The doors are all open," Nigel replied, staring at the large Cotswold stone dwelling they were passing. "And the windows. Every single window is open."

"What are you talking about?" Uros looked more closely at the houses and reduced his pace. They came to a halt by the stone war memorial on the edge of the village green and looked around.

"What do you want us to do first, Uros?" asked Brett, who was just behind his leader.

"Hold on, mate. Let me look around."

Brett held up his hands and told the men to wait. Uros and Nigel wandered over to the nearest house and were just about to push open the garden gate as a man came around the corner carrying some logs. Uros pulled out his gun and the man looked up to see it pointing at him. He dropped the logs and put up his hands.

"Hamish?" Nigel said, confused. "Is that you?"

"Nigel? Yes, yes, it's me." Hamish looked nervously at the gun. "I waited here to talk to you. I want to help."

"You know this bloke?" Uros asked.

"Yes, this is the person I was telling you about. Hamish Dacourt. You can put your gun down."

Instead, Uros stepped forward through the gate and pointed the gun at Hamish's face. "What's going on here? Where is everybody?"

"D-d-don't shoot," he replied fearfully, holding his hands up higher. "I'll tell you anything you want to know."

"So tell me."

"Tell you what?"

Uros sighed. "Where the fuck is everybody?"

"They've all left."

"The whole village?"

"Yes, they knew you were coming and left at about ten o'clock this morning."

"What? How did they know we were coming?" Uros asked, looking around the village.

"John, one of the men on the so-called village council and his son, Mark, were on the hillside near Briddip from dawn this morning watching out for you. All the others were already packing up their things just in case. John and Mark got back at half past nine – they looked like they'd been running – and said they'd seen about a hundred men marching along the road out of Gloucester towards Briddip Hill."

Nigel stepped forward. "Where have they gone, Hamish?" he asked.

"They all went off in different directions. Some said they were going to stay with friends in neighbouring villages, but others had tents." Hamish lowered his voice to a conspiratorial whisper. "I think they're planning to come back after you've gone. I overheard John talking to Peter the village leader. Not that he should be the village leader – I was voted in as chairman of the parish council."

"I wonder why they left you behind," Uros said, his words heavy with sarcasm.

Misunderstanding, Hamish replied: "I wanted to stay to talk to you." He turned to Nigel. "I wasn't around when you arrived yesterday, but I tried to persuade everyone that we should have an alliance with you. It seems like the most sensible move – we should be working together."

"Exactly what we were suggesting," Nigel replied.

"Unfortunately John's daughter, Sophia, said she came across your colleague a few weeks ago. Uros isn't it?" He looked at the man pointing the gun at him.

Uros didn't say anything, but Nigel replied. "That was just a misunderstanding. The girl just got the wrong end of the stick."

"I knew it," Hamish said. "I told them that you wouldn't associate yourself with someone who … well a person that …"

Uros ignored him and, lowering his gun, turned to the large group of men, who were trying to listen to the conversation.

"Did you all hear that?" he asked loudly. "They were scared of us and they've run away. Feel free to go into the houses and help yourselves to whatever food is left."

"There isn't any food," Hamish said before anyone could move.

"What are you talking about?" Uros demanded.

"They took it all with them."

"They took it with them? All of it?"

"Yes, I think so."

Uros turned to the men. "Okay, lads, let's see if he's right. Have a look in all the houses."

The men headed off in different directions to search the village.

Uros turned back to Hamish. "You'd better get cooking," he said.

"Pardon?"

"If the men come back empty-handed then you're going to give them lunch. We've had a long walk and the men are very hungry."

"What? I can't feed a hundred men. I'll have no food left."

Uros simply lifted his gun and pointed it at the man's face.

"Okay, okay," Hamish, replied lifting his hands, "I'll go and sort something out."

"Go," Uros snarled and Hamish scampered back towards his house.

Uros and Nigel stood alone in the middle of the village. Uros turned to the other man. "So Mr Mayor, what are we going to do now?"

27. My Enemy's Enemy

It is a competitive world where ferocity is a virtue and immediate action a necessity. Show any hint of weakness and you may as well roll over and bare your throat.
My father appreciated the rules of the game more than most and he realised that Brenscombe could not just wait for their enemy to withdraw. He knew that we needed to bare our teeth and, if possible, draw blood to make them think twice about challenging us again.
While the people of Gloucester stood in our village, searching through our homes, my father had put our reprisal in motion. At that moment four conversations were happening concurrently within a few miles of the centre of Brenscombe.

John and Sophia entered Cranwold and walked down the steep road through the centre of the village towards the home of the man they had appointed as village leader, Imre Varadi.

His home was perched on a ridge, overlooking the rest of the houses scattered haphazardly around the sides and floor of the steep Cranwold valley. The larger village of Prinswick could be seen in the far distance to the left.

John knocked at the house and presently the door was opened by the village leader. The man smiled and put out his hand in welcome.

"John," the former dentist said. "Good to see you. I wasn't expecting you until the village meeting next week though."

"Sorry to turn up out of the blue, Imre, but we need your help."

"Certainly," he replied, his speech still containing traces of his Hungarian origins despite having lived in England for twenty years. "Would you like to come in?"

"To be honest, we don't have much time. I'd like to gather your people together in the village hall and tell you all the full story. With your permission of course."

"Right now? It must be something serious."

"It is," John nodded. "An army of a hundred men has come up from Gloucester to attack us this morning and we've been forced to leave our homes. Sophia and I came ahead, but a few dozen others from our village are following behind with their belongings. We need a place to stay for the night and I was hoping that we could use your hall."

"Of course you can." Imre thought for a moment. "Hold on, this army isn't following you, is it? Might they come here?"

"That's what I want to talk to your people about," John replied, shaking his head. "We've scattered in different directions, but the army from Gloucester could go anywhere next. We'd like you to provide some men to help us make a counter-attack. We want to kick them out of our village and send them back to Gloucester before they make a move on somebody else."

"A counter-attack? You mean against a hundred men?"

"We have around fifty to sixty men and women who are willing to fight. If you can supply us with perhaps twenty men that would help, but we're also asking Dowley for assistance."

"I'm not sure if we can do that, John. What if this army knows we've helped you? They'll come here next."

John was momentarily stunned at the negative response and then realised he should perhaps have expected it. "I thought we had an alliance," he said weakly.

"Absolutely we do," Imre replied. "However I need to consider the safety of my people."

"But we need you. And they might come here next anyway. We're just asking for twenty men – and hopefully they won't even have to fight. I have an idea for – "

"Just a minute, John. Why is this army in your village? Who are they? What have you done to antagonise them?"

"We didn't antagonise them. They came to us yesterday asking for a share of our food in exchange for protection, but we didn't agree. So today they came back in force."

"I'm sorry, John, but I don't think we can help you. We don't have an army here. We can't fight against a hundred men. I think that our best option is to keep a low profile."

"But together, we can – "

"John, you're suggesting that I ask the people of Cranwold to fight for your village when we have only just emerged from hiding in our own homes a few days ago. We're just dentists, accountants and business managers. What do we know about fighting? I can't do it and I'm surprised that you're even asking me for this."

John didn't know what else to say. He opened his mouth and then simply closed it again.

Sophia looked at her father struggling for words and stepped forward slightly. "Can I point something out?" she said to Imre. "We can't tell your village what to do, but to me it is obvious that there are two paths forward from this point. We have the advantage of knowing the man who's leading this army, we understand how he thinks and what he wants. I need to tell you that if you sit back then he'll grow stronger, if nobody stands against him now then he'll gather more men, more weapons, more power. Then he'll be able to do what he wants. He'll be able to walk into your village and kill someone if he doesn't like the look of them – or just take all of your food, leaving your people to starve. Is that the future you want for your community?"

"Of course not, but – "

"The alternative path is to stand alongside us and create a larger, stronger community that this man cannot subjugate. We want to create an alliance with more villages around this area, perhaps twenty or thirty ultimately so that we can build a force that he can't defeat. We've already helped you and now it's your turn to help us, and we're not asking you to put yourselves in danger. Our fighters will take the front line in the attack, but we need the enemy to believe that our force exceeds theirs in terms of overall numbers."

Imre didn't respond, but John could see he was wavering. His daughter continued: "If you choose not to join us now, then you are in effect siding with this other man. There's no middle ground. We are at a junction, a tipping point. Your decision now, in this moment, will shape the future of your family, your village, this whole area for years to come. We simply ask for an opportunity to put this to your neighbours and see if some of them will stand alongside us. We can't force anyone, but I'll tell you, simply and honestly, about our enemy and ask your friends to help us if they want to. Does that sound reasonable?"

Imre didn't reply, but simply nodded slowly.

"Let's gather your people together," Sophia continued, "and I'll explain the situation to them."

She turned to walk back along the garden path and Imre, nodding again to himself, pulled his door closed and followed her. John fell in behind them, smiling in a mixture of surprise and pride at his daughter's words.

-o-o-o-

Reid entered Neville Forrester's workshop in Dowley followed by his brother Lewis and also Tim from the Brenscombe village council. Neville looked up from a bow that he was shaping and glanced at the faces that were standing in front of him. He didn't seem surprised to see them – Reid always thought that the old man seemed ready for anything.

"Good morning, Reid," Forrester said. "You've never been late before so I assumed it must have been something important."

"Hi, Neville. This is my brother Lewis and this is Tim Butterworth from our village council."

"You need something?"

"It's good to meet you," Tim replied, stepping forward and shaking Forrester's hand. "And yes, we do need your help please. This morning an army of over a hundred Gloucester men marched on Brenscombe forcing us to abandon our homes, but we're now attempting to pull together a force to win back our village. John has gone to Cranwold to ask them for support and he suggested I come and talk to you."

"No problem. How many men do you need?"

Tim smiled, surprised and pleased that the man had agreed so quickly. "It's good of you to be so helpful, Neville," he said. "It means a lot to us. We'll take however many men you can spare. It's your archers that we're particularly interested in, to be honest."

"We have nearly thirty men and women that we've been training up to be archers, but only two dozen bows. We should leave some men here to defend our village," he stroked his chin, thinking, "but you can have twenty archers if you can use them."

"That would be excellent. Thank you so much."

"I should check with Jonathan, our chairman, but I'm in charge of defence so it should be no problem."

"Thank you," said Tim. "I thought you might ask who we're fighting?"

"If Reid is asking for help that's good enough for me. I'm sure you'll fill me in on the details later. When do you need the men? Now?"

"No, no. We have some other elements to get in position first. We're aiming to make our assault at midday tomorrow and therefore would ask you to be over in Brenscombe in the morning."

"Okay, we'll set off just after dawn. What else do you need?"

Tim turned to Reid. "I like this bloke," he said with a smile. Turning back to Neville, he said: "We have around twenty families on their way here and we were hoping that they could stay the night somewhere. Reid said you have some large storerooms and other outbuildings."

"They can stay here in the house," Neville replied. "There's only me and my daughter. And we'll ask Jonathan to put a few of your friends up – he's got half a dozen spare rooms. It's about time he put his big house to good use."

"Some of the women will stay here tomorrow with the younger children if that's okay?"

"Sure. Whatever you need." Neville turned to Reid. "So, young man, you and I are going to use our longbows in anger then?"

"I guess so," shrugged Reid.

"I've been looking forward to a moment like this," Neville smiled. "Now, why don't you come along and explain things in more detail to Jonathan, myself and the other members of our village council …"

-o-o-o-

Rachel and Mark walked into the stable yard of Langdale Polo Farm, half a mile from Brenscombe along the Cranwold road. All was quiet, a large modern barn on the left, the old Cotswold stone stables ahead of them and the red-brick farmhouse on their right.

"He was in here last time," Rachel said, leading the way into the new structure, the huge barn doors wide open. Inside, the building was split into a dozen low-sided compartments, each containing a horse. Their heads swung around to look at them as they entered, their large eyes studying the visitors.

Hearing a noise came from the far end, Rachel called: "Freddie? Hello?"

A man appeared from the farthest stable door at the other end of the barn. "Rachel?" he said, walking up the passageway between the stalls, brushing his hands on his trousers. He was in his late thirties, dark-haired, tall and slender.

"Hi Freddie, this is my boyfriend Mark."

"Good to meet you," the man said, shaking Mark's hand with a smile. He turned to Rachel. "Have you come to borrow Agassi again?"

"No," she replied. "Well yes, but we've got a problem. Actually we were wondering if we could borrow a few more horses?"

"A few more? What do you mean?"

"How many horses do you have?"

"A dozen in here, around fifteen in the stables next door and another forty out in the fields. Why do you ask?"

"Wow, that's a lot," Mark said.

"Their owners stable them with us," Freddie explained. "I'd actually like to keep them all in the barns at the moment, but we just haven't got enough room. Anyway what did you mean, Rachel?"

"Have you heard that an army has invaded Brenscombe?"

"Of course," he replied. "Most of our stable girls live in the village. I'm keeping my fingers crossed that they don't come over here."

"We want to kick them out," Mark said.

"Tomorrow," Rachel added. "And we wondered if you could help us, well your ponies I mean."

"What do you mean?" Freddie said unsurely.

"I hate to ask, but we really need them."

"Come on, Rachel. Tell me what you want."

She took a deep breath and started to explain their plan.

-o-o-o-

Peter Parlane was following in the footsteps of John and Sophia, leading over fifty of the Brenscombe villagers along the road to Cranwold in the hope that they could stay the night in the village hall. They were carrying as many of their belongings as they could manage and all of their food - Peter had not wanted to leave anything for their aggressors from Gloucester.

As they came around a bend in the road, Peter suddenly called a halt. There, fifty yards in front of them, were six people on horseback, five men and one woman, emerging from a track in the woods. The riders saw them and also halted. The two parties studied each other for a moment. Peter noticed that they all carried swords at their waists. Was this a unit of men from Gloucester? He didn't think that they had horses. John hadn't mentioned anything about horses when he returned from having observed them that morning.

"May I approach?" called one of the riders. He appeared to be the oldest and was presumably their leader.

Peter was surprised at the question, the non-aggressive protocol. He nodded and waved a hand to beckon him forward.

After some quick words to his colleagues, the man nudged his horse forward into a trot but was careful to stop ten yards away.

"My name is Warwick Yorath from Baxley. We're looking for the village of Brenscombe."

"What do you want with Brenscombe?" Peter asked.

"That's a matter between us and them," Warwick replied slowly. He looked around the large group of people.

Peter paused for a moment, then decided he may as well explain the situation. He didn't think that these men were working with the Mayor of Gloucester. "I'm Peter Parlane," he said, "the leader of Brenscombe. Our village is a couple of miles up the road behind us, but we've been forced to leave it. Temporarily, I hope."

Warwick looked surprised. "You've been forced out of your village?"

"A man called Nigel Barkley, who calls himself the Mayor of Gloucester, marched on our village with a hundred men and we weren't in a position to defend ourselves against a force of that size."

"Ah, the Mayor of Gloucester," Warwick nodded.

"You know him?"

"He's the reason why we're here. He's been visiting other communities all around Gloucester. Not ourselves as yet, but we thought he might call on us soon enough. We'd heard that you were forming an alliance of nearby villages and wondered if you might be better partners for us."

Peter smiled at the news. "Some of my colleagues from Brenscombe are visiting our friends in the local villages right now with a view to building a force that can win the village back. Would you be willing to join us? You look like a group of experienced soldiers."

"Not as experienced as I'd like, but perhaps we can help," Warwick nodded. "In fact, perhaps we should help. Like the old Arabic saying, my enemy's enemy is my friend. However I can't promise anything on my own. I have Deborah Baxley with me over there and she'll need to be part of any discussions."

"We're on our way to Cranwold, where we hope to stay the night in their hall. Perhaps we can talk there?"

Warwick nodded. "We need a place to stay the night ourselves. Let me explain the situation to Deborah."

Warwick wheeled his horse around and trotted back to his group. Peter smiled. *This might just work*, he thought, *if the others have managed to get help as well, then this might just work …*

28. Council Of War

That evening the people of Brenscombe stayed wherever they could find a place in the village halls of Cranwold and Dowley or in houses belonging to the local residents.

Peter sent word to Dowley that they were to assemble the next morning at Langdale Polo farm and thus it was at nine o'clock that fifteen people were squeezed into the dining room of Freddie's farmhouse.

Rising from his seat, Peter started the proceedings: "Firstly, many thanks to Freddie Cansdell-Sherriff for allowing us to use his house and of course the barn where we have 130 men and women waiting right now."

Freddie nodded in acknowledgement.

"Secondly, let me make the introductions around the room. Myself, Sandy, John, Sophia, Mark and Rachel from Brenscombe; Imre Varadi and his friends from Cranwold; Jonathan Deane, Neville and Caitlin Forrester from Dowley; and finally we are very pleased to welcome Deborah Baxley and Warwick Yorath from Baxley Castle.

"Thirdly," Peter continued, "can I say formally how grateful we are to all of you for helping us today." He nodded to Deborah, Imre and Jonathan. "We fully appreciate the magnitude of what you're doing for us and we hope to re-pay you one day. Many thanks." He paused for a moment. "I'll now hand over to Sandy, who is in overall charge for today."

Sandy Woodall stood up. "Thanks Peter. Most of you know the plan, but I want to go through it one more time now that we are all sitting in the same room. It's vital that everybody knows their roles. This plan has been devised by Warwick and Neville, and we are fortunate to have you both involved – the two of you are far more knowledgeable than me about this sort of fighting."

"It's not our idea," Neville said, waving a hand dismissively. "We've just stolen it from the Earl of Derby who used this strategy at the Battle of Auberoche in the Hundred Years War." Neville looked around the table. "He deployed cavalry, infantry and archers with simple, yet hugely effective tactics to destroy a much larger French force."

"Let's run through what each group is doing," said Sandy. "I will command the main unit of seventy five people. They are unlikely to be in the thick of the action, but will act as the lure for the Mayor of Gloucester.

"Mark will lead the smaller infantry unit of twenty men, but we need something to distract Nigel Barkley while they move into position. Peter and John have volunteered to do this. Thank you, gentlemen."

"We're just going to talk to him in the middle of the field," John shrugged. "Simple as that. Hopefully we can ensure that everybody's eyes are in our direction for a few minutes."

"Neville will lead the archery unit of course," Sandy, "along with his daughter Caitlin, John's daughter Sophia, and twenty other men and women from Dowley."

"That's correct," Neville nodded, "but I would also like to take Reid – if that's okay with you, John?"

"Reid?" John repeated hesitantly. "I've asked my two boys to stay here at the farm …"

"Only Reid and myself have trained with the longbows. If you give me Reid that will double our firepower at the longer ranges, which could be vital."

"Okay," nodded John uncertainly. "But please keep him safe. I promised my wife that they wouldn't be involved in the fighting."

The bow-maker nodded. "I'll keep him beside me at all times. You have my word."

Sandy continued: "Warwick will lead the mounted unit. His five men will lead the charge, supported by Freddie, Rachel and twenty other men and women from the three villages who have experience of riding horses. We're very grateful to Freddie again for allowing us to use his ponies."

"Please don't let any harm come to them though," Freddie pleaded. "Sorry to say this again, but they're not my horses. I'm simply looking after them on behalf of their owners."

"Don't worry," Warwick said. "My men will lead the way. We've trained for this and we'll put the fear of God into these boys from Gloucester. They won't be expecting an attack from a mounted unit and when they see twenty five horses charging at them they'll scatter like cockroaches when the light comes on."

"But we want them to scatter in the right direction," Sandy pointed out.

"Absolutely. If Mark is able to do his bit then we'll drop them right in Neville's lap." He looked over at Forrester. "We'll crush them between the hammer and the anvil, Neville. Just like Auberoche – the Earl of Derby would be proud of us."

Warwick and Neville grinned at each other across the table.

29. Meeting The Enemy

The men of Gloucester had found beds and sofas in the empty houses of Brenscombe, after Hamish Dacourt had used the last of his food for their evening meal. As a result, his wife Melissa had berated him at length for suggesting that they remain in the village when all their neighbours left – especially when Uros had announced that a dozen of the Gloucester men were going to be staying the night in their house.

The next morning Nigel woke up and, for a moment, wondered where he was. *Of course*, he thought, shaking his head, the spare room in Hamish's house.

He opened the curtains and looked out on another beautiful day. There was a light mist hanging in the valley below them, but the higher ground was bathed in bright sunshine.

On walking downstairs, he found Uros sitting at the kitchen table opposite their hosts, Hamish and Melissa. Uros was eating while the two owners of the house just looked on in silence.

"Is that porridge?" Nigel asked brightly. "I didn't think you had any food left, Hamish?" He looked more closely at the man. "What happened to your eye?"

A black bruise was forming around Hamish's right eye and there was a small cut on his temple. He didn't answer but simply looked across the table in the direction of Uros Viduka.

"While you were having your long lie-in, I was up early," Uros said, through a mouthful of oats. "And it was a good job. It turns out they did have a bit of food left. Funny that."

"You can't go beating up the man that we're leaving in charge here."

"He needs to know who he's working for."

"Uros, you need to leave people with something. You can't just take it all away or they won't have an incentive to work."

"I did leave him with something." He scraped up the last of the porridge from his bowl. "His life. And he knows that if he wasn't on our side then he wouldn't still be here sitting comfortably in his home. And Melissa and I would be upstairs right now. Wouldn't we, Mel?"

"My name is Melissa," she replied haughtily. "And I would rather die than go upstairs with the likes of you."

"I've known plenty of posh women like you, Melissa Dacourt. They're all looking for a little bit of Oliver Mellors in their lives." He smiled at her. "Did you know that DH Lawrence at one time considered calling his book *Tenderness* instead of *Lady Chatterley's Lover*?" Uros reached out to take her hand which was resting on the table, but she pulled it away in horror.

"Uros!" Nigel shouted. "Leave them alone."

The Serbian laughed. "She loves it." He stood up, the smile dropping from his face as he turned to face Nigel. "But don't ever shout at me like that again."

"But you can't – "

"You need to realise who is actually in charge here, Barkley. You call yourself Mayor while I allow it. The moment you're no longer useful then it will be time for a new man to wear the mayoral chains. Actually I might call myself Lord of Gloucestershire once we've got all of these hamlets under our control. Or perhaps – "

At that moment, there was a loud bang on the door and it burst open. It was his Brett. "Uros," he said breathlessly, "there's a group of people gathering in one of the fields outside the village. I think it's the Brenscombe people."

"Good," Uros smiled. "Go and get them. Nigel can tell them what friendly people we are, we'll let them back into their houses and get them back to work in the fields. Under the benevolent leadership of Hamish here."

"No, no, you don't understand. There's about seventy or eighty of them and it looks like they're going to attack the village."

Uros looked at him in disbelief. "What do you mean attack the village?"

"They're all carrying weapons. Swords, shotguns, farm tools."

"Right, get the men together. We'll go and talk to them."

"All the men?" Brett asked.

"Yes, all the bloody men. If they've got eighty then I want a hundred."

Brett left as quickly as he had arrived.

Uros turned to Hamish. "What are your friends doing? They can't really be planning to attack us."

"I don't know," Hamish replied quickly. "I thought they'd all gone to stay in other villages. They didn't say anything about coming back."

Uros stared at him for a few seconds, considering the honesty of his words, before turning to Nigel. "I don't know why you picked this bloke for village leader. I don't think they like him. They haven't told him anything about their plans."

"I'm not sure if popularity is a pre-requisite for leadership at the moment," Nigel replied looking him directly in the eye.

Uros laughed sharply and turned to walk to the door. "Come on, Mr Mayor. Let's see what these farmers want."

-o-o-o-

The main contingent of seventy five people from Brenscombe, Cranwold and Dowley waited at the western end of the huge polo field that was owned by Langdale Farm.

Peter had explained that their role was to look aggressive – much to the amusement of some of the teenagers who were making up the numbers – in order to draw their enemy out of the village into the open. They now simply had to wait.

Warwick had his mounted unit ready and waiting in the barn a few hundred yards away, but, for now, he had joined Peter, Sandy and John on the polo field in order to keep an eye on proceedings. Once the Gloucester army appeared, his intention was to quickly return to the barn in order to lead his team into position.

The four men were standing talking when Harry Barkley walked over to join them.

Warwick was the first to notice him and he barked angrily: "What are you doing here, boy? I told you to wait in the barn with the others."

"I wanted to speak to Mr Parlane." He turned to Peter. "We haven't met before, Mr Parlane, but I've just heard that you're going to talk to the Mayor of Gloucester when he gets here."

"Yes, that's right," Peter replied. "Why do you ask?"

"I'd like to come along when you talk to him."

"Go back to the barn, boy," Warwick interjected.

"Why do you want to speak to him?" John asked.

"Because I'm his son. My name is Harry Barkley."

Peter, John and Sandy looked at each other in astonishment, but Harry noticed that Warwick simply shook his head slightly.

"You knew?" Harry said to him, the realisation dawning.

"Of course we did, boy."

"When?"

"From the moment you told us your name. You think we didn't know the Mayor's surname? Lady Baxley has even met him a couple of times over the years and she said that there was a resemblance between the two of you."

"And why didn't you tell us about this?" Peter asked, turning to Warwick. "Didn't you think that was important information? That you have the Mayor of Gloucester's son here. Does Nigel Barkley know?"

"No, no, he doesn't," Harry answered. He explained: "He knows that I went to Baxley but he doesn't know that we're here. He sent me to spy on them, but I decided to stay because I liked the people of Baxley and I hated what my father and Uros were doing in Gloucester."

"So why do you want to talk to him?"

"I know it's a long shot, but I thought that if I talk to my father then maybe I can persuade him to leave your village without any bloodshed."

Nobody spoke for a few moments as they considered Harry' words. They looked at the village leader. "I don't know," Peter said slowly, turning to his colleagues. "What do you think, John?"

"I don't know the man, but I do know Uros Viduka. There's no way he's going to simply leave Brenscombe. And unfortunately, I think we *want* to have this fight. Sometimes you need to stand up to someone like this, show them your strength so that they don't attack again in future. Or at least make them think twice."

"I agree," Warwick added. "We need to show them we have teeth."

"However," John continued, thinking out loud, "if Harry came over to talk to them, it would certainly add to the distraction while Mark and his team get into position."

"That's true," agreed Sandy. "And, whilst he may not give up the village, Nigel Barkley will be reluctant to attack a group that has his own son in their midst. It may slow them down a little at least."

"I think we should do it," Peter agreed, "but do you trust him, Warwick? We don't want Harry giving away our plans to his father."

Warwick turned and looked Harry in the eye. Finally, he nodded. "I think we can trust him."

-o-o-o-

Mark led his team of twenty men along the narrow country road behind the tall hedge that ran along the southern side of the polo field. The warmth of the early summer days meant that the hedgerow was covered in lush, green leaves providing a dense barrier, but Mark moved cautiously and insisted that the men remain quiet.

As they neared the eastern end of the polo field, the side nearest to Brenscombe, they approached a gap in the hedge. Mark held up his hand and the men halted behind him. He glanced quickly around the greenery to see if their enemy was in position, but relaxed when he saw an empty field.

Turning back to his men, he said: "Okay, there's nobody there, but we still – "

He stopped because he heard footsteps running up behind them. He pulled out his sword and stepped out so he could see past the line of his men. It was a figure running towards them carrying a sword.

Mark was just about to leap forward and attack the character when he realised who it was: "Lewis!" he exclaimed. "What are you doing here? I almost killed you."

"You wouldn't have been able to," Lewis smiled, waggling his sword in front of him.

"You're meant to be with the main group. Why are you here?"

"Dad said we were unlikely to see any action down there so I thought I'd come and join you."

"Go back, you fool."

"No," Lewis said firmly, with a grin. "And you can't make me, big brother."

"Do you want me to take him back?" one of the men offered.

"I'll just come back again," Lewis said.

Mark shook his head. "He probably would. Leave him. Just don't get yourself killed or Dad will kill *me*."

"Where are we going then? What's the plan?"

His elder brother sighed. "Our job is to get round behind the Gloucester people when they've entered the field and cut off their retreat. We're to wait up here at the south-east corner of the polo field until they've gone in at the north-east corner. Then we slip along behind the far hedge."

"Sounds like great fun." Lewis glanced around the side of the hedge and then darted across the gap.

Mark watched him running ahead to the corner of the field and shook his head again. "I hope I'm not going to regret this."

-o-o-o-

"An army marches on its toilet," Nigel muttered to himself, as he waited by the war memorial in the centre of Brenscombe, becoming increasingly frustrated at how long it was taking the men to assemble.

"What did you say?" Uros asked. He was sitting on the low wall around the monument, also shaking his head at the delay.

"One group arrive, then another few people trickle in, then a few more, then the first lot need to go to the toilet, then the second bunch. They're like children."

"Let's get going," Uros said. "They can catch us up." He turned to his friend Lee. "Bring the rest of the idiots up to the field when they arrive. Brett – show us where these Brenscombe people are."

Brett set off up a small road called Knapp Lane which led to a small cluster of houses and then narrowed to a footpath at the end. The path was only large enough for the men to walk in single file and it meandered through the last couple of houses on the edge of the village and up to a gate which opened out onto a small field. Brett led them across the field and through a small plantation of young trees before stopping at the corner of the next field – a huge, wide expanse of grass that seemed to stretch for miles.

In the distance, Uros could see the Brenscombe villagers waiting at the far end of the field. Some of them had been sitting on the grass chatting to each other, but on seeing the Gloucester army they stood up to look at their enemy.

Uros looked scornfully at the ramshackle gathering in the distance. *Seventy to eighty country folk*, he thought dismissively, *and some are just teenagers and women. This should be easy.*

He stepped through the two horizontal bars of the wooden fence which bordered this section of the field and motioned for the others to follow him. They moved along the fence until they were halfway along the eastern end of the field, facing the people of Brenscombe at the western end.

As his men gathered around him, Uros assessed their surroundings.

"This is an enormous field," he said to Nigel, who was now beside him.

"And very flat," Nigel replied.

"It is, isn't it? And look at the grass." He turned to Brett. "This is better than those football pitches we used to play on."

"Yeah, it's like Villa Park or something. But you could fit twenty footie pitches into this field."

"I wonder what they use it for?" Uros mused out loud. "It doesn't look like they've ever had cows in here."

"Horses maybe," Nigel said, indicating a fifty-yard stretch of rope behind them which was held by a series of posts, loops of string tied to the rope at haphazard intervals. There was a scattering of straw and some aging piles of horse dung.

Uros nodded and looked around the field again. "There's a big hedge all the way round, apart from that short section of fence we came through."

"I hope they haven't got more men behind those hedges," Nigel said.

"They're not that clever," Uros replied, but he turned to Brett. "Send a few men over to the gaps in the hedges and check there's nobody hiding on the other side."

"It's a long way over there," Brett said.

"Well they'd better set off quickly then," Uros snapped.

Brett turned and shouted at a few of the men, who broke away from the group and started sauntering over to the side of the field.

"Somebody's coming over," Nigel said, pointing at the far end of the field. Three men had separated from the rest of the Brenscombe group and were walking towards them.

"Let's go and see what they want," Uros said. "Brett, the Mayor and I are going to talk to them. You keep the men here, but be ready to come up fast if I signal."

"What's the signal?"

Uros sighed. "You'll know."

He strode forward, looking ahead to see if their opponents were carrying any weapons. He touched the handgun that was tucked into the waistband behind his back.

Despite the clear day, he couldn't make out the faces of the people coming towards him, but he thought he recognised the outline of the village leader who they had met the day before.

"This is a big field," Nigel re-iterated, looking around.

"So you've said."

"What do you think they want?"

"I don't know," Uros said curtly. "But I don't really care. It's what I want that's important as they'll soon find out."

"Who do you think they are?"

"One of them looks like their village leader."

"Peter Parlane I think he was called," Nigel said, staring at the three men walking towards them. "Hold on, that looks like … no, it can't be …"

"Who?" Uros tried to make out the faces in the distance.

"I thought it was my … is it him? … what's he doing here? I thought you said you saw him in Baxley?"

"Who? Your son? Yeah, I did," Uros nodded. He squinted into the sunshine. "I think you're right, though." They were now close enough to see who it was. "What's going on here, Barkley?"

"Don't ask me."

They walked as briskly as they could over the remaining distance until they were face to face with Peter Parlane, John Strachan and Nigel Barkley's son Harry.

"What on earth are you going here?" Nigel said to his son.

"Hi, Dad," Harry replied.

"Are you okay? I thought you were in Baxley?"

"I hate to break up this family re-union," Uros interrupted, "but we have more important business to discuss." He turned to the village leader. "Have you come to announce that you would like to join the alliance with us in Gloucester?"

Peter snorted in derision. "Far from it. We want you to leave our homes and never come back. This is your one and only chance. You have two minutes to agree or we'll attack."

"Attack?" laughed Uros. "With what? A bunch of farmers? Or is that old man from Baxley here with you, Harry? A bunch of farmers and one old man. And some fat, old company directors who live in this pretty Cotswold village."

"So you're not going to leave?" Parlane asked.

"Leave? You've got to be – "

"Uros," interrupted Nigel, holding up a hand. "Let me handle this. Please. We want to work with these people, don't we? There's no point antagonising each other." He turned to Peter and John. "I know this is a difficult situation, but perhaps we can all put aside our grievances and sit down to talk. We all want the same thing, which is a secure environment to bring up our families and live in safety. That's right, isn't it?"

"Of course," said Peter, "but we don't feel too safe when an army of a hundred men marches towards us."

"I understand your feelings, but I'm sure we can work something out. We need food in the city and you produce it here. We have men that can provide protection for you so why can't we work together, trading what we have for what you have?"

"We can protect ourselves, thank you. All we ask is to be left in peace."

"What about the people of Gloucester who are starving? Surely a man of compassion would want to help someone else in need. We don't ask for much, but if each of the communities around the city can spare a little food then we would be extremely grateful. Can I suggest that we withdraw our men and return to Gloucester – and then perhaps return in a few days for a civilised discussion?"

"We're not withdrawing our men," Uros said emphatically. Nigel sighed but the Serbian continued: "We haven't just come for a walk in the Cotswolds, Barkley. I'm happy to reach an agreement with these people, but they must understand who is in charge."

"That's exactly our point," John said, looking directly at Viduka. "We don't want to enter a so-called alliance with you in charge. I've seen how you operate and we don't want any part of it. You're an amoral murderer and we could never trust you. We would rather die now, fighting for our freedom, than live under your evil dictatorship."

"*There is no evil angel but love*," replied Uros pensively, reaching behind him to pull out his gun. "My father was an English teacher in Serbia and was always quoting Shakespeare to us." He pointed the gun at John. "My dad is a clever man, but when he came over here looking for asylum during what you call the Balkans War, the only work he could find was as a dustbin man and then a gardener in the council parks. Thanks to people like you. He was a much cleverer man than you will ever be. I bet you don't even know what play that's from? Love's Labour's Lost. My father knows far more about your Shakespeare than you do. Even I do and I hate Shakespeare," he added, shaking his head.

"Uros, put the gun away," Nigel said desperately.

"We just came over to talk, Uros," Harry shouted. "You can't pull a gun on us."

"This isn't your time of chivalry when knights had a pleasant chat under a flag of truce," Uros sneered. "The time for talking is over." He was still looking at John, the pistol a few feet from the man's face. "It's time for you and the village leader to tell your people to go back to their homes. You're going to work with us or I'm going to shoot you. I honestly don't care which."

John didn't move. There was nowhere to run. He glanced at the gun and then looked into Uros' eyes, wondering if the man would pull the trigger.

30. Let Slip The Dogs Of War

Back with the main group of seventy five men, Sandy stood next to Tim, who had a shotgun crooked in his arm.

"Has he pulled a gun on John?" Sandy wondered, staring at the small group of figures in the middle of the field.

"It looks like it," Tim nodded.

At that moment, they saw a flash from the far end of the field, and then another.

"That was Mark's signal with the mirror," Sandy said. "He's in position behind the Gloucester men. Go for it, Tim. Announce the attack."

"While Uros Viduka is pointing a gun at our men?"

"We've no idea what he's going to do. He may be just about to shoot them but if we get things in motion it may stop him. Do it."

"Are you sure?" Tim said, snapping his shotgun closed.

"Yes, do it. Now. Before it's too late."

Tim nodded, lifted his gun, fired the first barrel into the sky, quickly followed by the second barrel. Swiftly he lowered the shotgun, broke it, reloaded and fired another two shots.

-o-o-o-

A few seconds earlier, to Tim's right, Warwick had been waiting with his unit out of sight. While the discussions had been taking place in the middle of the field, they had quietly walked their thirty horses along the back of the hedge in the same direction as Mark's team.

They had reached the gap where Mark had been fifteen minutes beforehand when Lewis had joined him, level with the ramshackle army of men from Gloucester.

Warwick glanced quickly around the corner of the hedge and was surprised to see four men walking towards him only fifty yards away. He ducked back quickly. Warwick didn't know it, but they were the men that Uros had despatched a few minutes earlier to check the borders of the field.

What was he going to do? They hadn't had the signal to attack yet, but they were going to be discovered.

Then, away to his left, he heard a double shotgun blast and then another pair of shots immediately after.

"That was the signal. We're going now," he announced to the men and women beside him. "There are four men about fifty yards away, walking towards us. Ignore them. We ride at the main body of their army. Mount up."

Placing his foot in the stirrup, he grabbed the pommel and pulled himself swiftly onto his horse. He glanced behind him. All were ready. Rachel nodded at him, a hint of a smile on her face alongside nervous anticipation.

"CHARGE!" he shouted, the excitement welling up inside him as he kicked his horse into motion and guided it into the gateway. His whole life had been lived in the wrong era. He had always wished that he had been born in the Middle Ages and now incredibly those times had returned. Here he was leading a cavalry charge into battle. If he died today at least his last few minutes would be a glorious crescendo.

"CHARGE!" he screamed again as he bore down on the four men who had been sauntering towards them, discussing where they were going to find some lunch out here in the middle of nowhere.

"Charge!" shouted Rachel and others in the group echoed the call.

The men from Gloucester scattered like frightened chickens as the thirty horses tore past them, hooves thundering on the hard-packed sand-rich earth.

-o-o-o-

"What was that?" Uros exclaimed as the two pairs of shotgun blasts echoed around the field. He kept his gun point at John, the muzzle a few inches from his face. "What are they firing at?"

Uros looked in the direction of the shots and to his surprise the people of Brenscombe began to charge up the field towards him. He didn't quite believe what he was seeing and continued to stare at them for a couple of seconds.

"What are they doing?" he demanded, looking back at John.

Before John could reply, Warwick's unit burst out from behind the hedge a few hundred yards to Uros's left, a little behind them. On hearing the noise of the horses, Uros looked over his shoulder without lowering the gun. His surprise of a few seconds before became amazement as he saw a cohort of horses burst through a gap in the hedge and start galloping across the field in the direction of his men.

"Horses?" he mumbled to himself, still looking over his shoulder. "Of course they've got horses." He nodded, thinking that he should have some of these animals in his own army.

He turned back to John. "You tricked me," he said angrily. "Lured me away from my men so that you could attack."

"As you said, we're not in the age of chivalry anymore," John smiled.

Uros hit him suddenly with the gun, almost knocking him over. John steadied himself and stood up again, putting his hand to the side of his head where blood started trickling down from his temple.

"Order them to stop," Uros demanded. "Tell them to stop or I'll shoot you."

"I can't," John replied. "They won't be able to hear me."

"You have one second to stop them or I'll kill you. Do it now."

"I can't. We don't – "

John never finished his sentence. Uros pulled the trigger, the bullet hitting John in the forehead, the impact throwing him backwards onto the ground. Peter gasped in amazement and despair, and Nigel Barkley uttered a cry of surprise.

While they stared in disbelief at the prone figure of John Strachan, blood seeping from the wound in his head, Uros looked quickly behind him and saw the old man from Baxley castle on the lead horse, a demonic grin on his face as he screamed "Charge!" The whole of the Brenscombe army were charging while his men were just standing there.

"Shoot the guy at the front! He's their leader." Uros shouted to Brett standing with the men a hundred yards behind him, but the noise of the horses drowned him out.

The Gloucester army were simply staring at the cavalry unit hurtling towards them which fanned out into a V-shaped wedge now that they were on open ground, Warwick at the tip, the riders crouching down low behind the horses' heads.

The huge tidal wave of horse flesh and thundering hooves was heading for his men and they started to back away. Someone screamed "Run!", others echoed his shout and suddenly the hundred men of Gloucester were sprinting away as fast as they could run, hoping to reach the safety of the fence they had crossed a mere ten minutes earlier.

The Gloucester army, ragged and chaotic, had to cover two hundred yards to reach the sanctuary of the fence and they were running and stumbling towards it as fast as they could.

At least if they get over there, thought Uros, *then we can re-group and attack them. Brenscombe is going to pay for this. I'm going to wipe them out, every last one of them, and then I'm going to burn the village to the ground.*

Uros whirled back round and pointed the gun at Peter Parlane. "You've seen that I don't muck about. You have one second to stop your men or I'll kill you as well."

-o-o-o-

"Dad!" Reid almost couldn't believe what he'd seen. He stared at the centre of the field for a few seconds, waiting for his father to move, willing him to move. Then he stood up from his crouch, revealing himself above the hedge running along the northern side of the field, and notched an arrow on the string of his longbow. His father had been killed and he was going to avenge him. He started to draw the bow.

"Wait," said Neville Forrester putting a hand on his arm. "We'll take him down, but we must bide our time."

"He just shot my father," Reid blurted, tears coming to his eyes as the spoken words emphasised what had just happened.

"I know, but we can't give away our position. Wait just one minute and, with Mark's help, Warwick will have him running towards you. He'll be sprinting into our arms as fast as his legs can take him and we'll both put arrows through his chest. I promise you."

Reid nodded, fighting back the tears. He crouched back down alongside the other twenty archers that were hiding along the northern border of the polo field. He could wait sixty seconds.

-o-o-o-

Mark hadn't seen what had occurred in the middle of the field because the Gloucester army was in his line of sight. He and his team were watching their opposition from behind the hedge that ran along two thirds of the eastern end of the polo field, near the section of fencing in the north-eastern corner that the Gloucester men had climbed through earlier. They were here to cut off their retreat.

A few seconds earlier Lewis had whooped with delight as they watched Warwick's horsemen erupt from the hedge on the southern side away to their left, scattering the four men who were walking towards them.

Lewis and Mark's whole unit had cheered as the cavalry charge put the men of Gloucester to flight, but that was quickly replaced by a sense of unease at the realisation that a hundred soldiers were sprinting towards them.

Perhaps we should have had more men in this unit, Mark thought to himself, making a mental note for next time. He glanced along at his brother who was smiling in anticipation, oblivious of any danger, but then suddenly Lewis whirled around to look behind him.

"Did you hear that?" he asked.

"Hear what?" Mark replied.

"It sounds like somebody's coming from the direction of the village." Lewis craned his neck to see over the plantation of young trees and then moved from side to side to look through them. "Yes!" he said. "There's a group of men coming. Looks like about a dozen. It must be more Gloucester men." He turned to Mark. "I'll go and hold them off. You only need thirty seconds, don't you?"

Mark looked quickly over his shoulder, through the hedge at the men who were running in his direction. "Yes, you only need to slow them down for a short while. Take two other men with you. Rich, Tom, you go with Lewis."

Lewis set off at a run with the other two men behind him.

"Fall back to here if you get into trouble," Mark shouted after him, but he didn't have time to worry about Lewis. His little brother was going to have to look after himself. Mark glanced along the line. He had seventeen men. *Not many*, he thought, *but it was going to have to be enough.*

"Remember," Mark shouted above the noise that was heading their way. "We're just here to scare them and send them towards Neville. When they're fifty yards away, we quickly spread out along the fence, but wait for my command. Those of you with shotguns, start firing when I drop my sword. The rest of you: just don't let anyone get over this fence."

Looking through the end of the hedge, he glanced over at the horde running towards him.

"Ready … ready … now!" He ran along the section of fence, the rest of his team spreading out behind him, just a couple of yards between each of them.

Mark raised his sword, paused for a second and then dropped it. Six of his men were armed with shotguns and they fired into the crowd, a number of Gloucester men falling to the ground. One of his men climbed onto the first bar of the fence, shook his sword and screamed at the enemy. A number of the other men followed suit.

Thinking that they were being attacked from the rear, the men of Gloucester veered off towards the northern side of the field, still running as fast as they could. The cavalry was behind them, close on their heels, this new force was on their right and the main Brenscombe contingent was still running towards them from the far end of the field to their left. Their only option was therefore the northern side of the field, where they couldn't see anything to stop them from escaping apart from a chest-high hedge.

-o-o-o-

"Order your men to stop," Uros repeated, his gun pointing Peter Parlane. "You've seen that I'm prepared to shoot." Suddenly he pointed the gun at Harry. "Or would you like another demonstration?"

"Uros!" exclaimed Nigel Barkley, moving towards his colleague. "Leave Harry out of it."

"He's with them, Barkley, or haven't you noticed."

"He's my son."

"Shut up, Barkley. We don't have time to debate this." Uros turned back to look at Peter, the gun still trained on Harry.

Nigel Barkley decided that he needed to do something to save his son. Uros wasn't going to listen to reason. The man may or may not shoot, but he couldn't take the chance. Suddenly Nigel leaped forward and grabbed hold of the gun. "Run!" he shouted to his son as he tried to pull the gun from Uros's grasp.

Harry and Peter took the opportunity to start running back to the main Brenscombe contingent as Uros tried to wrestle the gun free of the Mayor's grasp.

"Let go, you idiot!" Uros shouted.

Nigel didn't reply and continued trying to pull the gun away from the Serbian, but suddenly a shot rang out and Barkley sagged to the ground holding his chest.

Uros pulled his gun free and whirled round to point it in Harry and Peter's direction. He quickly fired a shot, but then realised that they were already thirty or forty yards away, too far for the accuracy of his handgun.

"You stupid fucking idiot, Barkley!" he shouted at the top of his voice and kicked the Mayor of Gloucester's motionless body.

Uros quickly turned his attention to his men at the north-eastern corner of the field, his eyes scanning rapidly over the scene that was unfolding before him. He saw his men veer away from the fence as some of the Brenscombe people started shooting at them.

"There are only about fifteen of them at the fence," Uros shouted. "They'll need to reload. Attack them at the fence and we can over-power them." He realised he was wasting his breath. They couldn't hear him amidst the havoc and the hurly-burly.

He calmed himself down and forced himself to assess again. The Brenscombe army was more intelligent than he had suspected. The cavalry unit was a good move against un-trained men from the city, but they were now slowing down. Why weren't they trampling over his men?

The men at the fence were also a good idea, cutting off the retreat, but why weren't they taking advantage of this move? What had it achieved? His men were running towards the northern side of the field where they would escape. If he had been in charge of the Brenscombe army, he'd have placed men there as well …

A sudden realisation dawned on him. His men were being shepherded towards something – and it was probably towards something far more lethal. They were being led like sheep to the slaughter.

"Stop, you fools!" Uros called at the top of his voice, but it was like shouting into a hurricane.

He stood watching for a second, powerless, and then looked around again. The time had come to save himself, he realised.

If Brenscombe wanted his men to go to the northern side then he was going to head in the opposite direction. He turned and started jogging away towards the now-deserted southern border of the field.

31. When The Hurly-Burly's Done …

"He's getting away," Reid said, peering through the spindly branches at the top of the hedge.

"I see him," Neville nodded. "He's further than I'd hoped, but we can take him. I make it three hundred yards. You agree?"

"Yes."

"There's only you and I that can hit him from this range. It's a good distance, but we've trained for this. However we can't give ourselves away too early. Their main contingent is nearly here, another few seconds. When I give the command we'll stand. You and I will both aim for Viduka and the others will aim for the bulk of their army as planned. Okay?"

"Okay."

"Right, here we go … everybody ready …. ready … STAND!" Neville Forrester shouted along his line of men and women.

They stood to reveal themselves above the chest-high hedge. Reid was to Neville's right, Caitlin and Sophia and twenty others to his left, nearer to the fleeing men of Gloucester.

"LOOSE AT WILL!" he shouted as loudly as possible, loosing his own arrow to confirm the command for those who hadn't heard.

Reid drew back as he had thousands of times before, focussed his aim and released smoothly as he had been trained. He watched his arrow arcing through the sky. He hoped it was on target.

"Don't wait," Neville shouted. "Fire again. All of you, keep firing. Bring them down."

This broke Reid from his reverie and he launched another arrow. Then he glanced at the running figure of Uros Viduka and saw their first two arrows slam into the man's right shoulder and left leg, knocking him to the ground.

"Yes!" Reid shouted and released a third arrow, just as the prone figure of Viduka was obscured from his view by the Gloucester men running across in front of him, screaming and shouting as the arrows thudded into them.

"Keep firing," Neville called and the carnage continued.

Reid drew back an arrow, but didn't fire. The Gloucester men in front of him didn't stand a chance. They were only fifty yards away and arrows were flying into them unerringly from all along the line of archers. He slowly returned the string to its resting position and lowered his bow.

Glancing along the line to his left, he saw that his sister had also lowered her bow, as had a couple of the others.

"HOLD FAST!" Neville shouted and all the archers stopped.

Over half of the men in front of them were on the ground, injured, dead or trying to hide from the arrows flying in their direction. Those who remaining standing had raised their hands in surrender.

Warwick cantered over along with the rest of his unit and they formed a circle around the Gloucester men to prevent them from escaping. He shouted at them to put their weapons down.

Reid pushed his way through the hedge, ran around the cavalry unit and the captured Gloucester army and out to the area of the polo field where he had last seen Uros Viduka. However there was no sign of his body. He looked around, turning and turning.

Sophia ran up behind him.

"Where is he?" asked Sophia breathlessly. "I saw you hit him. What a shot, Reid."

"I couldn't see because of all the fighting," he replied. "We definitely hit him though. Me and Neville. Did you see him hit the ground?"

"Yes, but then Warwick's horses were in the way."

Reid looked around. There were four arrows in the ground, two of Neville's and two of his. He pulled one out of the earth and looked at it.

"This was my second arrow," he said.

"Are you sure?"

"Yes, the fletchings are mine. So Uros Viduka should be right here."

The two of them turned in a circle, their eyes scanning the perimeter of the field, searching for Uros, but he was nowhere to be seen. Where could he be? He couldn't have run to the edge of the field so quickly, especially with an arrow in his shoulder and another in his leg. The man had just disappeared.

They continued to gaze around the field for a few more minutes, but to no avail. Finally they walked slowly over to the place where their father's body was lying, arriving just as Mark and Lewis ran over from their position at the fence.

32. When The Battle's Lost And Won

Later that day the people of Brenscombe moved back into their own homes and the village hall was transformed into a makeshift hospital in order to treat the injured from both sides of the battle. Yvonne and Sophia worked all day and late into the evening sewing up wounds, removing shotgun pellets and splinting broken limbs.

Eventually, after they had attended to all the people who were waiting, Sophia was finally able to walk slowly home through the darkness, weary both from the battle and its aftermath.

Lewis, Reid, Mark and Rachel were sitting in the kitchen attempting to comfort their mother. Sophia hugged her mother and drew up a chair.

"Why was he so selfish?" Emilia said angrily, tears rolling down her cheeks.

"What do you mean?" Mark said.

"Why did he always have to put himself in the front line? What about me? Why didn't he think about me?"

"He wasn't being selfish. He always wanted to do the right thing for everybody."

"But what about doing the right thing for me? What am I going to do now?"

"I know," Mark agreed. "I'm going to get that guy, Uros Viduka."

"I don't care about him," his mother said, holding her head in her hands. "If it hadn't been him, it would have been someone else. Your father just kept on putting himself in harm's way."

"He was doing it for the village, but most of all of he was doing it for us, Mum."

She nodded as the tears continued to fall. "I know you're right, but I don't know what I'm going to do. What am I without him? I feel like half of me died along with him today."

Mark didn't know what to reply to this. None of them did.

"I'm sorry," she said, attempting to dry her tears. "I know it's the same for all of you. You've lost your father." She stood up slowly. "Maybe I should go to bed now. I'll try to be stronger tomorrow."

She kissed and hugged each of them. "I'll see you all in the morning." She shuffled out of the kitchen and nobody said anything for a few seconds, each lost in their own thoughts.

Rachel finally broke the silence. "Have you been up at the village hall all this time?" she asked Sophia quietly.

"Yes," she nodded. "We must have treated more than thirty people and about a dozen have serious injuries that will need close monitoring. Yvonne is sleeping the night there so she can keep an eye on them, but she sent me home to look after Mum."

"Mum was talking like that the whole evening," Mark said. "Not that I blame her." He paused for a moment. "I'm going to find that Uros Viduka if it's the last thing I do."

"I found out how he got away," Sophia said. "I was treating a woman from Cranwold who had a broken arm. I asked her how she did it and she said that Uros pulled her off her horse."

"He pulled her off a horse?" Mark said in surprise. "But Reid and Forrester hit him with two arrows."

"She said that he was just getting to his knees as she trotted past him and he suddenly jumped up, grabbed her and dragged her off the horse. Uros climbed onto the horse and rode off."

"That's unbelievable," Reid said, shaking his head. "We hit him in the shoulder and the leg."

"He'll be back down in Gloucester now," Sophia said. "Somebody else told me that there was a group of a dozen men who didn't get to the field before the battle started. He probably joined up with them again."

"Yes, Lewis saw them," Mark said. "They were coming up behind us and, with Rich and Tom, he held them off for a couple of minutes. It was a good job he spotted them because it would have screwed up the whole plan otherwise."

"But I heard there were a dozen of them," Sophia said. "And there were just three of you?"

"Yeah, they were out-numbered, weren't they?" Lewis laughed. "I charged at them with my samurai sword and they just ran off. Well, at first there was one guy who stood his ground, but when all the rest ran away he didn't have much choice so he took off after them."

"They'll be back in Gloucester now," Sophia said. "And if Uros recovers he'll be back."

"At least the Mayor is gone," Reid said.

"I don't think he was the problem," Mark replied. "Uros Viduka is the one."

"I've been thinking," Sophia said. Everyone looked at her. "We need to be stronger if he's going to come back again. We've done well up to now, but he'll be better equipped next time and therefore we need to improve immensely. We need to train like a proper army, archery practice, training with swords, handling horses, everything."

"You're right," Mark nodded. "We could get Warwick to train us. He obviously knows how to handle a sword."

"And we need to continue what Dad started with forming alliances with the other villages. The larger the alliance, the better. At least a dozen villages, perhaps more. Each community needs to organise its own defensive force, but I was also thinking that there should be an elite unit of the best fighters drawn from all the communities."

"The best fighters?" Mark echoed, nodding. "I like it."

His sister continued: "We pick the best from each community for a core unit of fifty men and women. A rapid reaction force that is continually training and ready to defend any member of the alliance in as short a time as possible. If there's trouble somewhere then they need to arrive within an hour at the most."

"How are they going to move so fast?"

"It needs to be a mounted unit. That'll allow them to respond quickly, but it will also be the most formidable force when it arrives, especially if we can fire arrows from horseback."

"While we're riding?" Reid said in surprise. "It's hard enough when you're standing still."

"It just takes practice," Sophia replied. "Neville should be able to help us. I don't know if he's done it himself, but he probably knows the theory."

"He was telling me about the bows that Genghis Khan used," Reid nodded. "His tribes were nomadic, riding small, tough ponies from birth, often sleeping in the saddle on long marches. They were also trained to fire arrows from horseback from a very young age."

"The polo ponies we have are perfect. You saw how they operated today: quick, nimble, not afraid of the sound of battle."

"I like it," Mark agreed. "We've got all the things we need and the people who can train us. When shall we start?"

"Tomorrow," Sophia said. "We need to be ready the next time someone attacks us, Uros or somebody else. You need to talk to Peter first thing in the morning and let him know we're doing this."

"Me?"

"Yes, you," his sister nodded. "You're going to be the leader of this elite force."

Mark smiled. "That's the best idea you've had yet …"

That was the beginning for us, the moment our tribe was formed. And we have trained every day since.

Each and every day is preparation for a battle which we hope will never come. We train hard every single day of our lives, working with swords, training the horses, practicing with bows. When you run through your drills tomorrow, remember this tale.

We must never show weakness. We are stronger than our enemies, we are faster, we are more determined, we are better trained, we are harder.

We are Brenscombe.

The End

See below for details of other books by RR Gordon, including the next book in the Brenscombe series.

Author's Note

A couple of years ago I read a novel called Last Light by Alex Scarrow, which follows a woman trying to get back to her family in the collapse of society after the world's oil supply is severed.

My teenage children also read the book and, over the subsequent months, we often discussed what we would do if society collapsed. The boys obviously felt that they would be the best fighters, but my daughter and my eldest son's girlfriend felt that they would be just as good. I talked about keeping a stockpile of baked beans in the garage and wondered where on earth we would get our water, let alone soap, shampoo, toothpaste and all the other everyday items we take for granted.

The premise for my book seemed to almost materialise in 2012 and 2013 as Greece repeatedly went to the brink of collapse, with Italy, Spain and others looking like they might follow. Around this time I took my daughter Alexandra Sophia Gordon on a long drive from Gloucestershire to Newcastle – and back – so that she could look round the university there. For some unknown reason we decided to while away an enjoyable ten hours in the car putting some meat on the bones of a potential story – and here it is. This book is primarily for my children, but they said that you could share it with us! I hope you enjoyed it.

Here are a few notes which might be of interest:

The Hundred Years War started in 1337 and the Battle of Auberoche took place in 1345. With just 1,500 men Henry, the Earl of Derby, won a huge victory over the 7,500 French contingent led by Louis of Poitiers. The battle of Brenscombe was inspired by Henry's decision to launch a three-pronged attack using cavalry, infantry and archers supported by the element of surprise. This battle was a significant victory for England as they established a regional dominance in Gascony which lasted nearly a hundred years.

During the writing of this book my daughter and one of my sons were fortunate enough to receive some archery tuition from a man who represented Great Britain at the Olympics. I am grateful to him for some of the descriptions of technique, some old war stories (literally) and the opportunity to hold a longbow.

The Mary Rose was Henry VIII's warship which sank near the Isle of Wight in 1545 and was raised in 1982 in one of the most complex and expensive projects in maritime archaeology. You can visit the Mary Rose in Portsmouth. 172 longbows were discovered in the ship and some are estimated to have had a 170 pound draw weight. Only English archers would have been able to use the bows, partly due to their training from childhood and partly due to the technique of holding the string still while leaning into the bow with their body weight to push it forward. A difficult skill to master, especially with such powerful bows.

Baxley Castle is loosely based on Berkeley Castle which is twenty miles south of Gloucester. The castle has remained within the Berkeley family since they reconstructed it in the 12th century, except for a period of royal ownership by the Tudors. The castle has never been taken by force and if society was to collapse that's where I would want to be.

Where would you want to be? What would you do for food? Would you survive? Let me know if you have any suggestions for improvements to the book – or ideas for the other books in the series.

Rod Gordon
rod@rrgordon.com

P.S. By the way, if you liked this book then you may like to add a short review comment to Amazon – it would be much appreciated. Just go to the Amazon site, find the book and click on "write a customer review" near the bottom of the page. Many thanks!

-0-0-0-

We hope you enjoyed this book.

*Watch out for the sequel, **Cotswold Haven, Book 2 of the Brenscombe series**.*
Look for it now on Amazon by searching for "rr gordon Cotswold haven"

If you wish to be informed of the release of this book and others in the series,
simply email <u>subscribe@rrgordon.com</u> with the subject of "Subscribe"

You may also wish to read other books by RR Gordon:

***Gull Rock** – a man on the run falls in love while his hunter closes in*
***Meaningless** – a modern-day parable of a normal family struggling to find their way*
***Leap** – a thriller telling the story of a young man's desire to fight for his beliefs*

-o-o-o-

Gull Rock *by RR Gordon:*
(Book 1 in the Wish You Were Here series)

What would you do if you needed to disappear after stealing a million pounds? Unfortunately you don't have the money any more which makes it a bit trickier.

Dan Lawrie's solution is to keep on the move, working a few days in each place in exchange for food and lodging. He gives a different name each time and never uses his credit cards. And he never communicates with his family - well just once …

His itinerant lifestyle leads him to North Cornwall where he finds that he can get casual work in pubs and hotels without too many questions being asked. He works hard in each job, but then moves on after just a few days.

Unfortunately he gets stuck when he reaches a small place called Trebarwith Strand – and the reason is a girl by the name of Sophie. And while Dan stands still, the man who is chasing him is getting closer and closer.

Highest positions in Amazon Bestsellers:
#1 in Crime, Thrillers & Mystery Series
#1 in Crime, Thrillers & Mystery Anthologies

Praise for Gull Rock:
"An excellent read"
"I couldn't stop and had it finished within two nights"
"A real page-turner"
"This author clearly has a gift for creating fascinating and believable scenes";
Beth Townsend, The Kindle Book Review
"I read it at one sitting" - "gripping" - "cliffhanger"
Elizabeth Gowing, author of Travels In Blood & Honey

Thriller Of The Month: www.e-thriller.com

To purchase Gull Rock – or to read a sample chapter – then please go to Amazon and search for "rr gordon Gull Rock" or go to <u>http://www.amazon.co.uk/dp/B006KWAL2O</u>

-o-o-o-

Meaningless by *RR Gordon:*

An unusual, thought-provoking story from the bestselling author of Gull Rock …

Nick Jemand could be any one of us. His job's okay, not exactly fulfilling, but not quite bad enough for him to look for another one. However Nick knows that he has a good life really – a wife he's lucky to have, three lovely children and a nice house in a quiet little village in the Cotswolds. What could possibly be wrong with any of that?

Unfortunately one of the main pillars of his lovely life has slowly disappeared over recent years: his children have now all left home. He misses the time they used to run to the door when he arrived home from work. He misses playing football in the garden, hide-and-seek, feeling foolish in the dressing-up clothes his daughter made him wear – and he even misses getting up at six o'clock in the morning to build a tower of wooden bricks. His children were the reason he got up in the morning - and now?

Meaningless is a modern-day parable of a simple man struggling to divine the meaning of life as we all do. Will he find the meaning for him? Will we find the answer for ourselves? Whether this forthright, quirky tale is uplifting is ultimately down to you.

-o-o-o-

Leap *by RR Gordon:*

Just after finishing his engineering degree, Ben Smith meets his dream girl - and is offered his dream job: working on the next generation of engines to be used in the first manned expedition to another planet.

However his career is over before it's begun as he uncovers a conspiracy in his new company, involving those closest to him. For Ben the space mission was to have been an opportunity to reach to the edge of our solar system, but others see a chance for personal gain.

Set against the backdrop of exploration, Leap is a classic thriller, which tells the tale of a young man's desire to fight for his beliefs and his need to win the girl that he loves.

Praise for Leap:

"Fantastic book, with plenty of twists and turns and a shocking ending."
"A very enjoyable book, written by a natural storyteller."

To purchase Leap – or to read a sample chapter – then please go to Amazon and search for "rr gordon leap" or go to http://www.amazon.co.uk/dp/B005F6EBX6

Printed in Great Britain
by Amazon

65234236R00158